The Thrice Named Man

Part XVI

Palmyrenian

The Thrice Named Man

Part XVI

Palmyrenian

by

Hector Miller

www.HectorMillerBooks.com

The Thrice Named Man

Part XVI

Palmyrenian

All characters and events in this publication, other than those clearly in the public domain, are fictitious and any resemblance to real persons, living or dead, is purely coincidental.

Author: Hector Miller

Proofreading: Kira Miller

First edition, 2025, Hector Miller

Part XVI in the book series The Thrice Named Man

ISBN: 9798311456555

Text copyright © 2025 CJ Muller

All rights reserved.

No part of this publication may be reproduced, stored in a retrieval system, or transmitted, in any form or by any means, without the prior permission in writing of the author. Publications are exempt in the case of brief quotations in critical reviews or articles.

Contents

Chapter 1 – Enemy of my Enemy 1

Chapter 2 – Wall (September 271 AD) 27

Chapter 3 – Sallust 36

Chapter 4 – Friends 43

Chapter 5 – Somnus 55

Chapter 6 – Meal 70

Chapter 7 – Merchant (October 271 AD) 81

Chapter 8 – Tillers 91

Chapter 9 – Kindling 103

Chapter 10 – Devil's Dyke 112

Chapter 11 – Missive 122

Chapter 12 – Way of Fire 130

Chapter 13 – Sacrifice 139

Chapter 14 – Oath 148

Chapter 15 – Pursuit 163

Contents continued

Chapter 16 – Taifali 172

Chapter 17 – Bear 184

Chapter 18 – Lambs 195

Chapter 19 – The East (January 272 AD) 206

Chapter 20 – Merchant 216

Chapter 21 – Envoy 222

Chapter 22 – Gates 233

Chapter 23 – Reward 241

Chapter 24 – Tarsus (May 272 AD) 250

Chapter 25 – Lake 260

Chapter 26 – Antioch 272

Chapter 27 – Daphne 281

Chapter 28 – Dispute 293

Chapter 29 – Antilibanus 305

Chapter 30 – Emesa (July 272 AD) 315

Contents continued

Chapter 31 – Tanukh 330

Chapter 32 – Palmyra 339

Chapter 33 – Euphrates 347

Chapter 34 – Khamsin 359

Chapter 35 – Lice 372

Chapter 36 – Mercury 383

Chapter 37 – Coin 398

Historical Note – Main characters 403

Historical Note – Palmyrenian storyline 407

Historical Note – Random items 411

Historical Note – Place names 416

Chapter 1 – Enemy of my Enemy

Ctesiphon, the capital of the mighty Sasanian Empire.

Outside the cover provided by the enormous vaulted chamber, the stone walls of the White Palace shimmered under the relentless onslaught of the midday sun. The day had started out pleasantly cool, but as the hours dragged on, the hot desert air slowly seeped into the great reception hall. Come afternoon, even the sweet-smelling incense burned by the priests of Ahura Mazda had taken on a nauseating quality.

From amongst the folds of his voluminous robes, the ambassador produced a thrice-folded cloth onto which he sprinkled a few drops of frankincense. He used the perfumed linen to dab pearls of sweat from his brow, taking great care not to smudge the kohl that his body slave had meticulously applied around his eyes in the early hours of the morning.

It was his fifth straight day of waiting in line. Four days in a row he had arrived well before sunrise, only to be sent back to his accommodations late in the afternoon, exhausted and dispirited.

Gaius Hairan glanced up at the hundred-foot-high domed ceiling and mouthed a prayer to the supreme god of Palmyra. He not only thanked the lord of heaven for the shade, but also beseeched the god to bring conclusion to his ordeal. A heartbeat later, a cool gust blew in from the south, convincing him that Bel had indeed heard his pleas. His suspicion was confirmed when a courtier called out his name and gestured for him to follow.

Before he entered the throne room he raised his arms, allowing the immortal guards flanking the arched entrance to search his person for concealed weapons.

Passing through the gilded doors, the ambassador prostrated himself and crawled across the marble floor to where Hormizd, the high king of all the realms of the Sasanian Empire, sat on an elevated ivory throne behind a veil of sheer silk. The envoy remained as he was for what seemed like an eternity before Kartir, the keeper of the veil, left the side of the king and ordered him to gain his feet.

The thin screen failed to conceal the shahanshah's gold-embroidered robes that glinted with precious stones and pearls. His hair and beard were blackened with henna and his face enhanced with kohl and gold dust - so much so that he appeared to be a god rather than a mortal. The magnificence of the high lord threatened to overwhelm Gaius Hairan and he was forced to fight the urge to drop down to his knees in reverence.

The dais of the great lord was flanked by lesser thrones representing all twenty-eight realms of the empire, their proximity to the king of kings a reflection of their worth in his eyes. The thrones were placed at a lower level than that of the god king's and occupied by representatives of the rulers of all the provinces who had sworn allegiance to the high king.

Only one throne, cast in solid gold, remained conspicuously empty.

"You may state your pleas to the ruler of the four corners of the world", the keeper of the veil stated haughtily, drawing the ambassador's gaze away from the unoccupied dais.

"Lord", Gaius Hairan said, "I come on behalf of Queen Bat-Zabbai of Palmyra. Her borders are threatened by the Roman Emperor who wishes to conquer the lands justly inherited from Lord Odaenathus, the legitimate king. She begs for your assistance and will gladly bow the knee to you if you agree to send your mighty army so that the invaders may be destroyed. As a token of her respect, the queen has gifted camels stacked with silk, gold and perfume."

At the mention of gifts, Gaius Hairan noticed a leer of greed flash across the keeper's face. It filled him with hope that an arrangement could be made with the Sasanians. Again, his gaze was drawn to the empty golden throne, an action that did not go unnoticed.

"It is reserved for the ruler of the last errant kingdom", the keeper of the veil enlightened him. "Soon, the emperor of Rome will take his rightful place as servant of the great king."

Before the ambassador could reply, the keeper stepped back behind the curtain to receive instructions from the high king of the realm.

He appeared again sixty counts later. Although he dutifully relayed the words of his lord and master it was evident to the ambassador, who was a perceptive observer, that Kartir did not agree with what was said.

"Why is Bat-Zabbai not here in person to prostrate herself before her rightful master? Why does she make demands when she knows that her unconditional fealty is required?"

It only took a heartbeat for Gaius Hairan to realise that his life hung in the balance, and he did well not to offer a reply. In an attempt to keep his head attached to his shoulders, he prostrated himself to show that he was at the king's mercy.

"Rise", the keeper commanded after he had conferred with the god-king behind the veil. "The gifts of your so-called queen will be cast into the holy waters of the Tigris and your camels and servants put to death by drowning."

Silence descended upon the court as all waited with bated breath on the shahanshah's final judgement.

"The great king grants you your life, ambassador", the keeper continued. "You may spend the night in the comfort of the palace, but tomorrow morning at sunrise you will be given a mule from the royal stables so that you will not have to dishonour yourself by trudging through the dust." Then he raised his arms and spoke to all in the court. "Let it be carved in stone. The great king is merciful, even towards those who dare to insult him."

The ambassador dropped down onto his knees. "May you be immortal, lord", he said, and made sure to keep his face pressed against the marble as he crept backwards, eager to be gone before the king changed his mind.

Kartir, the keeper of the veil and high priest of Ahura Mazda, stepped inside the silk sanctuary. "Like that man, Rome is on its knees, lord", he said. "Should we not use this Bat-Zabbai and the army of Palmyra to crush the last of the Empire's resistance? Soon, the Roman Emperor could be your vassal."

Hormizd scoffed at the priest's words. "I have seen Lucius Domitius with a blade in his fist. Have you, priest?"

The high king continued without waiting for an answer. "The Roman Emperor serves the lord of the field of blood, Arash the Destroyer. Even if we amassed the armies of the dark lord, Ahriman, we would fail. Only a fool would doom his forces to destruction against a warrior king who is unconquerable. Why would I provoke him if he has extended the hand of fellowship?"

Kartir lowered his gaze, not only to show that he accepted his lord's judgement, but also to hide the resentment in his eyes. Shahanshah Hormizd, like his father Shapur, was tolerant towards most religions, a trait despised by the high priest. But unlike his son, Hormizd, Kartir had feared Shapur more than he loathed the false religions, so he was never willing to risk offending the ruler of the land. As he backed out through the slit in the veil, the high priest said a silent prayer to Ahura Mazda, asking the god to give him the strength and courage to find a way to purge the realm of the agents of darkness.

* * *

Once evening had descended over the city, the high priest made his way to the place of fire - the temple dedicated to the lord of wisdom, Ahura Mazda. Tired after the long hours spent in attendance of the great king, he slowly laboured up the long flight of stone steps. He paused halfway, not only to catch his breath, but also to take in the splendour of the magnificent domed roof resting on four pillars of white limestone, one at each corner of the thirty-pace square elevated platform. Each column represented one of the four elements that were sacred to his religion - air, earth, water and fire, but above all, fire.

At the centre of the square, a large bronze vessel housed a blazing hearth. Kartir watched in silence as the keeper of the Eternal Fire diligently fed the flames with logs of seasoned, sweet-smelling cedar. When he was done, he replenished the fuel and oil of the silver incense burners that were set into recesses in the stone columns - aniseed for air, oakmoss for earth, cardamom for water and cinnamon for fire. The high priest waited patiently for the aromas of the four elements to combine before drawing a deep breath. He felt the power of the spirit of light rejuvenate his tired body, and walked up to the priest with a spring in his step. "Go home. I will attend to the prayers and offerings", Kartir said, and placed a comforting hand on the man's shoulder. "You are blessed, brother, it is good to toil for the sake of one's soul."

Once the acolyte's steps had faded into the distance, Kartir went down onto his knees and reverently recited the mantras as prescribed by the prophets of old.

In conclusion of the ceremony, the high priest was about to commit the fatty tail of a sacrificial sheep to the fire when he heard a footfall behind him. He spun around to face whoever dared to intrude upon the sacred fire rites, and came face to face with a hooded figure. As if at the command of the god himself, the flames of the Eternal Fire flared and the features of the man became distinguishable.

Kartir's first thought was to call out for the temple guards, but then he felt a strange sensation well up inside, one which he chose to interpret as a divine sign.

"The high king does not share your fervour for Ahura Mazda", Gaius Hairan said. "It is well known that he protects the ones who spread the heresies of the dark one. It is a pity that the great king does not walk along the path of truth."

Kartir sensed that he was facing a pivotal moment in his life and that his reply would determine both their destinies. He drew a deep breath to calm himself and showed that he was a man of wisdom by reining in his tongue and issuing only a near imperceptible nod.

"I have heard whispers that the shahanshah's older brother, the true heir to the throne, is a warrior, dedicated to the way of light", the Palmyrene ambassador whispered.

Again, Kartir nodded.

"Do you believe that Bahram will support my queen against the Romans?" Gaius Hairan asked.

"The Romans serve Ahriman and his demons", the high priest hissed. "A true follower of the light will draw courage from his faith."

Gaius Hairan leaned forward until his lips were a handspan from Kartir's ear. "One drop in a cup of wine is enough. The symptoms are much like that of dysentery. It takes days, even weeks, to take effect, so you will not be implicated." Then the ambassador pressed something into the high priest's hand, turned about, and walked away.

He paused at the top of the steps and glanced over his shoulder. "I will call upon you when the legions arrive", he said.

"Where are you going?" Kartir asked.

"I am on a journey to visit Palmyra's allies."

"I did not know that Palmyra had many allies", Kartir replied.

"We do not", the ambassador confessed with an amicable smile. "But Rome has many enemies."

Then he turned around and melted into the night.

* * *

The endless plains of Scythia, west of the northern shore of the Dark Sea. The lands under the dominion of the Goth king, Cannabaudes the Crow.

The two hundred warriors escorting the dignitaries were all clad in the plate and scale of Palmyrene cataphracts. It was due to the presence of the armoured horsemen, not the heavily loaded cart, that the progress of the convoy had been little more than twenty miles a day.

Neither Gaius Hairan nor his companion complained about the slow pace. Unlike the men accompanying them, the two envoys were not accustomed to spending long periods on horseback. Twelve days earlier, during the middle hours of the night, four Aegyptian galleys had beached on the northern shores of the Dark Sea, somewhere south of Olbia, to deposit them onto a remote beach, far from prying eyes. After almost two weeks in the saddle, the sinews in their legs, backs and arms still ached with every step their horses took.

"How far are we from the camp of the king?" the ambassador asked the guide. The question had become a daily ritual and the reply was always evasive, so much so that he had started to doubt the abilities of the man.

To the ambassador's dismay, the guide steered his horse next to his, so close that their knees almost touched. He leaned over in the saddle, and although Gaius Hairan turned his head away, he still caught a whiff of the man's putrid breath that reeked of rotten cheese and sour wine. "For all I know, it could be on the other side of that hill over yonder, highborn", the man said, indicating a slight incline on the far side of an overgrown ravine.

They had procured the services of the highly recommended half-breed on the outskirts of Tyras. Ennius Illadianus had the name of a Roman and features of a Scythian, but seemed to be able to converse in Greek only.

"Why are we paying you if you do not know the location of the king's camp, Greek?" Hairan asked.

"I am no Greek, highborn", Ennius replied in Greek. "My father was a *medicus* on double pay in the Fifth Macedonian and my mother was a Bastarnae whore. I was raised on the backstreets of Tyras, lord."

"How come you are a guide if you grew up in the city?" Rahim, Gaius Hairan's companion, asked.

"After my father was expelled from the legions for no good reason, he decided to earn his coin by trading with the tribesmen. He took me in when I was eight or nine", he said. "But on our first trip north he ran into a warband of Goths, so I never learned the Roman tongue."

Ennius started picking his teeth with his soiled nails rather than to offer any further explanation.

"What happened?" the ambassador asked.

"Them Goths slit his throat, they did", the guide snickered, and spat out a piece of gristle which he had liberated from somewhere amongst the rotting stumps.

"What did they do to you?" Rahim asked.

"They let me live", he said, and smiled in a way that could have meant almost anything.

"So why are we paying you?" Gaius Hairan asked, returning to his original question.

"To make sure the same doesn't happen to you when them Goths arrive", the guide replied.

Ennius had hardly uttered the words when an arrow slammed into the side of his head, the armour-piercing tip passing straight through his skull. At least two handspans of the shaft exited on the other side, showering Gaius Hairan with a fine mist of blood. The guide's eyes glazed over and the corpse, still frozen in a smile, slid from the gelding's back and tumbled facedown onto the ground.

The heavily armoured cataphracts reacted immediately, forming a ring of iron around the ambassador and his companion, their long, thick lances levelled, shielding the envoys from any further attacks.

Gaius Hairan was still wiping the red stains from his face when a lone horseman appeared at the crest of the incline which, ironically, the late Ennius had indicated earlier. Moments later, two more riders appeared, flanking the first.

"I may have underestimated the abilities of the scout", Hairan admitted, his eyes fixed on the horsemen.

The black rider nudged his massive stallion and approached at a walk, the other two warriors following close behind. They exchanged words along the way, showing no apparent concern for the iron-clad riders who usually put the fear of the gods into all who faced them.

The lead rider was dressed in a loose-fitting black robe and a matching wolfskin cloak was draped around his broad shoulders. His hair was black as a raven and his clean-shaven face almost handsome were it not for an old, white scar that ran from above his right eye all the way down to the corner of his mouth.

Gaius Hairan's occupation had taken him to many royal courts and it only took a moment for him to realise that the rider was no ordinary barbarian. "Lower your lances", he snapped, and the officer of the cataphracts reluctantly passed on the command.

The ranks of armoured horsemen parted and the rider reined in a pace in front of the ambassador, his horse brazenly stepping on the body of the guide as he did so, causing the ambassador to glance down at the corpse.

"He was of the Bastarnae, I am told", the Goth said in a grating voice. "They are one of the few tribes who refuse to pay fealty to me, so bringing the enemy into my lands is treachery, is it not?"

Gaius Hairan felt his throat constrict with fear as he met the rider's gaze. Unlike his dark hair, his eyes were light grey, almost white, which endowed his glare with an unsettling, corpse-like quality.

The ambassador was not fool enough to let the death of a lowly guide threaten the outcome of his mission. "It is as you say, lord king", he said, inclined his head and pressed his right hand against his torso in the way of the tribes.

But the Goth lord was not through. "Why do you bring soldiers into my realm?" he growled in passable Greek, his hand coming to rest on the hilt of the blade strapped to his waist. As if by pre-arranged signal, hundreds, if not thousands, of barbarian riders crested the high ground to the west, their ranks almost spanning the horizon.

"The soldiers are required to protect your gifts from the predations of bandits and thieves, Lord Cannabaudes", Hairan answered.

"My gifts?" the Goth asked, clearly amused.

"The queen of Palmyra wishes for an alliance", Hairan said.

"An alliance against who?" the king asked.

"The Roman Emperor", the ambassador replied.

In response to the revelation, the muscles in the jaw of the Goth king clenched and unclenched, his fist tightening around the leather-bound hilt of his blade. For a heartbeat Hairan feared that he had somehow managed to offend, but then the black rider seemed to relax and he turned his mount about. "Come, Greek", he growled. "Any man who considers Eochar the Merciless an enemy is my friend."

* * *

Augusta Treverorum, the capital of the breakaway Gallic Empire.

Gaius Hairan wished for nothing more than to feast his eyes on the magnificence of the procession of dignitaries entering at the far side of the sixty-pace-long audience chamber, but he steeled himself and kept his head bowed, his gaze fixed on the designs adorning the marble floor.

Every few heartbeats, his beady eyes darted across to his companion, Rahim, to ensure that he, too, adhered to the strict decorum of the Roman court.

Satisfied that all was as it should be, he resumed studying the intricate mosaics depicting the nine muses, and noticed that his left foot rested on the face of Melpomene, the muse of tragedy. Overcome with a sudden concern that he would bring down a curse upon himself, he slowly and imperceptibly slid his red leather boot a few inches backwards, only to reveal a bloody dagger that the goddess clutched in her right fist. Gaius swore under his breath, chastising himself for making the inauspicious omen worse. To remedy the situation he tried to move the foot back to its original position. So caught up was he in the furtive toil, he failed to notice that the emperor and his entourage had taken their seats which, he had been told earlier, would be the signal for the envoy to approach.

He was saved by Rahim, who softly cleared his throat.

Subjected to the piercing glares of the imperial entourage, the two men made their way towards the throne. The hollow echoes of iron hobnails striking marble reminded them that spear-wielding imperial guardsmen remained but a few paces behind.

"Behold, Emperor Gaius Pius Esuvius Tetricus, ruler of the Roman Empire of Gaul!" the imperial chancellor boomed when the two foreigners were ten paces away.

The representatives of the Palmyrene Empire came to a halt in front of the raised dais occupied by the self-styled emperor of the northern Roman provinces.

Both men saluted in the way they had been instructed. "Lord, I am Gaius Hairan of the Attar", the ambassador said in Greek, pressing an open palm to his chest and making sure to address the imperial chancellor rather than the emperor himself, "and my interpreter is Rahim, who belongs to the same clan."

Although the ambassador and his companion were fluent in Greek and Latin, they, like the chancellor and emperor, who also spoke both languages, observed the unwritten rules of negotiation and waited patiently for the discourse to be translated. The real reason being that it allowed them more time to contemplate the other party's words.

"The proud history of the Attar is well known even in this distant land", the emperor replied via the chancellor. "What brings you to my domain?"

"I carry a scroll from Septimia Zenobia Augusta, queen of the Roman East", Gaius Hairan said, and again waited patiently for Rahim to translate.

An underling detached from the troop of courtiers and hurried to collect the proffered scroll from the hand of the ambassador. The secretary carried the sealed document with great reverence and presented it to the chancellor on outstretched open palms who, in turn, signalled for a scribe to take the letter in hand.

Before the functionary could read the missive to the court, Gaius Hairan intervened. "My Lord Emperor", he said, his tone respectful. "I wish to caution that the missive is of a, er…, sensitive nature."

The chancellor nodded and immediately barked an instruction to the scribe. The scribe broke the seal but returned the scroll to the chancellor who, being of inviolate character, approached the dais and read the words so only the emperor could hear.

When he was done, the emperor whispered a curt reply.

"The request of Queen Zenobia requires careful consideration", the imperial representative announced. "Tonight, after our Lord Emperor has taken council, you will be summoned."

"Palmyra is in your debt, Lord Emperor", the ambassador replied, inclining his head in respect.

The entourage waited until Gaius Hairan and Rahim had backpedaled to the far side of the chamber before the emperor rose from the dais and led the richly adorned imperial procession back to the comfort of the palace.

* * *

Back in his well-appointed chamber, Gaius Hairan carefully removed his pride and joy - the pearl-studded cap that displayed the seal of the Attar tribe and placed it on a low table beside the bed. Then he spread his arms wide to allow his mute body slave to undo the square Heracles knot of the yellow sash from around his waist before the bondsman lifted the knee-length green silk tunic from his deceptively muscular torso. He waved away the servant before he could be relieved of the large egg-shaped earrings and matching necklace, both items exquisitely crafted from garnet-inlaid gold. The ambassador treasured the comforting embrace of the jewellery that marked him as an aristocrat of high rank, sworn to the throne of Palmyra.

Gaius Hairan was not only a learned noble of the desert tribes, but also someone adroit at removing obstacles from the path of his king, or queen, for that matter. He wore no armour nor carried a sword, but preferred to keep the tools of his trade away from the eyes of others. Once the slave had departed, he extracted a thin-bladed dagger concealed in his boot and carefully pried the assassins' ring from the index finger of his right hand before stowing both items in the hidden compartment of his bronze-bound coffer. He doubted whether his special skills would be required during his visit to the Gallic Empire, but he had learned that preparedness was rarely a waste of one's time.

His thoughts were interrupted by a knock at the door that separated his chamber from that of Rahim's. He had been waiting on his brother for some time and had become slightly annoyed at his younger sibling's uncharacteristic tardiness.

"You are late", he barked, and turned away to fill two goblets with ice cold white wine.

To show his irritation, he left Rahim's wine on the serving table and walked out onto the balcony. Gripping the hand rail of the marble balustrade, he took a long, slow swallow, savouring the delicate flavours of lime and apricot while drinking in the view across the sprawling city bordered by the great wall on the banks of the river.

"I am sure that the Romans chose our accommodations with care", he said, and took another sip. "They wish to humble us with a show of greatness."

"Well, is it working?" a female voice replied from behind in fluent Greek.

The ambassador suppressed the urge to swing around and confront the intruder. '*If the emperor wished me dead, there is nothing I can do about it anyway*', he thought, his left fist tightening around the handrail.

He took a deep breath to calm himself and chugged the wine remaining in his cup, his agile mind working through the possibilities. "Yes, Lady Vitruvia", he replied a few moments later. "It is working."

It was well known that Vitruvia, the mother of the former emperor, was the power behind the throne of the Gallic Empire. Years earlier, during the chaos following Postumus's murder, Vitruvia had used her considerable wealth to purchase the loyalty of the legions of Gaul. She had been trained as a druidess of the old gods and applied her skills to further cement her influence with the soldiers, so much so that they referred to her as the *Mother of the Camps*.

"Do not fear for your companion", she said to put the ambassador at ease. "He will not be harmed."

"Thank you, lady", he said, feigning meekness.

"I have the utmost respect for Lady Bat-Zabbai", Vitruvia said, using Zenobia's Palmyrene name. "She rules an empire, yet, because she is a woman, she cannot take credit for it."

"She is much like you, lady", Gaius Hairan replied, and turned around to see what reaction his words solicited.

His first emotion was that of relief, as a smile spread across her lips. But then he noticed that it failed to reach her eyes, that were fixed on him like an adder on its prey.

Vitruvia walked over to Gaius's leather-bound baggage chest, lifted the lid without asking for permission, and reached inside. With a metallic click the secret compartment slid open, revealing the dagger and ring. "We all play our part in the theatre of power, is it not, *ambassador*?" she asked.

Although there were no guards inside the room, Gaius harboured no doubts that the hallways outside were teeming with trained killers. For a moment he weighed up his chances of escape should he snap her neck, but immediately discarded the thought when she turned her back, her supreme confidence serving to cower him.

Vitruvia took the dagger in her fist. While tapping the blade on a palm she turned to face the ambassador.

"Your queen wishes for an alliance against Rome", she said. "She must have the courage of a lion."

Gaius nodded in relief, sensing that Vitruvia was not only gloating that his duplicity had been exposed, but that she *wanted* something from him. "She is fearless, majesty", he confirmed.

"Have the tales of the deeds of Lucius Domitius not reached the Land of Palmyra?" Vitruvia asked. "Have you not heard how he defeated almost two hundred thousand Goths, how he slaughtered the Alemanni and the Semnones, the most feared tribes of Germania? Are you deaf to the cries of the widows of the warriors north of the Danube?"

He had heard of Emperor Aurelian's exploits, but was convinced that much of it was propaganda, tall stories spread by the agents of the Empire to conceal its growing weakness.

"I see that you doubt the tales?" Vitruvia said, and was rewarded by a curt nod from the Palmyrenian.

"My spies have confirmed that the stories are indeed inaccurate", she continued, but rather than smile, her eyes hardened, revealing a burning hatred that made Gaius retreat a step. "The tales fail to give Aurelian the credit he deserves. He is a merciless, cold-blooded killer - an unconquered general who walks in the shadow of the god of war."

Gaius Hairan swallowed away the yellow bile of fear that crept up from his stomach. "What do you wish of me?" he asked.

"Tell your queen that Aurelian is preparing to march east", Vitruvia said. "Inform her that while her armies are engaged with the emperor, the legions of the Gallic Empire will attack and conquer the Eternal City. This, I will give to you in writing."

The ambassador felt relief at her words, but then he noticed the look in the Roman matron's eyes.

"You wish for me to deceive Lady Bat-Zabbai?" he asked.

Vitruvia ignored the Palmyrenian's words. "Soon, Aurelian will be marching east to subjugate all who stand against the Empire", she said. "Once he has razed Palmyra to the ground he will come to the walls of Augusta Treverorum. Serve your sworn lady and kill him before he destroys all that you hold dear."

"But how will I manage that?" Gaius Hairan asked, his tone tainted with a whining quality.

She offered the dagger hilt-first to the Palmyrenian, a warm smile on her lips. "You are a resourceful man, no doubt. I am sure you will find a way."

"Then we will depart with haste, Lady Vitruvia", Gaius Hairan said. "So that the necessary preparations may be made. I swear that I will not disappoint you."

"You are free to leave whenever you like, ambassador", she replied. "But your brother, Rahim, will keep me company until I receive confirmation that you have been true to your oath."

Chapter 2 – Wall (September 271 AD)

The Imperial Palace in Rome.

For many days, I had been beset by a dark mood which morphed into bouts of excruciating headaches, so much so that I started to suspect that my humors were out of balance. Segelinde ascribed my condition to the aftereffects of the long months of campaigning against the Germani, followed by the violent riots in the streets of the Eternal City. Although I kept my counsel, I suspected that it had more to do with the fact that I was not doing the bidding of the god of war, and that I had become ensnared by the day-to-day administration of the Empire, or rather, what was left of it.

I disdained summoning the imperial physicians, opting to follow Cai's advice, who prescribed abstaining from food and wine. The remedy alleviated the headaches but seemed to worsen my ill temper, up to a point where the slaves and servants were, in my opinion anyway, openly avoiding me.

It was the Ides of September, nearly a month after the onset of my ailment, when Diocles cautiously woke me up earlier than usual to inform me of what he referred to as 'sporadic outbreaks of violence' that had occurred during the hours of darkness.

"I know how the mob thinks, Domitius", Hostilius said when he joined us on the balcony a while later. He pointed at the top floors of the high-rise *insulae* just visible above the early-morning smog. "Yes, you've placated the *head count* for a while with daily rations of pork, oil and wine, but when Rome's grain stores run empty they'll burn the city to the ground."

"I agree with Tribune Proculus", Diocles said. "Ever since the usurpers have split the Empire into three parts, trade has been restricted. Many craftsmen and merchants have lost their livelihoods. The situation is exacerbated by the major barbarian invasions that resulted in many small-time farmers abandoning their fields. A large portion of those families have ended up in the larger cities."

"The Greek's right. Half of the starving, out-of-work bastards in the Empire end up on the streets of Rome", Hostilius muttered.

"Why not draft them into the legions?" I suggested. "Surely the treasury is overflowing after the massive amount of loot we recovered from the Germani and the property confiscated from the traitors in the Senate."

"Overflowing is a term that will surely give rise to unchecked spending practices if interpreted out of context, Lord Emperor", Diocles admonished me. "I prefer the word 'healthy'."

"It doesn't matter if the treasury is healthy", Hostilius said, and gestured towards the city. "The peasants that end up on the streets are the runts of the litter. The only thing they're good for is making trouble."

The Primus Pilus paused for a span of heartbeats, his eyes fixed on the faraway Tiber while he sipped on his watered wine.

"My *ava* used to say that if you don't find work for idle hands, Hades surely will", Hostilius growled. "Don't draft the useless scum into the legions, rather find something else for them to do."

"How much gold do we have in the *healthy* treasury?" I asked my aide.

"The amount fluctuates day to day", Diocles replied with the haughty arrogance administrators are prone to, "but, let's just say that we could build a stone wall around the city twice over and there will still be enough left to pay the legions for three years."

I exchanged glances with the Primus Pilus, who shrugged in reply.

"Please don't tell me that you are considering it, Lord Emperor", Diocles said, a hint of panic discernible in his voice. "Such a wall will have to be twelve miles long."

"My best guess is that it would take a single legion five years to build a proper wall", Hostilius said. "But these good-for-nothings will probably take twice as long."

"Or", I added, "we could employ fifteen thousand men to work on the wall and attempt to finish it sooner."

Diocles's expression slowly morphed from one of panic into a sly grin. "Mayhap the Semnones have done us a favour", he said. "If the *head count* believe that they are in a race against time to safeguard the city against barbarian invasion, we will be able to pay the labourers the bare minimum."

"Every evening they will waste the coin they've earned toiling on the wall to buy wine and women at the nearest drinking hole", Hostilius said. "And the tax the Greek levies on the *tabernae* will go straight back into the treasury."

Diocles found it impossible to suppress a smile. "You have a remarkable grasp of economic principles, tribune", my aide complimented. "The coin will indeed circulate through the economy quickly and end up back in the fiscus."

"I want it to be constructed with concrete and clad with bricks", I said. "The wall must be four paces thick and the height of four tall men. If we are going to spend the Empire's coin on a wall, we might as well do it properly."

"If you want a proper wall, you'll need towers that protrude at least three paces", Hostilius said. "Every hundred feet will do nicely, so that once the ballista bolts are exhausted, the boys can skewer the attackers with their *pila* or cave in their skulls with rocks."

Diocles was taking notes. "How high?" he asked.

"Didn't you hear Domitius say that the wall's got measure twenty-five feet?" the Primus Pilus replied.

"I meant the towers", my aide clarified sheepishly.

"Then why didn't you say so?" Hostilius snapped. "You want the defenders at least thirty feet above the wall walk, just in case the attackers gain the rampart or a traitor opens the gates. Mind you, make a note that the battlements should only be accessible via the stairs in the towers. That way, if we have a repeat of the recent riots we don't have to worry about the street scum getting up onto the wall."

Diocles nodded, all the while scribbling profusely on a clay tablet. "This will be the biggest construction project that the Empire has undertaken in centuries", he said. "And will require months, if not years of planning."

"Unfortunately, we don't have the luxury of time", I said. "I wish for it to get underway sooner."

"Mayhap the design can be fast-tracked", my aide speculated, "so that work can begin early next year."

My lack of response made Diocles issue a sigh. "When do you wish for the work to commence, Lord Emperor?" he asked.

I smiled in reply. "I would have liked for it to start tomorrow, but the beginning of next month will suffice, I suppose."

Diocles issued a curt nod and hurried from the chamber, nearly bumping into Gordas who was coming from the direction of the stables.

"Where is the Greek going?" the Hun asked, and poured himself a cup of neat wine.

"He's on his way to build a wall", Hostilius said, and popped a fresh date into his mouth.

In reply, Gordas shrugged noncommittally, as the tribes of the Sea of Grass cared little for walls or anything else that hemmed them in.

In any event, there was something more pressing weighing on the Hun's mind. "Are you planning on taking Kasirga's son into battle, Eochar?" he asked, and spared me the embarrassment of an answer. "If that is so, you are not spending enough time in Intikam's saddle."

Of course my friend was right, but although the imperial palace was enormous and well-equipped, it lacked one crucial element - a facility where I could train with the bow, sword and spear while mounted, away from the prying eyes of others.

I noticed a look pass between Hostilius and Gordas, which made me suspect that they had been conspiring.

"The Greek tells me that the late Senator Bassus owned a magnificent estate on the northern slopes of the Quirinal Hill", the Primus Pilus remarked offhandedly. "Maybe we can go and stretch Intikam's legs when you're not too busy building walls."

Gordas issued a grunt of agreement.

* * *

Early afternoon, my aide informed me that our meeting with Titus Flavius, who wielded much influence in the Senate, had been postponed at the senator's behest. Apparently he had fallen ill with some malady or other, leaving my schedule wide open.

As coincidence would have it, Hostilius strolled into my chambers moments after Diocles made the revelation. "We're about to ride out to the property I mentioned earlier", the Primus Pilus said. "We just came to see whether you're busy."

"Incidentally", Diocles said before I had a chance to react, "the afternoon meeting has just been cancelled."

Hostilius took me by the arm - not in a forceful manner, but his grip was firm nonetheless. "It's time we get you back on a horse, Domitius", he said.

We made our way to the imperial stables where Gordas was waiting with three saddled horses and an escort of thirty mounted praetorians.

"If I didn't know any better, I would have thought that you were expecting me to join you", I said as I swung up into the saddle.

"Bollocks", Hostilius replied. "You're imagining things."

Surrounded by the praetorians, we rode out the gates, descending the Palatine Hill in the direction of the Sacred Way. Our escort led us through the Forum of Nerva, past the stalls of the booksellers onto Long Street. Everywhere we went people stopped to stare. They cheered me with shouts of 'Germanicus Maximus' or raised their hands in a salute.

"The people love you, Domitius", Hostilius said as we turned left, heading towards the temple of the goddess of wellbeing.

"It is the free wine I distribute", I said. "They are a fickle lot. Their adoration can turn into hatred within heartbeats."

"The senators fear you, Eochar", Gordas remarked in an attempt to lift my mood. "Unlike love which is fleeting, fear is enduring. Don't be concerned, they will still dread your wrath long after the peoples' affection for you has dwindled."

"It is comforting to know", I replied.

Chapter 3 – Sallust

Near the temple dedicated to the bearded god, Quirinus, we turned the corner onto the High Path that ran along the spine of the Quirinal Hill. At the summit, just past the Temple of Fortuna, Hostilius led us to the left, onto a narrow street winding down the northern slope until we arrived before an arched entrance set in a twenty-foot-high stone wall. Interestingly, two praetorians manned the thick oak and iron gates that swung open at our approach.

On the Primus Pilus's command, the mounted praetorians who escorted us remained with their comrades. Hostilius, Gordas, Diocles and I continued along the path bordered by towering chestnuts, oaks, beeches and poplars that must have been planted even before the time of Caesar Augustus. Shrikes and bee-eaters fluttered in the canopy, their chirps muffled by the sound of a stream cobbling beside the track. Up ahead, a fallow deer darted from our path and an otter scurried down the bank to seek refuge in the water. It felt as if we had been magically transported to the forests of Germania or Pannonia.

"Do you wish to inspect the villa, Lord Emperor?" Diocles asked.

"For the first ten years of my life I lived in a room no larger than Intikam's stable, and for the next ten in a tent that was significantly smaller", I said. "Do you really believe that I ascribe value to stone and mortar?"

I saw Gordas suppress a grin. Only Scythians understood the ways of a man born to the Sea of Grass.

The path broadened as we passed through a gap in a low stone wall that demarcated the section of the garden dedicated to fruit trees. Neat rows of meticulously pruned orchards ensured that an abundance of different varieties of figs, apples, plums, cherries and peaches were available to the wealthy owner throughout the season. The extensive vineyards were sufficient to supply enough grapes to the cellar so that neither the host nor his guests would want for wine. The centuries-old olive trees framing the garden were already heavy with black fruit that would soon be pressed to fill the stores with amphorae of golden oil.

"If we get the slaves to chop them down immediately, the fruit and olive trees will make good firewood for next season", Gordas advised. "I've heard that boar grilled on an applewood fire has a pleasant taste."

Diocles rolled his eyes as he swung down from the saddle and strolled towards ornate iron gates set in a wall of neatly dressed travertine. "Mayhap, Lord Emperor, this will serve to pique your interest."

My aide pushed open the double doors and gestured for me to ride through the archway.

I complied.

I had to blink twice. A large oval field, three hundred paces across at its narrowest point, had been terraced into the slope of the hill. On the far side of the field a dozen horses grazed on the lush green grass of an enclosed paddock, close to beautifully decorated stone and wood stables. Abutting the lodging for the horses, a colonnaded portico, enclosed on three sides, housed a large stone hearth. Thick logs of seasoned beech and oak lined the far wall.

"So what do you think, Domitius?" Hostilius asked. "Gordas showed them how to build the stables and I oversaw the firepit and colonnade." Then he strolled towards Diocles and slapped him on the back. "But, truth be told, the whole thing was the Greek's idea."

"The legions laboured almost a month to construct it", Diocles said. "The men needed no encouragement when they were told that it was meant as a gift for their emperor."

I waited until my throat cleared before I spoke. "Do I have to go back to the palace or can I stay here and get my things delivered?" I asked.

"No need to go back to that prison", the Primus Pilus replied with a grin, dismissing my words with a gesture. "Your wife and the Easterner have already brought along your weapons and armour."

Moments later, Segelinde and Cai appeared at the top of the steps of the covered porch of the villa and started to descend towards the field.

* * *

I spent the remainder of the afternoon riding Intikam, honing my skills with the help of Gordas, Hostilius and Diocles.

When evening came. we dismissed our guards, slaves and servants and held an impromptu feast around the hearth overlooking the field. We spoke of our plans, but as the night progressed and the wine flowed, we remembered our friends who had crossed the river. I knew that Nik, Bradakos and

Marcus were at peace, but Kniva's murder remained unavenged.

When all had retired to their beds I committed more logs to the hearth, pulled my fur cloak tight around my shoulders, and filled my soldier's cup with wine. When the flames were at their highest, I poured half of the blood-red liquid onto the embers as a libation to Arash. While the hissing coals consumed the offering, I drank the remainder and renewed my oath of vengeance to the god of war and fire.

I could not help but wonder whether he had heard my words. And if he did, would he give heed to the pleas of a mortal?

Unbeknown to me, my sacrifice had indeed drawn the gaze of Arash the Avenger… but, in time, I would come to suspect that other, less benevolent gods had also been listening.

* * *

On the morrow I woke up long before dawn. I slipped from underneath the furs without disturbing Segelinde's slumber, dressed, took an apple from a fruit bowl, acknowledged the two praetorians outside the door with a nod, and made my way to the stables with the guardsmen trailing at a respectable distance.

Of the dark mood that had plagued me for weeks there was no sign, and I suspected that it had been banished by the excitement of spending time with Intikam. The more familiar I became with the horse, the more I realised that in many ways he was even more powerful than the stallion who sired him. Whether we would form the same bond I had with Kasirga, only time would tell.

The guardsmen at the entrance to the stables stepped to the side and saluted in the required manner.

My horse greeted me with a little whinny of recognition and I, in turn, curried his favour by presenting him with the apple, which he greedily consumed, muzzling me afterwards to check whether I had another hidden under my cloak. As a quid pro quo the stallion allowed me to saddle him without nipping at my torso as he had the day before. I coaxed him from the stall and found Gordas leading his mare along the central aisle.

"A warrior without a horse is only half a warrior", the Hun grunted, clearly pleased to see that I was bonding with Intikam.

"But in the saddle, a warrior is as good as two", I said, completing the saying that must have been as old as the steppes.

Gordas slapped me on the back as he passed. "You truly are a son of the Sea of Grass, Eochar", he said. "Come, we will work on your form with the bow."

Just after sunrise a third of a watch later, Hostilius strolled onto the field. I reined in beside the Primus Pilus, using his arrival to cut short the session with Gordas as the sinews in my back burned like the fires of Hades.

I noticed then that he clutched two wooden training swords in his left fist. "Let's train with the sword", he said, offering me one of the *rudes* hilt first. "It's good to see you and the Hun enjoying a relaxing ride, but that's not going to help you when things get nasty, eh?"

I sighed on the inside, dismounted to accept the sword from my friend, and assumed a high guard.

Chapter 4 – Friends

Diocles leaned over the table to accept Hostilius's empty cup. Rather than have it refilled, my aide used it to weigh down a stubborn corner of the large vellum map detailing the entire Empire, which earned him a scowl from the Primus Pilus. "How am I supposed to strategise with a parched throat?" he asked, and beckoned to a pouring slave, who rushed to hand him a vessel brimming with wine.

"What will we be up against when we face Zenobia's army?" I asked Diocles, who had earlier been briefed by our spies in the East.

"The last time that the Palmyrenians amassed their forces was when they conquered Aegypt", Diocles said. "At the time, reports mentioned a mounted force numbering seventy thousand."

"We're not interested in the past. How many men are we going to face come spring next year?" Hostilius growled.

"The Palmyrene military bases are spread out over an extensive area, some of which are situated in remote locations", Diocles said. "It makes an accurate estimation of their strength challenging."

"Give us your best guess, then", the Primus Pilus sighed.

"The core of their army is built around the heavy, Sasanian-style cataphracts", my aide said. "Zenobia inherited twelve thousand of these armoured riders from Odaenathus. She has since expanded their numbers to twenty thousand."

"The large warhorses and comprehensive, heavy armour make cataphracts inordinately expensive to arm and keep in the field", I said. "Zenobia has conquered Aegypt and I have no doubts that the Empire's gold that is traded for Aegyptian grain ends up being used to equip the Palmyrene army."

"We have been financing the expansion of Zenobia's forces", my aide concurred. "She needed our coin to build her army before suspending the sale of grain to Rome."

"Apart from heavy cavalry, Palmyra has a host of mounted bowmen", Diocles continued. "Most of these warriors are mercenaries recruited from amongst the desert-dwelling tribes that inhabit the vast lands of the East."

"How many?" Hostilius asked.

"Twenty-five thousand, but maybe as many as thirty thousand", my aide replied.

"How many Roman legions does she command?" Hostilius asked.

"Four", Diocles replied. "*Legio I Parthica, III Cyrenaica, III Gallica* and *VI Ferrata.*"

"I don't mind so much killing savages who are intent on ravaging Roman lands", Hostilius said. "But slaughtering the Empire's legions doesn't sit well with me."

"Our legions will do their bit when we have to reclaim walled cities, but they will not play a significant role when we engage the Palmyrene army", I said. "Zenobia and her generals will face us on the flatlands where they can bring their cataphracts to bear. They will hound us with their mounted archers, and once they have drawn us into a pursuit they will try to crush our cavalry with their iron-clad horsemen. Only when they have destroyed our cavalry will they whittle down our infantry like the Parthians had done to Crassus's legions all those years ago at Carrhae."

"Vibius has brought the strength of the Illyrians up to ten thousand", Hostilius said. "Could we counter the Palmyrene heavy horse with the black riders?"

"The heavy riders of Palmyra will annihilate the Illyrians", Gordas stated in his matter-of-fact way. "Our black riders are skilful and well-armoured, but the cataphracts with their Nisean mounts are clad in thick iron from head to toe. Our light lances will shatter on their iron, but their heavy, two-handed spears will punch through the armour of the Roman riders."

"So what will we be taking East?" Hostilius asked, which was the pertinent question.

It was an issue that I had mulled over for many weeks and I was ready with an answer. "We will need six legions", I said. "Four to counter the infantry of Palmyra if it comes down to that, and two more so that we may garrison the cities along the way to secure our supply route." That was the easy part of the answer to the Primus Pilus's question.

I took a swig from my cup before I continued.

"Vibius will command the Illyrians - all ten thousand of them. I have sent a missive to my daughter requesting five thousand of her best mounted archers and I have no doubt that, for the right price, Naulobates will let us have five thousand of his men to fight alongside the Scythians. In addition, I will approach the Yazyges and the Carpiani to further bolster the numbers of our light horsemen to ten thousand."

"Even if the Yazyges and the Carpiani were to provide us with half their fighting men we will still be ten thousand riders short of Zenobia's numbers", Hostilius said, showing that it was not only my aide who was skilled at mental arithmetic.

"That", I replied, "is why I have sent for an old friend. And a not-so-old friend as well", I added with a grin.

"I have a feeling you're not going to tell us, are you?" Hostilius scowled. "How can we plan when you're keeping things from us? We only have two weeks left before we've got to take the Illyrians over the passes."

"You won't have to wait long", I said. "I'm expecting my friends any day now."

* * *

They arrived six days later.

I made sure that Hostilius, Gordas, Cai and Diocles were present when the men I had sent for many weeks before were ushered into my private chambers. Judging by their appearance and by the way they held themselves, they could easily have been father and son, but many thousands of miles separated their arid homelands.

The elder of the two was clean-shaven with grey curls, dark brown eyes, and an olive skin. A genuine smile split his lips as soon as he laid eyes on me. The other man was at least thirty years his junior, with the same olive complexion and dark eyes, but his neatly oiled hair and beard were as black as the night. He, too, failed to suppress a grin of recognition.

Both men averted their eyes and went down onto one knee.

I walked over, indicated for them to rise, and embraced them in turn.

"You do not look like an emperor", the elder of the two said in heavily accented Latin. "You look like a warrior who spends his days in the saddle."

I had known Adherbal for longer than thirty years and he, too, appeared as wiry and fit as when I had first met him. "And you do not look like a man who has retired from the auxiliaries, a man who drinks away the days", I replied.

"Even though I enjoy wine more often than I should, I still ride every day and train with the javelin", he said. "Once war is in your blood, it stays there until you cross the river."

While my friends greeted the commander of the Berber cavalry, I turned to face the younger man. More than five years earlier, I had saved Amr and his uncle Jadhima from the sword of the murderer of Odaenathus. Shortly after, they had reciprocated the favour by freeing me from Zenobia's dungeon where my friends and I were awaiting certain death. Jadhima had been a powerful lord of the desert tribes, and after his passing Amr had taken his place.

I knew that Amr and his people followed the teachings of Mani, the holy man of the East. "I am sorry for your loss, Lord Amr", I said. "Your uncle was a man of reputation. I believe that he has ascended to the eternal light."

"Thank you, lord", Amr replied. "I, too, pray that he has passed from darkness to light."

I guided both the Berber and the Arab lord to the couches arrayed in a corner of the room. Once our glasses had been filled by pouring slaves and we had toasted our good fortune, I addressed them. "Zenobia has been a thorn in the side of the Empire for years", I said. "Lord Odaenathus was a man of honour, a man who I am proud to have called a friend. He was a warrior-king without equal and remained humble in victory. But Zenobia is a scheming miscreant who gained her throne through spilling the blood of Odaenathus. Rome extended the hand of friendship, and in return she sunk her teeth into the flesh of the Empire and tore the ravaged limb from the body."

"Zenobia is of the darkness", Amr replied, slowly nodding his head. "She mourned the passing of her husband in the way of the tribes and convinced many that she had no part in his death."

I gestured for Amr to continue, as I wished to know what transpired after the Lord of Palmyra's demise.

"Lord Odaenathus united the tribes of the *Tanukh* under his banner", Amr said. "During the time of his rule, the clans of the desert were at peace with one another, but in the aftermath of his death, all changed. Many of the tribes believed Zenobia to be the reincarnation of the great Cleopatra, while others, including my uncle, suspected that she was to blame for Lord Odaenathus's murder. My people were divided along this line, with half of the tribes supporting Jadhima, and the other, Zenobia."

"War broke out and the trade routes became increasingly dangerous. Silk caravans from the East were attacked and the merchants slaughtered. Soon, the river of gold that flowed into the coffers of Palmyra slowed down to a trickle, impacting all in the land. Zenobia sent a scroll to my uncle, proposing that they unite Palmyra by marriage. Jadhima was fooled by her honeyed oaths and agreed to her request."

"Man who accepts word of enemy is doomed to death", Cai said.

Amr nodded. "I, too, cautioned Jadhima against it, but he told me that he was willing to risk his life so that peace may once more reign in the lands of the desert tribes."

"How did the witch kill him?" Hostilius asked brazenly.

"My uncle partook in a great feast prepared by Zenobia", Amr growled. "When he was under the spell of the vine, she opened his veins, drained his lifeblood into a golden vessel, and offered it as a sacrifice to Bel, her ghastly god."

"Come spring, the Empire's forces will march east to reclaim that which Zenobia has stolen", I said. "Do you wish to fight at our side, Lord Amr?"

"I do not wish, Lord Emperor", he replied. "I *insist* to be at your side when you engage the murderer of my uncle. The debt of blood needs to be repaid."

Amr took a sip from his cup to wet his throat. "I heard that Zenobia has sent ambassadors to the king of kings of the Sasanians", he said. "If the great king enters into an alliance with Palmyra, their combined army will be enormous and very difficult to overcome."

"Lord Shapur was an enemy", I admitted with a nod, "but I am well-acquainted with his son, Shahanshah Hormizd, who has taken the throne recently. I wrote to the great king when we started planning the campaign and he has given his oath that the Sasanian Empire will not meddle in the internal politics of Rome if I, in turn, gave my oath that the legions will remain west of the Euphrates."

Amr pursed his lips and it was clear that something was amiss. "You have not heard?" he asked.

I turned to Diocles for an answer, but all my aide could offer was a shrug.

"The day before I took ship to the West, I received tidings of King of Kings Hormizd's passing", he said. "Some say that he died of poison, but others believe it was dysentery."

I felt a stab of worry in the pit of my stomach, but managed to keep my composure. "Who has taken the reins in his stead?"

"Bahram, his elder brother", Amr replied, and by the look in his eye I knew that he harboured the same concerns that I did.

I took a deep breath and moved on to more practical issues. "How many men can you field?" I asked.

"The clans have ten thousand riders who wield the Parthian bow from the saddle", he replied.

It was fewer than I had hoped for, yet I kept my counsel.

"But", he added with a mischievous grin, "if you want them, the lords of the *Tanukh* can contribute five thousand mailed spearmen who are also capable of wielding horn bows. They, however, are not mounted on horses, but fight from the backs of camels that are clad in felt and boiled leather."

"No self-respecting lord of the Sea of Grass would be caught dead on the back of a camel", Gordas growled. "Besides, their foul smell makes cavalry skittish."

The Primus Pilus ignored the Hun's concerns. "Your camels are armoured?" he asked.

"My people value camels above horses", Amr replied. "We keep them safe because once the fighting is done, they will go back to doing what they do best - lugging heavy loads across the arid lands without the need for much feed or water."

"We will take them with pleasure", I said, drawing a scowl from Gordas. "And I look forward to fight by your side."

"What do you expect of me, Lord Emperor?" Adherbal asked.

"You will return to Africa Proconsularis with chests of coin so that you may bribe the chieftains of the Mauri, Musulamii, Gaetuli and Garamantes and convince them to give you the best of their seasoned warriors - men who know the ways of war and have fought by your side under the standard."

Adherbal inclined his head and pressed his right fist against his heart in the way of his people. "You honour me, Lord Emperor", he said. "I understand and I will obey."

Chapter 5 – Somnus

"Is there anything else that you would like to discuss?" I asked in the hope that we had worked our way through the long list of issues that, according to Diocles, required to be addressed prior to our departure.

"Almost done", my aide replied.

Hostilius shifted on the couch so that he could reach his cup. "That is what you said a watch ago."

Diocles issued a sigh and laid down his stylus next to his clay tablet, locking me in a piercing gaze that reminded of the way that Nik used to glare at me before I received a tongue lashing.

I scowled and gestured for him to continue.

"There might be, er…, issues in the city if the warehouses and pits run dry", Diocles said. "We will have to leave strict instructions for the prefect of the grain supply."

"Just make sure there are enough amphorae of wine in stock", Hostilius suggested. "Besides, most of the *head count* sell their free bread and oil to have more coin to spend at the drinking holes in the Subura, so they won't mind now, will they?"

"I believe that the campaign will be concluded before the stored grain is exhausted. Just in case the gods will it otherwise, I will leave most of the praetorians in Rome to ensure that order is maintained", I said. "The praetorian prefect, Julius Placidianus, is an honourable man who has earned my trust. I have no doubt that he will quickly stamp out any unrest."

"I agree", the Primus Pilus said. "I, for one, will feel much better if Placidianus stays in Rome to make sure that our families are safe."

"I don't think it is wise to depart on campaign with great fanfare", I said, and took a swallow of purple *basarangian*. "But we cannot leave without the blessing of the gods."

"You've got that right", Hostilius said. "The problem is once you involve priests, the whole city will know before the sun rises the next morning."

"We could perform sacrifices in the Temple of Janus", Diocles said. "Moving through the doors while chanting the verses will ensure that Fortuna smiles on our venture. The senator and his wife who are the keepers of the sacred rites will surely be discreet if that is your wish, Lord Emperor."

"Good. That's settled, then", Hostilius said. "Are we done?"

"No", Diocles replied, and moved on to the next item. "Only this week there were eight instances of bakers selling loaves weighing less than what the law states."

"Execute one of the culprits, that'll fix the problem", Hostilius said, dismissing the issue with a wave of a hand. "What else is on your list, Greek?"

Diocles rolled his eyes and traced his index finger down his tablet. "We need to address the rising price of eunuchs, the clothing of senatorial runners, and the use of silver leaf on the coaches of commoners."

"Is that all?" the Primus Pilus asked.

"The last item on the list is a plan of action to revive the viticulture in Northern Italia", my aide said.

Hostilius stood to leave. "Let's deal with that one before I get going", he said, and finished the wine in his cup in one long swallow. "My *ava* was in the wine business, so I can give you a few pointers."

"What about the escalating cost of eunuchs?" I asked.

"Unfortunately I've got urgent military matters to attend to", Hostilius replied. "But I will send Gordas up from the stables.

As far as I know, the Hun's got some strong views on the subject."

* * *

Two days later, after having concluded the ceremony in the temple of the two-faced Janus, my wife and I retired to our chambers for the evening.

"You must be careful, Lucius", Segelinde said once we were both in bed. "Zenobia is not the same as the enemies you have faced in the past."

I nodded, indicating that she should elaborate.

"Men are proud by nature, not willing to share glory with other men, but Zenobia is not constrained by her ego. She will not hesitate to trade glory for victory. You would do well not to underestimate her."

"She has already demonstrated her martial ability by capturing much of the East, as well as Aegypt", I said. "I will be vigilant when I meet her army on the field of blood."

She reached out and put a hand in mine. "You will have to do better than be on your guard", she said. "From what I have heard, the queen has little regard for honour. Zenobia will try to defeat you long before you reach the walls of Palmyra. She will foster an alliance with Hades himself to achieve her goals."

"How will I know who has sided with her?" I asked.

"All those who are not friends to Rome you must treat as if they are aligned with Zenobia", she said.

"That, my love, is a very long list", I said.

"True", she confessed, "but there is good news as well."

"And what is that?" I asked.

"You will not have to wait long for Zenobia's friends to reveal themselves", she said. "You are marching east the day after tomorrow, so they will not have any choice but to try and stop you along the way."

I did not doubt that Segelinde was right, but what I could not have imagined was how soon her words would come to fruition.

* * *

Although I was tired, Segelinde's words kept me from rest. I wondered whether my hubris had caused me to embark on a campaign that was doomed to fail. Had I underestimated Zenobia? Was my desire to reunite the Empire blinding me to the obvious? Should I not have waited another year to allow my weakened forces to rebuild their strength?

Sometime near the middle hour of the night, fatigue got the better of my concerns and I slipped into Somnus's comforting embrace.

Mounted on Kasirga, I thundered across the fallow fields of Roman Moesia at the head of a contingent of at least a thousand Illyrians. We passed the ruins of yet another ravaged farm, while all along the northern horizon tendrils of black smoke rose to the heavens.

"Come!" I shouted, and dug my heels into my stallion's sides. "We must catch the raiders before they cross the Mother River!"

I lowered myself in the saddle and gave Kasirga free rein.

My powerful horse easily outpaced the mounts of my men. The hoofbeats had hardly faded away when I became aware of something approaching from behind. The rhythm was that of a cantering horse, but the hooves struck the ground with the power of Vulcan's hammer, the beats reverberating through my skull.

I glanced to the right and for a moment I was blinded by the sun reflecting off burnished silver armour.

"Why are you in such a hurry?" the god asked, fixing me with a glare of his piercing blue eyes that shone with the brilliance of a thousand stars.

"I wish to overhaul the men who have ravaged my lands, lord", I replied. "And I need to catch them before they cross the river."

"Surely you can do that tomorrow", he said, and I believed that there was a mocking quality to his tone.

Before I could answer, Arash snapped his fingers and we were magically transported to the wide plains of the lands of my youth.

He reined in and Kasirga dutifully came to a halt beside the god's mount.

"How do the horse lords of the Sea of Grass deal with incursions into their lands?" he asked, his arms folded across the front of his saddle.

"The Scythians will chase the men who have wronged them until they are caught", I said. "Never mind whether they have to pursue them to the very ends of the earth."

Arash nudged his massive horse closer, and I was cowered by the overwhelming presence of the lord of the field of blood. He reached out and placed a comforting hand on my shoulder. "Then do not forget who you are, Eochar the Merciless."

I woke with Segelinde's hand resting on my shoulder. "Was it him?" she asked.

"Yes", I said, still in awe of the god.

"Did Arash the Avenger tell you what needs to be done?" she asked.

"Yes", I confirmed.

"I suggest you heed his words", she said, turned onto her other side and went back to sleep.

* * *

The following morning, Diocles, Hostilius, Gordas and I were making the final arrangements for the campaign when a messenger was brought into our presence.

The dusty cavalryman was glaringly unsure as to the decorum, and kneeled when he entered the room. I waved him to his feet and ordered a servant to hand him a cup of wine diluted with water.

He drank greedily, passed his cup back to the waiting pouring slave, and saluted in the way of the legions. "Decurion Tiberius Hispo, second *turma*, *Legio VII Claudia*, Lord Emperor", he said.

"Where do you serve?" I asked.

"I am stationed at Singidunum, lord, but we patrol the *limes* as far west as Sirmium", he said.

"Report, Decurion", I said.

"My unit intercepted a group of Scythians near the legionary fort of Singidunum", he said. "We took them to the legate because they carried a message from the queen of the Roxolani."

My aide stepped closer and accepted the scroll, which was adorned with a seal I immediately identified as my daughter's.

I held up a palm to stop Diocles from reading it. "When did you receive it, Decurion Hispo?" I asked.

"Five days ago, lord", he said.

"Make sure this man gets a good meal, wine from my cellar and a comfortable bed", I commanded a guard, and dismissed the messenger before waving the slaves, servants and attendants from the room.

I nodded to Diocles.

Queen Aritê to her father.

My lord, I write to you so that you may know that the army of the Crow has attacked and scattered the forces of the chieftains whom you allowed to settle on the plains of Oltenia, north of the Mother River. The warriors of Respa and Veducus have been defeated and thousands fled into the forests. The horde of the Crow is creeping towards the Pass of the Wolf - no doubt heading to the plains that we call home. Naulobates and I have no choice but to gather our forces and ride east to fight side by side with our allies. Only if the people of the horse stand together will we have a chance to defeat the dirt eaters. Where the River of the Oak Forests meets the Tibiscus, the three tribes will gather to make our final stand.

Although my husband and I have pledged our warriors for your campaign in the East, we cannot allow our people to be annihilated by the Goths.

I wish you well, Father. May Arash watch over you and give you victory in war.

"Bastard", Hostilius growled.

Given Segelinde's words and the vision I had received from the god, the tidings from my daughter came as no surprise.

Gordas must have noticed the knowing look on my face. "You have been forewarned?" he asked.

"Segelinde believes that Zenobia has courted the enemies of Rome", I replied, my answer not quite convincing the Hun.

"It may well be", Diocles said, "but the fact of the matter is that without the warriors of our allies north of the Danube, we will have twenty thousand fewer horse archers."

"Maybe we could recruit more horsemen from amongst the wild tribes in Africa?" Hostilius ventured.

"It will take many months, even years", I said.

"Should we delay the start of the campaign?" my aide asked. "What use is it to march to war with an insufficient force?"

"I suggest we place our trust in the gods", I said, leaned back, and took a sip from my cup.

Hostilius narrowed his eyes. "What aren't you telling us, Domitius?"

"We cannot take on the armies of Palmyra without the Scythians", I said. "Neither can the Empire afford to delay the campaign until our grain runs out."

"What do you suggest?" the Primus Pilus asked.

"Tomorrow we will go north to rendezvous with Vibius and his Illyrians at Aquileia", I said. "Meanwhile, I want an urgent missive dispatched to the commanders of all legions on the Danube."

"Every one?" Diocles asked. "There are ten legions stationed along the length of the river."

"Every single one between the mouth of the Danube and as far west as Vindobona", I confirmed.

"What are your commands to the legates?" my aide asked.

"The three least experienced cohorts must remain on garrison duty", I said. "The seven best cohorts of each legion must march for Sirmium within two days", I said.

"But how will they protect our borders against incursions if they are undermanned?" my aide asked.

"I am tired of receiving news that the tribes have crossed the Mother River into Roman lands", I said, and slammed a balled fist onto an open palm. "We will take the legions north into the lands of the Goths and deal with them so harshly that they will cease to be a threat for three lifetimes. Dead men do not make incursions."

I could not help but notice that both Gordas and Hostilius were suppressing grins.

* * *

When we arrived in Aquileia eight days later, we found ten thousand horsemen camped outside the walls.

"Looks like he beat us to it", Hostilius said as we neared the sprawling camp on the bank of the Natiso, close to where it spilled its water into the large lagoon.

We left the contingent of mounted praetorians at the city gate and advanced towards the base of the Illyrians. On the outskirts of the camp a unit of veteran horsemen were performing drills. I had recruited and trained many of them myself and after they called out greetings, they fell in ahead of us to provide an impromptu escort of sorts.

The guards at the headquarters saluted in the way of the legions and parted to allow us to enter.

We found our friend pacing around the room, dictating to a scribe. "It is good to see you", I said, and embraced Vibius like one would a brother.

"It is good to see you too, Lucius", he replied, a genuine smile on his face.

"Are the Illyrians ready?" Hostilius asked.

"Ready enough to get to Aquileia ahead of you", Vibius jested.

"We had to accommodate the praetorians", Gordas replied.

"Jests aside", Vibius continued. "Thanks to Diocles's consignments of gold, my men are better armed and armoured than they have ever been. The new recruits lack battle experience, but it is something that cannot be trained."

"Domitius has made arrangements to remedy that, I believe", the Primus Pilus said, which caused Vibius to frown.

"We are taking a detour on our way to Palmyra", I replied, which only served to deepen my friend's wrinkled brow.

"We're going to cross the Danube and attack the Crow and his Goths", Hostilius explained.

"Ten thousand Roman horsemen against more than a hundred thousand barbarians", Vibius mused while thinking on my words. "I guess we've faced worse odds."

I slapped my friend's back. "I've called for the help of the legions", I revealed.

"How many legions?"

"All of them", Hostilius replied.

Chapter 6 – Meal

On the morrow, Hostilius, Diocles and I led the Illyrians north into the passes. Cai chose to ride with the pack mules while Gordas accompanied Vibius, who had sought his advice on some issue or other concerning the horses.

"It will take three days for the messenger to reach Vindobona in Pannonia, which is the home base of the legion stationed farthest to the west, and six days for our missive to arrive at Oescus near the mouth of the Danube", Diocles said.

"How long for those legions to get to Sirmium?" Hostilius asked.

"Twenty days from Vindobona and seventeen from Oescus", my aide replied. "If you add the time they require to mobilise, the last of the legions will arrive twenty-eight days from today, maybe even sooner. We, however, will be in Sirmium within fifteen days."

"So, to answer your question, tribune", Diocles concluded, "we will definitely have time to spend a night in Siscia. Besides, it is along the route."

"As if you don't want to, Greek", Hostilius countered.

"Let's just say that the emperor craves after his favourite dish", I said.

"Which is gossip, I assume", Diocles ventured.

"Of course", I replied.

* * *

We arrived in Siscia two weeks later. While Vibius and his commanders set up camp, the rest of us entered the city.

"Lord Emperor", Hortensius called out while I was still in the saddle, walking my horse towards the stables. Our host waddled towards us, all the while shouting for a stable hand to attend to the honoured guests. "Forgive me, Lord Emperor", the portly innkeeper said, and went down onto one knee, a toil which took considerable effort.

"My apologies, lord. I am breaking in new Germani stable slaves", he explained when he had caught his breath.

"You should have rather forked out a few silvers more and procured Scythians", I said as I swung down from the saddle. "They are much better when it comes to caring for horses."

"I know, lord. I know", Hortensius admitted, "but unlike Germani who can be tamed, Scythians are notoriously difficult to domesticate."

"True", I replied. Still holding Intikam's reins, I extended a hand to assist our host to gain his feet.

"Thank you, lord, I am afraid I am not getting any younger", he said while trying to smooth the wrinkles from his tunic.

"Nonsense", I replied. "You look as vigorous as you did ten seasons ago, my friend."

It was no lie. Hortensius appeared to be in no worse shape than he had been years before, mayhap because of his plump frame.

The innkeeper beamed at the compliment and my chosen form of address.

"There will be no charge for the emperor and his entourage. No charge at all", he proclaimed.

I nodded my appreciation.

"I must confess that I have heard rumours of a campaign", he said, lowering his voice. "For that reason, I have been expecting your lordship to grace us with your presence. Knowing that you appreciate the finer things in life, I have taken the liberty of procuring ingredients that are, er…, suited to your exalted status."

"I hope that includes chicken", Hostilius said from the other side of the courtyard.

"A host worth his salt never reveals the composition of the menu before the feast has commenced", the innkeeper replied.

"Just make sure there's Parthian chicken on the table", Hostilius warned.

Hortensius pursed his lips and raised an open palm. "I cannot make a promise that I may not be able to keep", he scolded the Primus Pilus, but smiled to show that it was in jest. "But what I can do, tribune, is give you my oath that you will not be disappointed."

* * *

Once Vibius and Cai had joined us, we visited the private baths of the inn to rid ourselves of the sweat and grime of the day's ride. After stripping off our armour and washing away most of the dust in the warm room, we moved on to the *caldarium*.

I felt my aches and pains slowly dissipate as I immersed my tired sinews in the hot water.

"Tell us plan, Lucius of Da Qin", Cai said from where he was lounging beside me.

We were interrupted by a servant bearing a tray. Without speaking a word he handed each of a us a finely crafted glass goblet filled with iced wine.

Before I replied to Cai's question, I savoured a sip of the golden liquid that tasted of fresh baked bread and walnuts. "I believe that my daughter is right and that the Crow is on his way to the fertile homeland of the Scythians", I said. "It makes sense that from Oltenia the enemy will move north into the passes and then east along the Tibiscus Valley, passing by the Iron Gates to reach the plains of the Roxolani and the Yazyges."

"Sounds about right", Hostilius said, and chugged the wine in his glass.

"In any event", I continued, "we need to halt the advance of the horde before they spill onto the open plains west of Dacia to massacre the Scythians. There, in the Valley of the Tibiscus, I plan to trap the Crow between the hammer and the anvil."

"Who will be the anvil that will halt the Goths' advance?" the Primus Pilus asked, and gestured for the slave to refill his glass.

"The Scythians will be swept aside by the sheer numbers of the horde of the Crow", I said. "Five Roman legions should be able to hold them."

"Remember that the legions are not at full strength", Diocles pointed out. "Five legions of seven cohorts each barely make up twenty thousand men."

"Your concerns are valid", I said. "But we will have our barbarian allies fighting by our side."

"And the second force - the hammer?" Vibius asked.

"The remaining five legions and the Illyrians will cross the Danube at Drobeta and advance north along the Iron Gates to emerge in the valley of the Tibiscus, behind the advancing Goths. They will be the hammer that will crush the Crow."

"And where will you be?" Hostilius asked.

"I will be riding with the Scythians to harass the horde as they move towards the lands of my mother's people", I said.

"The rightful place of the emperor is at the head of his legions", Hostilius stated.

"Someone recently told me that I am a Scythian and that I should never forget it", I replied.

"Who?" Vibius asked.

"The god of war and fire", I said, climbed out of the hot water and lay down to subject myself to the ministrations of a strigil-wielding slave.

* * *

Under the watchful eye of our host, a troop of kitchen slaves carefully placed four extraordinary large silver cloches onto the low table. Once the wine had been decanted into two exquisitely decorated craters, he waved the servants away and filled our goblets with the help of an ornate dipper crafted in the image of a stork.

"Which one is the *falernian*?" Hostilius asked.

Hortensius ignored the Primus Pilus and placed an open palm on the wine crater on his right, calling to mind the way one would introduce a favourite son. "The *caecuban* is from the vineyards overlooking the poplar swamps near Capua. It is the cool breeze that blows in from the Tyrrhenian that endows the wine with such delicate aromas."

The innkeeper paused for a span of thirty heartbeats. Some would say it was for effect, but I believe that he was forced to take a moment to gather himself.

My suspicion was confirmed when he said, his voice hoarse with emotion, "It is the last of a batch I have kept safe for twenty years."

He retracted his right hand and placed his left palm on the other vessel. "The vineyards that produced this *setinian* overlook the Appian Forum. It is said that the divine Augustus favoured it above all others. I traded eight amphorae of *falernian* to get my hands on this special vintage."

For once I was at a loss for words, but Hostilius muttered some comment or other like, "We will decide for ourselves", which Hortensius shrugged off before continuing.

"I know that you are warriors on your way to war so there will be no dainties to compliment the wine", he said. "I give you meat so that you may fortify your bodies for the upcoming campaign."

He lifted the lid of the first cloche with an accompanying flourish. "Whole roasted milk-fed lamb, boned and stuffed with gravy, wine, honey and fresh dates."

Even the Primus Pilus was silenced by the aroma that filled the room.

He lifted the second lid. "Whole roasted suckling pig, boned and stuffed with figs drenched in raisin wine and spiced with pepper and lovage."

Hortensius met Hostilius's gaze, a smile playing around the corners of his mouth. "And for my special friend, chicken prepared in the way of the Parthians", he said, and opened a cloche to reveal half a dozen fowl drenched in a dark aromatic sauce.

Our host nodded his head in Gordas's direction. "Last but not least, a few delicacies for those amongst us whose tastes are more orientated to the exotic", he said, and removed the final lid, revealing two serving plates filled with steaming dishes. "Pig liver marinated in mead, milk and eggs, and stewed in peppered wine", he said, and gestured to the other dish, "and boiled sheep lungs filled with egg, honey and spices."

"I have called down the blessing of my household gods on the food", he said, bowed low, and made to leave.

I stopped him with a raised palm. "Hortensius", I said. "You have proven yourself to be a loyal and trustworthy friend not only to me and my companions, but also to my father. Tonight, you will join us and partake in the feast."

"Lord, I am here to serve you", he said. "I am not worthy to dine with the favourite of Mars."

"Do not disobey a direct order of your emperor, innkeeper", Hostilius growled, and took a swig from the priceless *caecuban*.

I moved up, closer to Cai, indicating that Hortensius should join me on the couch.

"If word gets out, and it will, I will be famous throughout all of the land", the innkeeper muttered, and hesitantly reclined beside me.

* * *

By the time that we had sampled all the culinary delights, Hortensius's tongue had been loosened.

"What news is there from north of the Danube?" I asked as I leaned over to tear a piece of crackling from the roasted pig.

"I have a friend, a merchant, who vends wine to the savages up and down the Alutus, lord", he said. "He's had a river boat and the same two Thracian slaves for as long as I care to remember. Only two days ago he returned from up north and spent a night here in the inn. He is my age, and because of what happened he is considering taking his stash of coin and settling down somewhere in the south, probably on a farm in Dalmatia."

"So what has unsettled him so?" Vibius asked from across the table.

"One of his slaves took a shaft in the neck and did not return, while the other made it home and is fighting a corrupted arrow wound. My friend narrowly escaped with his life", the innkeeper said, and took another sip of *setinian*. "They were attacked by mounted bowmen - most probably allies of the one they call the Crow."

"Does he know which tribe the attackers belong to?" Diocles asked.

"I did not ask", Hortensius replied.

"Then on the morrow we will put the question to him ourselves", Gordas said, for the first time that evening more interested in the conversation than in the liver and lungs.

Chapter 7 – Merchant (October 271 AD)

Judging by his reaction when he was escorted into our presence, it was evident that the vendor harboured concerns regarding our motives.

"Lord Emperor", the merchant said once he had gained his feet, "I can assure you that I have the highest regard for the laws of the Empire."

Hostilius narrowed his eyes. "That's not what we're interested to know, but since you've mentioned it - I've spent years north of the Danube and I'm yet to meet a merchant who trades in Barbaricum and doesn't keep a chest of second-hand weapons hidden under a goatskin somewhere in the back of his wagon. Every vendor knows that savages covet Roman iron even more than they love our wine."

"I have never sold weapons to our enemies, tribune", the merchant insisted. "Although, on occasion, I may have used an old rusted sword or dagger to lubricate the palm of a chieftain."

"Of course", the Primus Pilus replied.

"Tell us of the men who attacked you, trader", Gordas said.

"The warriors were bearded brutes mounted on steppe horses and armed with horn bows", he said. "Their torsos were covered in scale and their heads protected by conical helmets."

"That's what most Scythians look like", Hostilius sighed, and turned his head to address me. "Probably a handful of Yazyges or Carpiani bandits if you ask me."

"Anything more specific?" I asked the merchant.

"Their faces and exposed limbs were covered in blue-green tattoos", he replied.

I shrugged. "It is the way of many tribes."

"Maybe this will help", he said, and extracted the back end of a broken arrow from a leather pouch attached to his waist. "This is the shaft that stole the life of my slave", he said.

Gordas took it in his fist. He inspected the bone nock and ran a finger across the feather fletching. While he studied the patterns inked into the wood, his countenance became increasingly sombre.

Eventually he handed back the shaft to the merchant and his eyes met mine. "North of the Dark Sea lie endless open plains bordered by putrid swamplands", he said. "The forests farther to the north are infested with tribes who fear the light and choose to serve their dark gods in the land of eternal shadow."

"The people of the Sea of Grass avoid the shadow dwellers", Gordas continued, "and the forest people never venture onto the plains. But at the edge of the trees, where there are neither forests nor grasslands, a tribe of bastards have made a home for themselves. They till the earth like Germani, ride like Scythians, and grow rich by trading with both the horsemen of the plains as well as the hunters of the greenwood." The Hun lifted the arrow while running a finger across the fletching. "Only the Taifali use the tail feathers of waterfowl. Unlike the other tribes of the plains, they fashion their shafts from birch and decorate them with the shapes of the forest."

"Never heard of them", Hostilius said, no doubt concerned because of Gordas's grim demeanour. "Are they feared warriors?"

"The Urugundi do not fear them", he replied offhandedly.

What Gordas failed to add was that the Huns feared no one.

"Good to hear", the Primus Pilus said.

But the Hun was not through. "What they lack in skill, they make up for in numbers", he said. "If the Taifali have come under the dominion of the Crow, we will be facing many thousands of horsemen armed with the bow."

* * *

To cater for the large contingent of horses, we took the southern route out of Siscia, heading for Marsonia. The Roman road followed the course of the Savus, which meant that it took two days longer to arrive before the walls of Sirmium. We found that the legions based in Singidunum and Viminacium, the *IV Flavia Felix* and *VII Claudia*, had beaten us to it and were already camped on the bank of the river, upstream of the city.

I halted at the track heading towards the legions, intent on inspecting the camps.

Divining my intentions, Hostilius reined in beside me. "It's not your job anymore, Domitius", he said. "Besides, I'm better at it."

"Take Diocles along", I said, conceded with a nod, and passed the Primus Pilus my ivory rod of imperial authority.

Hostilius, in turn, handed the sceptre to Diocles. "I don't need it", he said, and started down the path. "You can use it to pull rank if you want to, Greek."

Diocles rolled his eyes, accepted the carved ivory baton and secreted it away in a pouch attached to his saddle before following the Primus Pilus to the gates of the nearest camp.

* * *

In the days following our arrival, Sirmium became a hive of activity. Almost every day a legion arrived at the gates, until ten days later, ten sprawling camps lined the northern bank of the Savus, upstream of the city.

I spent my days briefing the legates of the legions and resolving disputes, which, I believe, are unavoidable when so many thousands of battle-hardened soldiers descend upon a city. I had just delivered another verdict when Hostilius stormed into my quarters and poured himself a cup, which he chugged. "We have to march tomorrow, Domitius", he said, "or there will be no one left in the legions who hasn't been striped by the lash."

"Give the order", I said, sharing the Primus Pilus's frustration. "We leave at first light."

The following morning the legions broke camp. We said our goodbyes to Vibius and Diocles and watched them lead the Illyrians and five legions east, heading for the valley of the Iron Gates, the age-old route into Dacia. Shortly after, we led the remaining five legions towards a ford in the Danube.

* * *

Three days later, Hostilius, Cai, Gordas and I watched from the ramparts of Rittium as thousands of legionaries made their way across the shallows. The Roman fort was built on an elevated embankment to overlook a ford, just upriver of where the Tibiscus spilled its waters into the Danube.

"Are you going to war against the Scythians, Lord Emperor?" Gallonius, the prefect of the auxiliary cohort asked. He commanded a mixed infantry and cavalry unit recruited from Chalcis in Bithynia on the southern shores of the Dark Sea.

"No", I replied in Greek. "We are on our way to render assistance to the barbarian horsemen."

"Lord?" he asked, clearly confused.

"We will be facing the horde of the Goths", I said. "They are moving west through the lands of the people of the horse."

At the mention of the name of the tribe, a sneer appeared on the prefect's face. Absentmindedly he reached for his ivory talisman of the axe-bearing god, Jupiter Dolichenus, that adorned his bull-like neck. "Goths murdered my family when they raided Bithynia years ago, lord. Many of my men have similar scores to settle", he said. "Will you not take us with you?"

"We will be facing many thousands, prefect", I said, and gestured to the two dozen bolt throwers lining the walls. "If the Goths break through our lines, I expect you and the brave men of the *First Chalcidenorum Cohort* to prevent them from crossing the ford."

Prefect Gallonius set his jaw and saluted in the way of the legions. "You can count on me and my men, Lord Emperor", he said. "I understand, and will obey."

* * *

We kept to the western bank of the Tibiscus as we made our way north onto the great plain, following the dirt tracks that the men of the tribes had used since time immemorial.

For four days we traversed the hinterland, guided north and east by the river. Apart from almost twenty thousand pairs of legionary hobnailed boots grinding away at the dirt, it was eerily quiet on the plains. There were no travellers on the road and neither did we encounter the usual warbands of mounted warriors patrolling their lands.

Shortly after sunrise on the fifth day, a cold northerly breeze picked up. It gusted straight into our faces, which made talking difficult, and there was little of the usual banter. I rode in silence, my thoughts dwelling on my sword brother, Kniva, and how the Crow had treacherously murdered him. For years I had prayed to Arash to give me vengeance. Had the god finally answered my pleas? Or was I leading the legions to their doom?

Over the course of the morning the wind increased in intensity. Fortunately, the track which followed the left bank of the river slowly gave way to the right, until we were travelling almost due east, sheltered from the worst of the blow by a low ridge to the north.

"I wonder how Vibius and the Greek are getting on", Hostilius said when we were out of the worst of the storm.

"The Illyrians and the other five legions should be at Drobeta on the Danube by now, entering the Iron Gates", I said, and pulled my fur cloak tight around my shoulders in response to a freezing gust. "If the weather holds, it will take them two weeks to get through the pass." I stole a glance at the darkening sky. "I suggest we pray to Fortuna that this blow doesn't draw in early snow from the north."

"How far to where the tribes are camped?" Hostilius asked.

Before I could offer a reply, an outrider appeared at the top of the ridge, galloping towards us. He was intercepted by a handful of praetorians, who escorted him into my presence. The decurion saluted, and I gestured for him to fall in alongside me.

"The tribesmen are camped five miles upstream, lord", he said. "It is close to where another river spills into the Tibiscus."

"What are their numbers?" I asked.

"As many as fifteen times a thousand, lord", he replied, and asked, "Are we to conceal our presence from the barbarians, lord?"

"No", I replied, and dismissed him with a wave of a hand.

When he had gone, Gordas steered his horse abreast of mine. "You have seen them too, Eochar?" he asked, clearly surprised at my level of awareness.

"No", I admitted, "but we are five miles from my daughter's camp. You are the one who taught her the ways of war, so I am sure that we've had eyes on us for at least a watch." I studied the surroundings, but was none the wiser. "Where are they?" I asked.

"Concealed in the shrubbery near the bent oak over yonder", Gordas replied.

"Bring them to me", I said.

The Hun grinned and nudged his mare to a canter.

Chapter 8 – Tillers

"Do you know who I am?" I asked the two Roxolani scouts who followed Gordas from the undergrowth.

"You are the father of Queen Aritê, lord", the nearest man replied, inclining his head to show respect. "The one they call Eochar the Merciless."

"Return to your camp and inform the queen that I will seek her out soon", I said.

As soon as the scouts had gone, I turned Intikam's head to the north.

"Where are we going?" Hostilius asked.

"I do not wish for the legions to draw water downstream of where fifteen thousand barbarians and the gods know how many horses perform their ablutions", I replied. "Four miles to the north there is another river, the Bega. It feeds the putrid swamplands to the west, but here, close to the passes, it runs clear."

"Good point", Hostilius replied, his frown indicating his annoyance at not thinking about it himself.

We arrived on the banks of the Bega at the start of the last watch of the afternoon.

Once I had approved the location of the legionary camp and the engineers and *immunes* had started marking out the ditches, Gordas and I rode towards the barbarian camp, leaving the Primus Pilus to keep an eye on the works.

"Lord Eochar!" a warrior exclaimed as I walked my horse into the sprawling camp of the Scythians. The hulking Roxolani oathsworn approached slowly, pressed his right fist against his armoured chest, and inclined his head in the way of the people of the horse.

"Well met, Burdukhan. You look as formidable as ever", I said.

"I am on my way to inform the queen of your arrival, lord", he replied. "She and Lord Naulobates are leading a hunting party in the southern hills." He gestured towards the interior of the camp. "But the kings of the Yazyges and Carpiani are both present. Although they are bathing, they are expecting you."

"Bathing in the river?" I asked, perplexed at the strange behaviour.

"No, lord", Burdukhan replied. "In the tent, of course."

* * *

As was the way of the tribes, the tents of the kings and their closest ringmen were situated at the centre of the sprawling camp. The two Scythian axemen flanking the door of the smoke tent stood aside when they noticed our approach.

Gordas remained with the guards, while I pushed aside the thick felt flap and ducked into the gloom. The pungent, woody scent of hemp seed vapour overwhelmed my senses and I burst into a coughing fit, much to the amusement of the two men seated beside the glowing embers.

Thiaper set aside his cup, gained his feet with a sigh, and embraced me like one would a brother. "Come, my friend", he said. "Join us."

"Well met, Lord Banadas", I said, and inclined my head at the greybeard king of the Yazyges seated across from Thiaper.

"We thought it prudent to purify our bodies before we meet the Goths in battle", Banadas said while Thiaper poured me a cup.

"The priests say that it eases the passing across the bridge of stars", the Carpiani king added as I accepted wine from his hand.

"Why are you expecting to cross the river?" I asked.

"Our scouts have laid eyes on the army of the Crow as it moves through the eastern passes", Banadas said. "Their campfires light up the mountains for twenty miles like a giant glowing serpent that has wrapped its coils around the peaks. Never before have they seen such a host."

I pictured the size of the horde in my mind's eye. Were it not for the calming effect of the hemp, I would have felt the grip of panic. Just to be sure, I took a long draught from my cup. "Let us not talk of war, then", I said. "Let us reminisce about the best of our memories."

"Then I have nothing to talk about," Thiaper replied sheepishly. "All my best memories are of war."

We exchanged glances, realising the truth of his words.

Banadas was the first to burst out laughing, and soon Thiaper and I followed suit.

* * *

"I expected your forces to number more than fifteen thousand", I said after I had welcomed Aritê and Naulobates to my tent.

"The Roxolani and Heruli contributed five thousand warriors each", she said. "We dared not leave our winter camp undefended in case the northern allies of the Goths attack during our absence."

I nodded, as it was a sound strategy. "So the Yazyges and the Carpiani have only brought five thousand warriors in total?" I asked.

King Banadas of the Yazyges led three thousand warriors into camp, but Thiaper only two thousand.

"The Carpiani should be able to field at least five thousand horse archers, if not more", Gordas said.

"Did Thiaper tell you about their encounter with the Goth horde?" my daughter asked.

"I did not wish to talk of war", I said.

She raised an eyebrow. "When the Carpiani departed Transsilvania, they rode south through the valley of the Marisus, where they left a thousand men to garrison the hillforts that guard the narrow corridor that gives access to their lands."

"A wise decision", Hostilius said.

"Rather than journey directly to our place of meeting, Thiaper decided to be bold and take his army south. His scouts had told him that, although numerous, the Goth horde is a slow-moving beast that is ripe to be ambushed."

"The Carpiani lay in wait in the Valley of the Rabon, just north of the Pass of the Wolf, and fell upon the Goths while they crossed the river. They struck with the speed of a viper and killed many, almost five hundred", she said. "Before the Goths could regroup and launch a counterattack, Thiaper led his men back the way they had come."

"Why are you frowning, Father?" my daughter asked.

"Because, from what you have told me, I find it difficult to fault the Carpiani king's actions", I said.

She issued a snort that could have meant anything. "The Crow had expected an ambush and he, in turn, sent a force along a nearby ravine to block the escape of the Carpiani. Almost half of Thiaper's warriors were slaughtered."

It was not good news.

"Worse than the loss of the warriors are the tales of the survivors", Naulobates said. "To hide their shame, they have inflated the prowess of the enemy."

"At least now, with your arrival, the morale of the men is much improved, even though we still face overwhelming odds", my daughter added.

"I believe that twenty thousand Roman legionaries would have that effect", Hostilius said with pride in his voice.

"That is not the reason, tribune", Naulobates said, and accepted a cup from a servant.

Hostilius must have frowned.

"There is a rumour spreading through our camp that yesterday, when Lord Eochar was told of King Thiaper's defeat at the hand of the enemy, booming laughter could be heard from inside the kings' tent", the Herulian said. "Some swear that Arash himself had joined you and filled your hearts with iron."

"There no smoke without fire", Cai remarked.

My daughter rolled her eyes, but before she could issue a retort I changed the subject. "I wish to behold the army of the Crow with my own eyes", I said. "Do you know where they are?"

"Yes", she said, and stood to prepare. "Pack seven days' rations and leave your Roman guards in the camp."

* * *

A third of a watch later, Gordas, Naulobates, Aritê and I rode from camp.

"Tonight we will sleep near the Roman stronghold of Tibiscum", my daughter said once we were underway. "After Rome had withdrawn its legions, the warriors of Respa and Veducus garrisoned the fort."

"Are they still there?" I asked.

"The scouts report that the fort has since been abandoned", Naulobates replied. "Everything of value has been looted. Even the gates have been burned to extract the iron."

I sighed.

Gordas must have noticed my reaction. "If you had not given up Dacia, our bleached bones would have littered the battlefield at Naissus", he growled. "There is always a price to pay for victory."

"The Empire should never have set foot in Dacia in the first place", Aritê said. "Nik always said that it was Emperor Traianus's lust for glory and treasure that caused him to cross the Danube. After the loot taken from Decebalus had been spent on lark tongues and acrobats, the Empire started to pay the price trying to defend Dacia's borders."

I had long before made peace with my decision and did not wish to be dragged into a discussion about it. "Isn't the fort on the far bank?" I asked, suggesting that we should cross to the other side of the river.

My daughter shook her head. "Do not be fooled", she said. "Here, on the plains, the Tibiscus is deep and treacherous. We will be able to cross upstream, near the fort, where there is a fork in the river. The Bistra flows in from the east, from where the Crow will come. The Tibiscus points the way south, to the Gates of Iron."

* * *

The sun was rapidly descending towards the western horizon when we eventually arrived at the confluence of the rivers where the Bistra spilled into the Tibiscus. On the far banks, a mile or two distant, the abandoned stone battlements of a Roman fort were visible above the treetops.

Naulobates indicated the dark forest of lime and ash on the southern bank. "It will be better if we spend the night between the two rivers", he said. "Few scouts will cross unknown waters in the dead of night."

Soon, he guided us across a shallow submerged bank of gravel and sand to the southern bank of the Bistra. While Naulobates set up the tents near the water's edge, Arîtê secured the horses. Gordas moved along the riverbank in search of something for the pot, leaving me to gather wood for a fire.

Two hundred paces into the gloom I came across the largest lime I had ever laid eyes on. In awe of the forest giant, I paused for a span of heartbeats to run a palm across the ridges in the grey-brown bark before I continued deeper into the greenwood, only to stumble upon an even larger lime. I squinted into the darkening woods and noticed the line of massive trees. Like an army of giants waiting on a command, they stood stark and silent.

The wind whispered in the canopy above, and a sudden chill travelled down my spine.

From deep within the thicket I heard the rustle of leaves and a thin mist spilled from amongst the lichen and moss-covered trunks, its wispy tendrils creeping across the forest floor like a serpent from the scrolls of old.

A dark, stooped figure materialised from the fog and slowly limped closer. *"Why is your fist clamped around the hilt of your blade, Roman?"* the old lady of the forest hissed. *"Do you wish to wield it?"*

I released my grip on the pommel of my sword.

The crone stopped five paces from me, the fog following her like an obedient hound shadowing its master. Apart from a gnarled hand gripping a linden staff and lank grey hair protruding from underneath the hood of her cloak, her features were obscured.

"That which was never yours to take, you have returned", she said, and I believe I discerned a hint of amusement in her voice. *"Have you come to claim it back again?"*

"I have come to assist the people of the land beyond the forest", I replied. "If we do not defeat the invaders, the people will trade one master for another. And the Goths are harsh overlords."

She tilted her head and I suspected that the reason was to listen to the whispers of the earth and the trees. Slowly her purple-black lips parted and morphed into a sneer. *"You are right, Roman. They come"*, she said, and shrugged her bony shoulders.

"Can they be defeated?" I asked.

"Why would I help you, Roman?" she sneered.

"The invaders are tillers of the earth. Your groves will soon fall prey to their axes", I said, and gestured to the ancient trees around us. "Here, between the rivers, they will plant millet and einkorn once their fires have burned the boles from the earth."

The last rays of the setting sun pierced the canopy, illuminating her old, weathered face, and I noticed sadness in her rheumy eyes. Without a word she turned her back to me and started to limp back the way she had come.

Before the veil of white enveloped her, she paused. *"Look to the ancients, Scythian"*, she croaked. *"They will show you the way."*

And then she was gone.

Chapter 9 – Kindling

"There is not enough wood to last throughout the night, Father", Aritê reprimanded me once Gordas had lit the cooking fire. "The wolves will come once the flames fade away."

My son-in-law stood, took a flaming brand from the fire and hefted his axe. "I will get more", he said.

Just then, a faraway screech emanated from the dark wood, one I doubted belonged to an animal.

I waved him back to his seat. "Not tonight", I cautioned. "Out there in the darkness are creatures far more dangerous than wolves. Besides, they will not bother us this night."

For a span of heartbeats Naulobates eyed the shifting shadows cast by the flickering flames. "I will not gainsay the man who walks in the shadow of Arash", he said, and reached for an amphora instead.

Gordas weaved another willow branch through a plucked pheasant and carefully positioned the fowl beside the others, close to the edge of the fire. "You spoke with the one who commands the trees?" he asked, a hand searching for his wolf's foot amulet.

I nodded.

"Did she offer you advice?" he asked.

"She spoke in riddles", I replied, and accepted a cup from Naulobates.

* * *

On the morrow we followed the Bistra east along a valley bordered by steep slopes covered in near-impenetrable forests of pine, rowan and larch. Late morning, the valley narrowed and the slopes closed in around the Roman road. Ten miles down the track, Gordas raised an open palm and I called a halt.

The Hun sniffed the breeze. "Fire", he said. "It is the stench of a town burning."

He had hardly uttered the words when half a dozen fingers of thick black smoke billowed from the eastern horizon.

"Ulpia Traiana is ablaze", Aritê said. "The city where Traianus settled his veterans after the Dacian wars."

"It appears that we have found the Goths", I said, and nudged my stallion off the cobbles and into the undergrowth.

For two miles we struggled through the forest until the valley flared and the slopes became less dense. It afforded us a view across the large plain created by the junction of three vales. We dismounted, tethered our horses and stealthily made our way towards a rocky outcrop farther down the hillside.

My daughter pointed towards the left. "That road leads to Transsilvania, the land beyond the forest", she said, then indicated straight ahead. "The eastern pass leads to Oltenia."

We hardly paid Aritê any heed because less than half a mile below us, the warriors of the Crow were putting the great city of Ulpia Traiana to the torch. The sprawling barbarian camp was spread out across the flat ground, almost filling up the entire plain. Tens of thousands were ravaging the city, while others were still toiling to bring the last of the carts and wagons through the eastern passes.

"How many are there?" I asked.

"At least a hundred times a thousand", Naulobates said. "But one hundred and twenty thousand is probably more accurate."

In silence we watched as the flames leaped to the heavens, the savages destroying in an eyewink that which the Romans had built up over two hundred long years.

"The Crow has come in force", Gordas whispered, and gestured to the many large banners in the barbarian camp.

"Do you see the standard of the Taifali?" I asked, as I noticed few horsemen amongst the host sacking the city.

Gordas studied the sea of tribesman. "No", he said. "The Taifali are not there."

I issued a sigh. "At least we will not be facing horse archers", I said.

We watched in grim fascination while the horde devoured the Roman settlement until I could bear it no longer. "Come", I said. "I have seen enough."

* * *

There was no need for caution so we thundered back the way we had come, returning to the same place where we had camped the previous evening.

"Do you need help with the firewood, Lord Eochar?" Naulobates asked as I strolled off.

"Not tonight", I replied, hiding my scowl.

Not long after, I returned with a large haul of thick oak branches, silencing my critics. While Gordas butchered the roe deer that had fallen to a well-aimed arrow, I split the wood and lit a cooking fire. Once the carcass was roasting above the flames and Naulobates had filled our cups, we congregated around the fire.

"We will not be able to check the advance of the Goths", Aritê said. "Thirty thousand warriors cannot hold back four times their number."

"How long until the enemy arrives at our camp near the two rivers?" I asked no one in particular.

"I have seen their ox wagons", Gordas said. "They will struggle to advance more than twelve miles a day, which means that it will take them five days to arrive at the place where the legions are camped. If the queen's horsemen harass the advancing horde, add two more days, three at best."

"We will spend most of tomorrow on the road", I mused, "which leaves five or six days to prepare."

"Where the valley of the Tibiscus spills onto the great plain, the approach is bordered by two rivers", Naulobates said. "The Tibiscus to the south and the Tissus to the north. We can make our stand there, with our flanks anchored against the banks."

"The legions could build fortifications between the rivers", I suggested.

"Underneath the thin layer of fertile black soil, the earth is hard as rock", Naulobates said. "It will take the legions weeks, if not months, to dig a trench."

"We dug the trenches for our camp easily enough", I countered.

"You made camp on the banks of the Bega where the earth is dark and soft", Naulobates replied, sounding much like a farmer.

"Did you try to till the earth?" Gordas sneered, clearly disgusted at the wolf warrior's revelation.

"Early in the season the queen and I led a warband in pursuit of a raiding party of hillmen - bandits who make their home in the mountains to the south", he said. "We caught up with them between the rivers."

My daughter placed a gentle hand on Naulobates's armoured shoulder. "I remember, my love", she cooed. "I was the one who suggested we impale them to serve as a warning not to trespass on the territory of the Roxolani."

Naulobates issued a sheepish grin. "No matter how hard we tried, we could not hammer the stakes deep enough into the soil", he admitted. "The impaled filth kept on falling over so we ended up having to settle on cutting their throats."

Gordas nodded, his faith restored in my son-in-law.

When all had retired to their furs, I remained at the fireside, staring into the flames. In my mind's eye I relived the carnage I had seen inflicted by the Crow on the Roman city of Ulpia Traiana and wondered whether I had made the right choice to abandon Dacia to the tribes.

While I fed the flames, I prayed to Arash to help me crush the Crow's army before they, too, consumed the lands of the Scythians like the insatiable fire consumed the logs.

*　*　*

Mid-afternoon the following day, we were still ten miles from the legionary camp when we noticed a rider galloping towards us. It did not take long for Aritê to identify the man as Burdukhan, one of her ringmen.

The hearth warrior reined in and greeted us in the way of the tribes. "Lord Eochar", he said. "A man arrived from Roman lands carrying a message from your oathsworn."

I issued a nod.

In reply, the warrior reached into his saddlebag and handed me a scroll carrying a seal I immediately recognised as belonging to Vibius.

Greetings Lucius.

Fortuna having blessed us with good weather, we arrived at Drobeta on the Danube one day ahead of schedule. The crossing of the river was without incident.

We were about to march north along the Iron Gates when we were informed that a large host of barbarian horsemen had breached the limes somewhere east of Ratiaria and are ravaging Moesia north of the Thracian mountains. Reports indicate that their numbers are somewhere between twenty and thirty thousand.

I had little choice but to take all but a few hundred of the Illyrians back across the Danube to face the threat. In addition, the men of the First Italian Legion accompany me, as they are acquainted with the invaded lands.

Diocles and the legions are continuing north, through the Iron Gates. Although his army has been greatly diminished, he is confident that the numbers will be sufficient to strike the death blow to the Goths.

May Mars bless you.

Chapter 10 – Devil's Dyke

"We were going to be a brave wolf attacking a bear", Thiaper said. "Now it seems we will be like a little mongrel dog nipping at the ankles of a hulking beast."

I knew that my friend was right, so I offered no retort but rather decided to clutch at the straw the old crone of the woods had dangled before me. "Tell me of the ancient ones who dwelled on the great plain of the Yazyges", I said.

"My grandfather told tales of a time when the tribe lived on the northern shores of the Dark Sea", Banadas said. "In those days, wave after wave of clans were moving west, fleeing a great evil that stirred on the Sea of Grass far, far to the east."

I suspected that the Huns might have been the great evil the king referred to, but wisely kept my counsel.

"At first my forebears fought the tribes in an effort to preserve their lands, but soon they were threatened from all directions by hordes as numerous as the stars", he said. "Traders spoke of a fertile plain lying far to the west - an open grassland that is protected by snowy peaks and watered by many rivers."

"Did they find the plain deserted?" Thiaper asked.

Banadas issued a chuckle. "The Yazyges were almost destroyed by the local tribe who defended Hades's Dyke to the death", he said. "But in the end my people prevailed."

"Tell me of Hades's Dyke", I said, and took a swallow from my cup.

Banadas gained his feet, and for a moment I believed that I had offended him, but he was only reaching for his fur cloak. "I will do better than tell you about it, Eochar", he said. "Ride with me and I will show you."

* * *

For obvious reasons I asked Hostilius to accompany us.

Banadas reined in on the open plain bordered by the two rivers, about six miles west of the camp. Apart from a seven-pace-wide stretch of soil where the grass grew thinner, there was very little to be seen.

The Yazyges king must have noticed my confused expression. He swung down from the saddle and dropped his mare's reins. "Here, behind a great wall of earth, the Anartes made their final stand", he said. "My grandsire brought me here to show me when I was but a boy. With the help of their neighbours, the Dacians, the Anartes excavated a trench all the way between the two great rivers. The earthen rampart was twice the height of a man and the ditch ten feet deep and fifteen feet wide."

While I tried to imagine the imposing fortification, Banadas walked about as if searching for something. "Here we go", he said, and kicked loose soil from what appeared to be a length of firewood buried just below the surface. He went down onto his haunches and produced a piece of timber from the sandy soil. Although the rotting wood crumbled as he lifted it, I immediately recognised it for what it was - a fire-hardened stake.

"Thousands of Yazyges were impaled on the sharpened timbers", he said. "But they had little choice - conquer the Ditch of Hades or perish at the hands of the invaders from the east."

"You see", he added, "my forefathers paid for these lands with the lifeblood of their sons and daughters."

I felt the presence of the god of war and fire knew what had to be done.

"We will resurrect the Ditch of Hades", I said. "We will defend it, and once again the Yazyges will live or die by the outcome."

Hostilius unlashed an iron mattock from his saddle. "Let me see what it's like", he said, and scraped away the thin layer of topsoil a few paces from the ancient ditch with the help of the adze blade. With a practiced hand he flipped the tool around to wield the iron pick, grunting as he slammed it into the earth. The spike failed to penetrate more than an inch.

Thrice he struck the rock-hard soil then took a step back, the mattock slung across a shoulder. "By the gods", he said, shaking his head. "Naulobates wasn't exaggerating. It will take the legions months to dig into this."

The Primus Pilus strolled to where the outlines of the ancient ditch could be seen and slammed the tool into the earth, the whole of the head disappearing into the soft sand. Again, he stepped back and glanced across the open ground between the rivers. "Two days", he said. "Every *contubernium* will be a team and we will have a competition between the legions with double wine rations for the winners. Don't you worry, Domitius, it will be done in time, although you will face a bigger challenge."

"And what might that be?" I asked.

"Your tame barbarians will have to cut the stakes and haul in the timber from the hills", he said.

"Leave it to me", I replied.

Banadas had been listening and asked, "Why do you think the ditch will halt the Goths when it failed to repel my forefathers all those years ago?"

"Because this time around, twenty thousand Roman legionaries will be manning the wall", Hostilius muttered, and swung up into the saddle.

* * *

It took the remainder of the day to move the camps seven miles west, causing both the Romans and barbarians to toil well into the hours of darkness.

When all had settled in for the evening, Hostilius, Gordas, Cai and I joined the leaders of the Scythians around a fire. Ten paces away, a handful of my daughter's oathsworn were tending to the carcass of a whole sheep spitted above the glowing embers of what had been thick oak logs. The aroma of the fat and juices that dripped onto the coals, mixed with the woodsmoke, reminded me that I had not eaten since early morning.

"You are welcome at my hearth, Father", Aritê said. In response, my companions and I lowered ourselves onto the furs beside the fire. A servant handed me a cup which I accepted gratefully, and I washed the dust from my parched throat with a long swallow of wine.

"It will take the Romans two days to clear the soil from the ditch and stack it on the far side to build a rampart", I said.

"While the Romans dig in the dirt, our brave warriors will ride east to slow down the Crow's advance", Aritê suggested.

"I have something less heroic in mind", I said. "I want each and every one of your men to ride into the hills tomorrow. Every warrior is to cut down three saplings of oak, beech or ash. Each one as tall as a man."

I noticed that Aritê's scowl was very similar to the ones worn by Naulobates, Thiaper and Banadas, but I ignored them and continued. "They are to be cut into three lengths, as long as a man's arm. One end must be fashioned to a sharp point, hardened in fire, and a notch cut a handspan below the tip."

"To fill the ditch with stakes will be a waste of precious time", my daughter opined. "The Goths will simply jump over them or cut them down with their axes. Besides, our men are warriors, not woodcutters."

I had little patience for the petty hang-ups of the tribes and was about to issue a retort when Gordas intervened.

"Where do your brave warriors get their arrows, Queen Aritê?" he asked.

"You know as well as I do", she said.

"Humour him", I said.

"They cut the timber themselves", she growled. "Around their cooking fires, while they tell tales of their feats on the battlefield, they carve the shafts of war from the seasoned wood."

"It is a toil required by Arash", Gordas replied with an accompanying nod. "Tell your warriors to do that which the god of the field of blood has whispered into your father's ear. There is no shame in heeding the commands of Arash the Avenger."

* * *

Mid-afternoon two days later, the Primus Pilus walked into my tent, his whole body coated with a thin layer of dust. I did not fail to notice that despite the cool and overcast weather, his hair was matted with sweat and his face streaked where droplets of perspiration had run down his brow - evidence that, as always, he had gotten his hands dirty.

He filled a cup from an amphora and chugged the contents. "The young officers aren't cut from the same cloth as the hard men of old, Domitius", he said. "They need constant supervision."

"Are you finished?" I asked, and refilled his cup.

He nodded his thanks and chugged the second cup as well. "Now that I'm less thirsty we can go and have a look", he replied.

Not long after, we rode along the two-mile-long fortification spanning the flat ground between the rivers. Apart from groups of legionaries levelling sections of the rampart to set up bolt-throwers, few toiled on the earthworks. Mid-way Hostilius reined in, dismounted, scrambled up the earthen wall, and gestured for me to join him.

On the other side of the rampart thousands of legionaries were still toiling, hammering stakes into the damp clay soil at the bottom of the ditch. The barbed tips not only pointed in the direction of where the attack would come from, but were positioned in pairs in the shape of an X.

"It's a trick I've learned when I campaigned under Maximinus Thrax's banner during the Germani wars", Hostilius said. "It keeps the vermin from running away once they've had a taste of Roman iron."

Other legionaries were planting stakes at the top edge of the rampart to create a low, but continuous barrier. "And that will help protect our boys when the fighting gets bloody", he said. "I've defended a rampart myself more than once. Savages like nothing better than to stick their spears into feet and legs."

We swung back up into our saddles and continued until we reached the area where the ditch intersected the riverbank. Under the direction of legionary engineers, a sluice had been installed.

"Are you ready to open it up?" Hostilius asked the man in charge.

"Ready when you say so, tribune", the man replied.

"Do it", Hostilius said.

On the engineer's signal, an *immune* removed a wooden board from the sluice and a steady trickle of river water started to spill into the ditch.

"How long will it take to fill up?" I asked.

"Could be as long as a day, Lord Emperor", he said. "But it's got to be slow else the walls may collapse."

I nodded to allow the man to continue his work.

"Do you have stakes left over?" I asked Hostilius once we were out of earshot.

"Thousands", he replied. "If I didn't know you any better I would have thought that you had calculated wrong." He issued a sigh. "Just tell me what you want me to do with them so I can get on with it."

Chapter 11 – Missive

Later that same evening, after Cai and I had trained with the sword and spear, we retired to my tent.

Gordas had insisted that the legionary carpenters cobble together retractable platforms that were wide and rigid enough to allow horses to cross the ditch in pairs. It would enable the Scythians to make sallies against the advancing enemy and return to the safety of the fortifications. He had earlier ridden out to join Hostilius on the rampart and the pair was yet to return.

On my request, the cook had prepared a simple meal of thick chicken and vegetable broth with freshly baked wheat bread on the side.

"Crow is clever and resourceful", Cai said once he had wetted his throat with a sip of wine. "Best not underestimate."

"Cannabaudes has to get past the fortifications to lay his hands on the fertile lands of the Scythians", I said. "The Goths and their allies are many, but it will not be easy for them to breach the ditch."

"Crow wants head of Lucius of Da Qin more than lands of Scythians", Cai pointed out. "Maybe Crow has strategy of own to get what he wants."

I nodded my agreement and took a sip from the bowl of broth. "But how will I know what to expect? How will I know his strategy?"

In a fluent motion, Cai moved his raised open palms to the right, then left and back again. "Everything in life has rhythm", he said. "Attack has rhythm. Defence has rhythm. One who breaks rhythm of enemy claims victory."

"How do I break the enemy's rhythm?" I asked.

"Best not defend if you want dictate rhythm", he said, and raised a balled fist. "Choose Way of Fire. Take initiative, strike hard and control enemy."

"It is easier said than done", I replied.

"Cai not say it easy", he said, and took another sip from his cup.

* * *

That night sleep did not come easy. I prayed to Arash and rolled around in the furs while I invented and discarded one plan after another. When I eventually succumbed to sleep around the middle hour of the night, I was yet to come up with a strategy.

Dawn arrived too soon and I woke up tired. I washed my face in a bowl presented by a body slave and dried it with a piece of linen before Cai assisted me to don my armour.

We had hardly arrived at the command tent when Hostilius and Gordas walked in. Moments later, a messenger was ushered into our presence by my praetorians. From his dusty, dishevelled appearance it was clear that he had ridden hard, probably throughout the night.

"Lord Emperor", he said, saluting in the required manner.

I extended an open hand to accept a scroll, but the messenger shook his head. "I am sorry, lord", he croaked. "But I carry no message, only tidings."

My first thought was to ask him to explain the difference, but instead I gestured for a pouring slave to hand him a cup of watered wine. The messenger, who was an Illyrian decurion, drank thirstily before handing the cup back to the servant.

"Tell us", I said.

"Tribune Diocles and the army are camped in the valley of the Iron Gates, fifteen miles south of Ulpia Traiana", he said. "I was sent out early yesterday morning to reconnoitre the area and found that most of the Goth horde had already moved on, west along the valley of the Tibiscus."

"Good news", Hostilius said.

"There is more, tribune", the decurion said. "When I wished to return to our camp I found that a large force of Goths, mayhap twenty-five times a thousand, was busy closing the pass of the Iron Gates with a triple line of ox-drawn wagons. The carts were being chained together and fortified with spears. The Goths had closed off my route back to camp and all I could think of doing was to make my way west through the woods."

"You did well, decurion", I said, and handed him a small purse of gold. "The legions advancing north through the Iron Gates will no doubt soon discover that their path is blocked. For us, it is extremely important to know that no help will be coming from the east."

I dismissed the man and took a long swallow from my cup, forcing myself to focus on the task at hand. Cai was right, I had indeed underestimated the foe.

"Diocles's legions will struggle to break through the *wagenburg* of the Goths", I said. "Even if they are successful, it could take them days to drive the barbarians from the mouth of the Iron Gates. We are on our own."

"If the Greek's force is not going to be the hammer that will crush the Goths, I suggest we just beat them to a pulp with the anvil", the Primus Pilus growled. "At least there will be twenty-five thousand fewer of them."

"If you were the Crow, what would you expect us to do?" I asked Hostilius, while servants arrived with platters of bread, cheese, olives and dates.

"Cannabaudes will know he's in for a tough fight", the Primus Pilus said. "Our Scythian riders will harry the vanguard of his army, whittling away at their numbers with bow and arrow. Once our mounted archers withdraw from the field, our bolt throwers will cut swathes of death through their ranks before they reach the ditch where our boys will be waiting on the rampart behind sharpened stakes." He popped an olive into his mouth and swallowed it down with a gulp of watered down white. "There's not a lot to it, eh? Only a fool would choose not to defend such a strong position."

Hostilius reached for a small round of cheese, stuffed it in his mouth, and took a bite from a loaf, all without breaking eye contact. "I know that look, Domitius", he said between mouthfuls. "It can only mean one thing, and that is that you're about to suggest something that I'm not going to be happy with."

"I fear you are right", I replied.

* * *

"Have you taken leave of your senses?" Hostilius asked once I had revealed my plan.

"The Crow is expecting an onslaught of arrows and bolts", I said. "If you were him, who would you put in the front ranks?"

"The expendable, poorly armed and armoured rabble of my allies", the Primus Pilus conceded.

"When our archers have expended their arrows, the ballistae have shot their last bolts and the sword arms of our men are tired, the Crow will unleash his best warriors against us", I said.

"Best defence is attack and best attack is defence", Cai said.

I chose to interpret the Easterner's words as support for my plan. "I agree", I replied.

"What do you think?" Hostilius asked Gordas.

"If we perish, it will be a worthy death", the Hun said. "For many generations warriors will share the tale of our demise around their cooking fires, and the glory of our deeds will echo through the ages."

Hostilius rolled his eyes and raised his open palms in defeat. "Alright, alright", he said, "we'll do it your way, Domitius. But if it turns out bad, don't say I didn't warn you."

"I won't", I replied. "Because we will all be corpses if my plan fails."

I could not help to notice the smile playing around the corners of Gordas's lips.

* * *

The following morning, we woke up to grey, overcast skies. I dressed and made my way under guard to the praetorium, arriving at the same time as Thiaper and Banadas

"Is everything in place?" I asked when all were present.

"A thousand of my horsemen have crossed the Tissus to gain the northern bank", Thiaper said.

"And I watched while the same number of King Banadas's horse archers swam their mounts across the Tibiscus, five miles downstream", Gordas confirmed, drawing a nod from the Yazyges king.

"And the ballistae?" I asked.

"We managed to get twenty *carroballistae* across both rivers using rafts and ropes", the Primus Pilus said. "We crossed far downstream and moved them to concealed positions after dusk."

"Are you certain that the enemy did not see you?" I asked.

"Mayhap they did, lord", Naulobates said, and shrugged. "But apart from the corpse-eating eels at the bottom of the river, the Goth scouts will tell no one."

"When will the enemy arrive before the fortifications?" I asked.

"In less than a watch", Hostilius replied.

"Then it is time", I said, gained my feet and donned my gilded helmet.

Chapter 12 – Way of Fire

The portion of the Devil's Dyke that we had resurrected spanned the flat ground between the Tissus to the north, and the Tibiscus to the south. The ditch was almost three miles long, meaning that the legions could only deploy three ranks deep. But rather than three ranks, only a single line of legionaries stood on top of the rampart, the bottom edges of their shields resting on the knee-high barricade of stakes and the hafts of their *pila* firmly grounded on the compacted earth.

Every hundred paces along the length of the wall, a platform made of wooden planks spanned the ditch. The makeshift bridges would allow the cavalry to retreat to the safety of the wall after engaging with the enemy.

Gordas pointed at the dust rising on the eastern horizon. "Here they come", he said.

Behind the rampart, Aritê, Thiaper and Banadas headed up a force of ten thousand horsemen, their mounts painted for war. The blonde hair and beards of the warriors were braided in the way of the tribes, while the exposed skin of their faces and arms were adorned with swirling blue-green tattoos depicting the animals and plants favoured by their clans. They were garbed in the loose-fitting robes of Scythians, with vests of scale armour worn underneath. Their iron or bronze helmets were still strapped to their saddles and their strung bows slung across their shoulders. Leather quivers bulging with poison-smeared war arrows dangled from their saddles. Many of the quivers were rimmed with pure white leather obtained from the tanned skins of vanquished enemies, marking them as warriors of renown. A variety of longswords, battle-axes and daggers hung from the broad leather belts around their waists.

I nodded to my daughter, who barked a command. In response, the Scythians fanned out along the wall and made their way across the wooden platforms that spanned the ditch. Once they had crossed, they formed up in a long line, two hundred paces in front of the fortification, facing the approaching enemy.

The departing Scythians revealed the presence of twelve thousand legionaries drawn up in their respective legions. I drew my sword and raised the blade, the signal for the heavy Roman infantry to advance.

In a show of supreme discipline, the cohorts moved into position, traversing the ditch and deploying behind the Scythian horsemen at the centre of the battlefield.

"By the gods, Domitius, I hope you know what you're doing", Hostilius said as he, Gordas and I walked our mounts across the planking and through the gaps between the blocks of infantry. The men saluted as we passed, but they made no sound. The banners of the centuries, cohorts and legionary standards were not held high and proud, but almost horizontal to hide them from the eyes of the enemy.

Gordas and I left Hostilius with the legions and continued until we had joined the kings and queen of the Scythians.

I leaned forward in the saddle and glanced to the right and left. "Where is Naulobates and his men?" I asked my daughter.

"The fact that you cannot see them does not mean that they are not where they should be, Father", she replied, her words reminding me of the fact that Cai had been her tutor.

"You know what to do?" I asked.

"My answer is the same as when you asked a third of a watch ago", she replied, and gestured with her chin to the expanse of flat ground.

What started off as a black line on the horizon slowly morphed into a writhing mass of men. The sea of banners they held high rose and fell with the contours of the land as they inexorably crept across the plain between the rivers. Unlike the disciplined legions of Rome who marched in silence, a low drone accompanied the approaching horde.

Although the enemy army consisted almost exclusively of infantry, most who considered themselves headmen of clans and tribes, were mounted. At the centre of their line, a group of black-clad riders, mayhap fifty or sixty, clustered around what must have been their king.

When six hundred paces separated us from the front ranks of the enemy, a black-robed rider raised a fist in the air. The shouts of the chieftains echoed the command along the Goth line until the horde trudged to a halt.

Just then, Hostilius arrived from the rear, pushing through the ranks of Scythian horsemen. Before he could comment on the sight of the enemy, three riders of the Goth command party separated from the horde and approached, reining in midway between the armies.

"Looks like the Crow wants to talk", Hostilius said. "He doesn't ride under a branch of truth though."

"Neither will we", I said, and nudged my horse forward at a trot.

* * *

Thirty paces from the three mounted Goths, Hostilius, Gordas and I pulled back on the reins, coming to a halt just in front of the enemy trio.

The horses of the Crow's ringmen were large animals, but the two hulking warriors flanking the Goth king still managed to dwarf their mounts, their legs dangling near the ground, the soles of their undyed leather boots bending the plumes of the ten-inch-high autumn grass. They were black-bearded brutes, their bare forearms criss-crossed with scars where iron had cleaved their flesh. The thick gold and silver torques clasped around their necks and upper arms were a testament to their prowess and experience in battle. Both were encased in fire-blackened armour, and aprons of thick chain were riveted to the rear of their open face helmets. Starting at the waist, their iron chainmail jerkins were split at the sides, allowing them the freedom to move in the saddle.

Although Cannabaudes had aged since I had last laid eyes on him, he was no doubt still a formidable warrior. There were grey streaks in his raven-black hair, but his arms, bull-like neck and chest were still thick and bulging with muscle.

"I have beseeched Teiwaz through prayer and sacrifice to be granted the opportunity to cross blades with you again, Eochar the Merciless", he growled.

"Likewise", I replied, and my hand went to the hilt of my sword. "Do you wish to do it now?"

The grim smile that split his clean-shaven face did not reach his cold, near-white eyes. "I have made an oath", he said. "First I must placate the lord of the field of spears with the lifeblood of the Scythians and the Romans. But have no fear, half-breed, before the sun sets tonight, my men will hack your corpse to pieces and feed what remains to the ravens."

While the Crow spewed his drivel, I felt the presence of Arash and a red-hot anger rose from deep inside, one which I battled to cage. Hostilius must have realised that I was a heartbeat away from violence. Without a word, he reached out and took my sword arm in a grip of iron.

"Do not waste your breath to beg for mercy when we meet again", I growled, and turned my horse's head back to return whence I came.

"Run, and hide behind your wall, cowards. It will help you naught against the wrath of the Crow", Cannabaudes sneered, and his guards spat out gobs of phlegm to show their contempt.

"Why did you restrain me?" I asked Hostilius while we trotted back to our lines.

"We serve Rome, not our own interests", he said. "If you wish to finish that which Marcus has started, killing the Crow will not suffice. We're going to have to do better than that."

"Like what?" I asked.

"Kill them all", he replied.

* * *

We had hardly reached the ranks of Scythian horsemen when a great cheer rose from the enemy ranks. The warriors banged the hafts of their spears and the blades of their swords against their round shields, working themselves up into a crazed frenzy.

"You know what that means, eh?" Hostilius said.

I nodded and turned to face my daughter. "We must take the initiative", I said.

She smiled sweetly, raised her strung horn bow above her head and issued a blood-curdling war cry. Moments later, a roar rose from the Goth ranks that shook the very foundations of the earth.

Forty thousand hooves pounded the dry earth to powder, and in our wake a great cloud of fine dust swirled to the heavens. A hundred paces from the front line of the onrushing horde, I put an arrow to the string, drew back, and released on Aritê's command. Ten thousand arrows flew high into the grey sky before plummeting down on the front ranks of the invaders.

Without breaking stride, the Goths raised their shields at an angle above their heads to receive the missiles. Most of the shafts embedded in laminated willow. Judging by the isolated screams of pain, only a few found flesh.

Seamlessly the Scythians wheeled about and cantered back the way they had come before turning to thunder down on the approaching enemy. Once again, ten thousand arrows rose from their ranks.

The charging Goths swatted aside the thin hail of shafts with contempt, their confidence growing with each step. As they passed into the veil of dust, it was clear that they no longer feared the Scythians, but wished to get to grips with the men who defended the fortifications - the last obstacle between them and the rich pickings beyond.

But unbeknown to the Goths, the Scythians' aim was to preserve their arrows while raising a screen of dust - a veil to cover the advance of the legions.

We reined in paces away from the lead cohort. "Do it", Hostilius commanded the *imaginifer*, the warrior who carried the image of the emperor. He saluted, raised the gold standard, and in response hundreds of banners were lifted high.

The Primus Pilus and I swung down from our saddles and handed our reins to Gordas. "Keep him safe", I said, accepted a shield from a guard, and fell in beside Hostilius at the head of a century of praetorians.

When all eyes were on me, I thrust my sword in the air.

In silence, the legions surged forward into the cloud of suffocating dust.

Chapter 13 – Sacrifice

As soon as the legions advanced, the Scythians split into two groups, each tasked to protect a flank of the infantry, leaving nothing but the swirling dust between us and the Goths.

We continued marching, Hostilius squinting into the haze, his face a mask of concentration. When the first dark shapes became visible, he nodded to the signifer and the shrill note of a *buccina* relayed his command along the Roman line.

As one, the legionaries came to a halt, hefted their *pila*, and twelve thousand iron-shanked javelins streaked into the fog. We were rewarded by screams and wails of pain as another volley of Roman spears were cast into the gloom.

We knew from experience what would follow.

"Testudo!" Hostilius boomed. He kneeled and slammed the iron rim of his shield onto the rock-hard ground. The second rank went down onto one knee, simultaneously sliding the bottom edges of their *scuta* onto the top rims of the front rankers' shields. The rear ranks followed suit to create a barrier resembling the overlapping clay tiles of a Roman roof.

A heartbeat later, thousands upon thousands of Goth spears slammed into the wall of Roman shields. I felt a stinging pain in my shoulder as two, maybe three thick-hafted spears struck my shield almost at the same time. The impact rocked me back on my feet, the steady hand of the praetorian behind me the only thing keeping me from falling over.

Hostilius stole a peek through the slit between our shields. "Hold!" he shouted, just as another volley struck.

On the Primus Pilus's command, the rear ranks yanked back their *scuta*. I drew my shortsword, raised my shield, braced my left shoulder in the curve of the plywood and rushed at the enemy, all the while making sure to retain the cohesion of the line.

The rim of my *scutum* deflected the honed tip of a spear and I buried my blade in the unarmoured stomach of its owner. The next warrior to face me wielded a longsword, which he swung with the grace of a woodcutter. In response to a clumsy cut, I lowered my shield and slashed my *gladius* across his throat, shoving the corpse into the man behind him, who lost his footing and tumbled facedown to the ground. Hostilius's blade snaked out, the tip of his *gladius* piercing the back of the man's neck.

"You were right, Domitius", Hostilius admitted as he punched the iron boss of his shield into the face of another helmetless Goth, pulverising the warrior's nose and shattering his teeth.

"They put the rabble in the front ranks", he added, and followed with a straight thrust to the groin that would have made Cai proud.

Suddenly the enemy warriors were reluctant to face us, causing a lull in the fighting. On Hostilius's signal, the men of the first-line cohorts retreated through the ranks, allowing the second- and third-line cohorts to relieve the tired men. Hostilius and I retreated as well, the praetorians forming a protective circle around their emperor.

"It felt good to get stuck in again", the Primus Pilus admitted while we waited for our horses. "It wasn't such a bad idea after all", he added, and used his bloodied sword to point at the dead and seriously wounded enemies littering the ground behind the advancing legions. "We must have killed ten thousand of the bastards."

I walked over to a dead Goth who was bare-headed and wore no armour. "We've been fighting the peasants, the ones the Crow wishes to sacrifice in order to rid us of our stores of arrows", I said. "Soon we will be facing the battle-hardened Goths, the warriors who have both armour and skill."

I noticed Gordas approach, leading Intikam as well as Hostilius's gelding. We mounted and took up our positions at the head of the command group, near the centre of the line just behind the rear ranks. The dust that had earlier shrouded the battlefield had settled, and being mounted afforded us a view across the plain.

"You put fire in the shades of your warriors by fighting by their side, Eochar", Gordas growled, and used his chin to gesture to where the legions were advancing, grinding away at the enemy.

His words filled me with pride, and for the first time I truly believed that the legions could overcome the overwhelming numbers of the enemy.

The feeling was not destined to last.

Hostilius watched the battle like a hawk. "Look", he said, indicating a distinct line in the Goth horde where the ranks of bare-headed rabble gave way to the shine of burnished armour and whetted blades.

Once the legionaries had cut through the last of the peasants, they came face to face with mail-clad Goths with good shields and well-crafted blades. The sounds emanating from the front ranks changed almost immediately. The constant cries of anguish and shouts of pain from the enemy were replaced by the ringing of iron on iron and the grunts of men pushing shield to shield while probing with their weapons, waiting for a careless moment so that they could bury their blades in flesh.

Many Goths still fell to Roman iron, but the injured and dead legionaries being carried to the rear by the *medici* also increased to a steady stream. Slowly but surely the overwhelming numbers of the foe began to tell, and the Roman line bent under the strain of their relentless onslaught.

Hostilius and I exchanged looks of concern. "There are just too many", he said, his lips pursed in frustration.

"Give the order to retreat", I said. "Signal to the crews of the *carroballistae* to send their bolts into the horde from across the rivers, and for Naulobates and his men to strike the enemy in the flanks."

The shrill notes of the *buccina* carried across the battlefield and the legionaries started to shuffle backwards. But the pressure on the front ranks remained. In fact, sensing victory in the legions' retreat, the Goths increased their efforts, putting even more pressure on the thin Roman line that appeared in danger of giving way at any moment.

I heard the familiar sound as a skein passed on its pent-up power to a ballista bolt, and a heartbeat later, forty three-foot-long wooden shafts tipped with broad-bladed iron streaked across my field of vision from beyond the rivers. The bolts cut swathes of death through the ranks of the Goths, but still they came on relentlessly, throwing themselves against the shields of the retreating Romans.

A ripple went through the Goth ranks and terrible screams emanated from the flanks. "Looks like Naulobates and his men have shown themselves", Hostilius said.

Then I heard the thunder of hooves as Aritê's warriors abandoned the flanks to the Heruli. The Scythians wheeled into formation and swept in behind the thin ranks of the Romans, darkening the sky with wave after wave of shafts. Almost ten thousand arrows at a time arced over our heads and slammed into the ranks of the Goths.

The warriors of the Crow were no strangers to battle, but faced with the onslaught of the Roman artillery combined with the attack of the Heruli and the arrows of the Scythians, they faltered, providing the legions with precious moments to withdraw into the dust cloud and cross the ditch to the safety of the walls.

* * *

A sixth of a watch later, Aritê and Naulobates joined Hostilius, Gordas and me on the rampart.

"We lost almost two thousand legionaries", Hostilius said.

"Five hundred of the Scythian warriors have made their wives widows", my daughter said.

"Three hundred of my men now feast in the mead hall of the gods", Naulobates added. "They died well, surrounded by the corpses of their enemies."

On the far side of the ditch, the Crow's warriors were regrouping. Thousands upon thousands were working up the courage to attack. Spurred on by chanting priests, they were screaming and striking their blades against their shields.

"We've killed so many", Hostilius said, shaking his head in disbelief. "But there must be sixty times a thousand left of the bastards while we've got almost no *pila* left."

"I am down to my last quiver", Aritê said. "And so are most of my warriors."

"When they come, join us on the wall and make every arrow count", I said.

"Once our quivers are empty, we will fight with our blades", she replied.

"And when our blades are broken", Naulobates added, "we will fight with our bare hands."

"Arash be with you", I said, and the two strolled off to tend to their men.

When Hostilius had left to do his rounds, Gordas remained beside me on the wall. "Do you fear that you will lose the battle against the Crow?" the Hun asked, his gaze fixed on the sea of enemy banners.

Before I could reply, he continued. "Romans fear the humiliation that comes with defeat", he said. "That is why they are often not bold enough to emerge victorious." He turned to face me and looked me straight in the eye. "You know as well as I do that the people of the horse have no fear of death or defeat. What one should fear most is the absence of a glorious death. What does victory bring but hubris? What worth is victory when one has to spend eternity in the shadows?"

He reached out and uncharacteristically placed a hand on my scaled shoulder. "Remember who you are, Eochar", he said. "Beseech Arash to grant you a glorious death in battle and leave the outcome in the hands of the god of war and fire."

Gordas's words rang true. I glanced up at the darkening sky and felt a great weight lift from my shoulders as I lay my concerns at the feet of the lord of the field of blood.

Chapter 14 – Oath

"Here they come", Hostilius said, and hefted his heavy stabbing spear.

I took a single arrow from my quiver and drew the string of my horn and sinew bow to my ear.

A wall of Goth warriors charged towards the ditch, their round, painted shields pulled tight against their torsos.

I sighted on a blonde-bearded brute clutching a longsword in his right fist. Spittle flew from his wide open maw as he bayed for the blood of the Romans. I exhaled slowly, and released. The fletching of the heavy tamarisk shaft brushed my left thumb as it fishtailed from the string, the laminated layers of hardwood, horn, bone and sinew endowing the deadly missile with incredible velocity.

The Goth must have caught a glimpse of the arrow and jerked his shield upward to protect his face. But my aim was elsewhere. The shaft cleared the rim and slammed into his black-plumed helmet, the tempered, armour-piercing tip splitting the riveted plate and lodging deep in his skull. The men flanking my victim slumped mid-stride, Aritê and Gordas's arrows sending them on their way to the afterlife.

The arrows of the Scythians killed hundreds, if not thousands, but still the foe came on. For every man we felled, two or three made it to the ditch. I took four arrows into my draw hand, and in so many heartbeats dispatched four Goths negotiating the dyke.

But our men were within spear range of the foe, and as the attackers streamed over the edge of the fosse, they cast their missiles. I stole a glance at the line of defenders to my right and saw a Scythian stagger backwards, his chest skewered by a javelin. Another fell to a Goth spear to the neck, the corpse tumbling down the incline to the bottom of the trench.

"Tell your warriors to fall back and release their arrows over our heads into the horde", Hostilius said to my daughter, rolling his massive shoulders. "The close-quarters work is about to start", he added with relish.

She was about to object, but before she could, the Primus Pilus lashed out with his shield to batter away a spear that would have pierced her flesh. Aritê nodded, shouted a command, and the archers withdrew, the wolf warriors of the Heruli stepping into the vacated spaces.

I stowed my bow in a pouch, took my *gladius* into my fist and hefted my shield as the barbarians waded through the muddy water at the bottom of the ditch.

Hundreds of the enemy fell to the sharpened timbers concealed by the putrid water until the impaled corpses rendered the stakes ineffective. Like a swarm of locusts, the invaders flooded into the fosse, clambering over the bodies of the dead and scampering up the slope of the rampart.

Hostilius blocked a sword-strike with his *scutum*, and using an overhand grip, thrust his spear into the face of a Goth who must have dropped his shield somewhere in the ditch. The broad iron head shattered teeth and bone and the man fell backward, taking three of his brethren with him as he careened down the rampart. Another took his place, but before he could bring his sword to bear, Hostilius clubbed him in the neck with the thick haft of his heavy spear. Clutching his ruined windpipe he, too, slid down the muddy incline.

Two men, one armed with a spear and the other with a longsword, used the corpses as footing and ran up the slope. The Sword-Goth won the race and cut at my legs with a low sweep.

I slammed my shield onto the dirt and leaned to the right to avoid the spear that was thrust at my face, turning my head to the side to present the chain apron of my helmet to the edge of the leaf-shaped blade. Relinquishing my shield, I gripped the haft of the Goth's spear, shoved him backward, and the snarling warrior tumbled from view. The other's blade was drawn back for the kill, but the honed iron of Gordas's battle-axe bit into his temple, laying open his skull.

I picked up my shield during the moment of respite and scanned the battlefield. All along the wall the Romans were fighting for their lives as ever-increasing numbers of the enemy streamed into the ditch. I heard the bellow of centurions as they called on the help of reserves where the Goths had gained a foothold on the rampart. Across the trench, thousands of the foe were still baying for Roman blood, eager to be the first to have the honour to claim and hold the wall.

And then, thirty paces into the press of savages, I noticed the Crow surrounded by his ringmen. Cannabaudes's lips were pulled back in a sneer of pleasure as he watched his slow but certain victory unfold. Although we had killed thousands of the foe, many remained, and I knew that eventually we would succumb to the onslaught. For so many years I had pleaded with Arash to give me the opportunity to avenge Kniva's death, and now, ironically, the Crow was within my grasp, fewer than thirty paces away.

But he could just as well have been on the other side of the earth.

I was distracted by a scream from my left, and another legionary rolled from the rampart, impaled by a Goth spear. His body came to a rest on the corpses of the invaders that, I noticed, threatened to fill in the trench. A sudden dread overcame me - a fear that I would lose not only the battle, but also be responsible for the demise of my mother's people.

Then I heard the words of Gordas echo inside my mind. *'Remember who you are, Eochar. Beseech Arash to grant you a glorious death in battle.'*

Unconcerned for my life I lowered my shield and closed my eyes. I heard a spear whoosh past my ear but paid it no heed as I begged Arash the Avenger to grant me a death worthy of a warrior.

The lord of war came to me then and I knew what had to be done.

I raised my shield, dispatched another Goth and turned to face Hostilius. "Assemble a hundred of the best men you can lay your hands on, tribune", I said. "Find Naulobates and tell him to do the same."

* * *

It was the last watch of the afternoon when I took up position at the front of a wedge of two hundred men, flanked by Hostilius and Naulobates, with Gordas guarding my back. We were barely holding on to the rampart, while the Goths, sensing victory, had intensified their effort.

I hefted my shield, gripped my *gladius* and vaulted over the low wall of stakes, only to land right in front of a large black-bearded brute wielding a war axe. The Goth had been using his weapon to aid his ascent of the slippery slope, his fist on the haft just below the head. Before he could change his grip and bring it to bear I landed a kick on the bronze boss of his shield. He tried in vain to hold his balance and ended up tipping over backwards, taking at least two others with him as he tumbled into the ditch. I took full advantage of the warrior's fall, followed him down the slope, and slammed the edge of my shield down onto his neck as he came to rest against the heap of bodies at the bottom of the fosse. Without getting our feet wet, we crossed the bridge of corpses and fought our way up the far side of the trench.

But the surprise of the sudden attack lasted only so long.

As we surged from the ditch onto the flat ground beyond, I heard the chieftains boom commands to their clansmen.

Fifteen paces away, the Crow sat atop his massive black stallion, his piercing gaze fixed on me.

Reacting to the orders of their war chiefs, the Goths who faced us suddenly turned tail and melted back into the milling horde, to be replaced by a line of hulking warriors who pushed their way to the front. Cannabaudes's ringmen were encased in scale and chain, their gold and silver armbands and crested helmets as much a sign of their loyalty to their sworn lord as it was a testimony to their skills with a blade.

A big man, no doubt a champion, with a neck so thick that it seemed that his head was directly attached to his torso, shoved another out of the way and stepped into my path. There were streaks of grey in his braided blonde beard and the exposed skin on his sword arm was criss-crossed with the scars of a man who lived by the blade.

I breathed deeply, felt my body relax, and focused my mind.

The Goth spat in contempt, rolled his massive shoulders and slowly raised his shield, grinning with relish at the inevitable confrontation. "You don't look like much, Scyth...", he said, but got no further as the tip of my *gladius* scraped over the rim of his shield and slid into his mouth. When I felt the slight resistance offered by the bone of his spine, I jerked the blade back and the corpse toppled to the side.

The brute next in line roared with rage at the demise of his sword brother. He charged with such ferocity that I barely had enough time to drop down onto one knee. I planted the bottom rim of the shield, lowered the top edge, and forced my left shoulder into the curve of the plywood. At the last moment I powered up with my legs and pressed forward with my shoulder, the bottom edge of my shield slamming into the warrior's shins.

He tumbled across my raised shield and I heard the thump from behind as he went to ground, followed by a gurgling scream as Gordas's axe bit deep into his neck.

A short and heavily muscled man came at me with a massive two-handed sword. The weapon must have been extremely heavy, but he wielded it as though it weighed naught, shattering my *scutum* with the first strike. I discarded the shield, flipped my *gladius* to my left hand, and drew my favoured sword.

The Goth swung again, his longsword sweeping from right to left like a scythe.

I moved forward into the parry, twisted my hips and felt the power surge through my arms as I met the warrior blade to blade. But Eastern smiths had crafted my sword from sky-iron, and the honed edge cut through the foe's sword as if it had been carved from wood. His eyes were still fixed on his ruined weapon when my *gladius* brushed across the vessels in his neck. The iron opened the flesh to the bone and I was showered with a mist of red.

On my left and right Hostilius and Naulobates were both roaring like beasts as they ground down the warriors facing them.

I was filled with the rage of the god of the field of blood and cut down another Goth, and another. Still our wedge edged forward.

And then only one man stood between me and the Crow.

The blonde giant was a foot taller than me, and in his fist was the biggest axe I had ever laid eyes on. Rather than readying the weapon, his eyes darted around like that of a scared animal. A frown split his brow and he cast aside the axe before darting into the press of the horde.

Cannabaudes's horse was trained for war and the big black beast reared up, its hooves powerful enough to crush the skull of a man with a single blow.

But I was no ordinary Roman, and dodged the club-like hooves as they clawed the air around my helmet. The blood of the horse lords of the Sea of Grass coursed not only in my veins, but it was even stronger in the man who was but a step behind.

"Duck!" Gordas shouted in the tongue of the Huns.

I obeyed and felt the air stir as the Hun's battle-axe whirred inches above my head. A heartbeat later, the honed iron spike slammed into the skull of the animal. The stallion screamed in pain and swayed on its feet, providing Cannabaudes with the opportunity to vault from the saddle, narrowly avoiding being pinned beneath the beast as it crashed onto its side.

The Crow proved to be as agile as a cat, landing in a crouch. He slipped his blade from the sheath and took his battle-axe in his left fist, while his remaining oathsworn rallied around their lord. "Today you will join Kniva in the afterlife, Roman pig!" he roared to be heard above the din of the raging battle.

"Widen the front!" I heard Hostilius boom.

I stole a glance across my shoulder, concerned that the Primus Pilus was sacrificing our men to save me. But our charge into the ranks of the enemy had fortified the resolve of the defenders. The legions and their allies were rallying behind us, streaming across the rampart to take the fight to the enemy.

Cannabaudes did not charge, but led his men forward at a walk, the flat of his sword resting on his right shoulder.

Although he appeared as relaxed as a high-born strolling to the forum, I knew from experience that he was using a guard favoured by the Goths.

I took five steps forward, bent my knees and drew back my right elbow, my weight on my rear leg. I held my sword in a high guard, the blade parallel to the ground and the tip a few inches from my ear.

"Be careful, Domitius", I heard Hostilius growl through gritted teeth. "These savages are treacherous snakes."

When I was within reach, Cannabaudes launched himself at me, sweeping his weapon down without warning, his sword flashing from right to left. It was an unremarkable stroke, but the blade moved in a blur of silver, so fast that I was forced to lunge backwards to prevent it from severing the sinews in my leg.

At the same time his men surged forward, and I knew that no help would come from my friends, who would be fighting for their lives.

The Crow stepped into my retreat, his long-hafted battle-axe following in the wake of his sword. I was late to defend, but still managed to block the blow with my *gladius*. The strike lacked the crushing power I had expected and I immediately surmised that it had been a feint. Meanwhile, my foe effortlessly reversed the path of his sword, ripping the blade upwards from low to high across my body - a difficult blow to execute and even more so to parry. I stood my ground and our blades met close to the hilts.

For a span of heartbeats we remained like two bulls locking horns, testing each other's strength.

"While your corpse is being picked clean by the crows, I will exterminate the horse-peasants once and for all", he sneered. "By the time that your bones have been bleached white by the summer sun, I will lead the horde to the gates of Rome. Once we have ravaged your women and looted your gold, we will set the city to the torch. I will not rest until nothing but dust remains."

"I have prayed to the lord of war and fire to deliver you into my hands", I growled. "In return, to honour him, I will litter these plains with the corpses of the Goth nation - a nation that you, fool, have led to death and destruction."

For a change, Cannabaudes used his head.

The Goth attempted to smash the brow ridge of his helmet into my unprotected face. I divined his intentions in time and jerked my head away, his nose guard striking the crest of my Roman helmet. Dazed by his own blow, he staggered back.

I moved with him, thrusting with my *gladius* as I did so, the tip of the shortsword aimed at his groin. He brought up his sword to push my blade from its path, but it was only a feint. Using my wrist, I whipped the edge of my favoured blade low, the honed edge splitting the iron of his greave and cutting deep into the flesh beneath.

The Crow roared in pain. In anger, he hacked down with the whetted spike of his axe, intent on burying it deep in the base of my neck.

Although his blade moved in a blur, I was faster. I gambled, stepped in, and felt a numbing impact as the haft of his weapon struck my armoured shoulder. A searing pain shot down my arm and my *gladius* fell from my left fist.

A sneer of triumph split Cannabaudes's lips. But it lasted only until the brow of my helmet slammed into his face, the blow bursting his lips and splintering teeth.

Disorientated, he staggered backwards and spat out a glob of blood and white shards. "I will flay you alive", he roared, and tried to split me in half with a massive overhead cut.

I stepped in close, met the blow with the flat of my blade, and used the power behind his strike to unbalance and push him back. The Crow stumbled and his injured leg gave way.

Cannabaudes's fate was sealed, my dagger already moving with the speed of a striking viper. The sharp point, designed to pierce armour, parted the links of his chain and slid in between his ribs.

The Crow gasped for breath, unable to accept the fact that his time had come, his eyes wide with shock.

I ripped the iron free, pivoted on my heel, and took the head of the man who had haunted my dreams for half a lifetime.

A collective sigh of dismay rippled through the ranks of the enemy, and the legions responded with an overpowering roar.

The Crow had subjugated countless tribes during his reign. The only glue that kept his forces together was their oaths to, and fear of, the man who had conquered them. I noticed a handful of warriors discarding their shields and pushing back through their ranks. Others followed, and within a hundred heartbeats, not a single Goth remained.

It is not uncommon for men elated by victory to pursue a routed enemy, but the legionaries and their allies were so close to total exhaustion that they collapsed where they stood.

"Signal for the men to return to the fortifications", I said, and noticed that Gordas had picked up Cannabaudes's severed head by the hair, no doubt to claim as a trophy.

"Leave it be", I said.

"Why?" the Hun asked.

"I gave an oath to give these corpses as an offering to Arash the Destroyer", I replied, and bent over at the waist to wipe the blood from my blade with Cannabaudes's fur-lined cloak.

The Hun shrugged, unceremoniously dropped the head, and continued to wrench his battle axe from the skull of the Crow's dead stallion.

Chapter 15 – Pursuit

The sun was low in the sky when Gordas, Hostilius and I eventually retired. Cai, who was a healer of renown, chose to remain with the wounded. We arrived at my tent, where Thiaper and Banadas were waiting for us. Soon we were joined by my daughter and her husband.

"We heard that you have issued orders not to loot the bodies of the dead", Thiaper said as I bade them to enter. "And why are you not pursuing the enemy?"

"Eochar has dedicated the fallen to Arash in return for granting us victory", Gordas said, the tone of his voice conveying his approval of my pious act.

All nodded their agreement as none wished to draw the wrath of the one who decided the outcome of battles.

I turned to face my daughter. "Apart from the wagons we need for our wounded, I give the spoils of the Goth's camp to the Roxolani, Heruli, Yazyges and Carpiani", I said. "Divide it as you wish."

"You honour us, lord", Naulobates said, and inclined his head as he knew that the loot would be significant.

"Tonight we will enjoy the protection offered by the fortifications", I said. "The enemy still outnumber us, and if they decide to attack it will not go well with us. Only a fool will sleep in the open with fifty thousand Goths roaming around."

Aritê issued a reluctant nod.

"Tomorrow when the sun rises, retrieve your useable arrows, take your horsemen and ride down the survivors", I said, indicating Thiaper, Banadas and Aritê.

"Should we take slaves?" Naulobates asked, and stood to refill his cup.

"Show them the same mercy as they would have shown you and your people", I replied, drawing a wolflike grin from my daughter that left little doubt in anyone's mind as to the fate of the fleeing Goths.

"Where will you take your men now that you have exacted vengeance on the Crow, Eochar?" Thiaper asked.

"Once we have sent our dead to the afterlife and cared for the wounded, we will hurry east to relieve Diocles's force that is being besieged in the Iron Gates Pass", I said.

"Do you still intend to march on Palmyra?" Banadas asked.

"It has to be done", I replied, and took a sip from my cup. "Will you be able to provide me with horsemen in exchange for gold?" I asked, and altered my gaze between the three Scythian leaders.

"We have taken heavy casualties, Father", my daughter replied.

Thiaper and Banadas averted their eyes and nodded their agreement with the words of the queen.

"Now that the Crow is no more, the tribal lands to the north will be in turmoil", my daughter continued. "Chieftains will vie with one another to claim disputed territories, and the more daring amongst them will wish to prove their courage by raiding our camps."

"Your concerns are valid", I conceded. I realised that, like Rome, the tribes had arrived at a critical point in their history, and stripping them of their warriors could doom their people to annihilation.

I raised my cup in a toast. "Let us not dwell on what is yet to come to pass, but rather share the tales of the victory that the lord of war and fire has granted us this day", I said, and poured the wine in my cup onto the ground as a libation to the god.

The sombre expressions around the fire morphed into smiles as they joined in the toast.

* * *

I cantered through a dark forest mounted on Simsek, the Hun horse gifted to me by the khagan of the Huns. Beside me rode a blonde man attired in the garb of a Goth noble, his fur-lined cloak fluttering as he skilfully weaved his mount around the moss-covered trunks.

We neared the edge of the greenwood. Beyond the shadows I saw luscious green meadows bathed in sunlight and teeming with deer.

My companion reined in, grinned, and hefted his spear. "It is a good day for a hunt, eh?" he said.

Although I had not laid eyes on him for many seasons, I would never forget the jovial features of Kniva, my sword brother. He leaned from the saddle and slapped my armoured shoulder. "Stop being so morose", he said. "You have done well today, Eochar."

"How can I not be concerned?" I said. "I am taking the legions east to pit them against a foe who fights in the way of the Scythians, and I have no mounted bowmen to call on."

"Our fate is cast in stone", Kniva shrugged, and then his expression turned sombre. "Now that my death has been avenged, I can go to the other side."

He started towards the sunlit fields.

I nudged my horse to follow, but Kniva pulled on the reins. "It is not yet your time, Eochar", he said.

I heard the leaves rustle and stole a glance over my shoulder. When I turned back, Kniva had ridden out into the sun.

* * *

It was the second day on the road and three days after the battle of the Devil's Dyke.

We had been riding at marching pace for the best part of a watch when Gordas pointed at a small plume of dust on the eastern horizon. "Riders", he grunted.

Hostilius squinted at what appeared to be a small group of horsemen approaching the marching column at a canter. "Doesn't look like savages", he said.

I was frustrated by the slow pace and itching for an excuse to stretch my stallion's legs. "I suggest we take a look", I said, and noticed that the Hun had already strung his bow. I gestured for my mounted guards to stand down and Hostilius, Gordas and I rode out to meet the approaching riders.

Intikam was at full gallop within twenty strides. I lay low in the saddle, relishing the wind in my face as my powerful warhorse's hooves slammed the earth like the hammer of Vulcan, his enormous lungs pumping like bellows. In his veins flowed the blood of Simsek, and I knew that he could maintain the pace longer than most, but we were interrupted by a thrill whistle from behind. I glanced over my shoulder and was surprised to find that Hostilius and Gordas were twenty strides behind. I pulled on the leathers to allow them to catch up.

Hostilius scowled and angled his head in the direction of the approaching horsemen. "It's not going to help our cause if they are a bunch of Goth bastards and you arrive without someone to watch your back", he scolded.

I slowed Intikam down to a trot.

"Illyrians", Gordas, whose eyesight rivalled that of an eagle, announced from my left.

Hostilius raised an eyebrow and kept his gaze on the riders. Slowly his scowl morphed into a wide grin. "I believe it's the Greek", he said.

Shortly after, Diocles detached from his Illyrian escort and rode ahead to meet us.

"It is good to see you well, Lord Emperor", Diocles said, and clasped our forearms in turn. "I feared that we had condemned you to the mercy of the Crow."

"We had word of your troubles", I said. "And knew that no help would be coming from the east."

"We tried to break the blockade of the Iron Gates", Diocles confirmed. "But we failed."

"So how in hades did you get here?" Hostilius asked.

"Yesterday, at dawn, we launched another desperate assault on the *wagenburg* when thousands of Scythian horse archers, led by their queen, suddenly appeared at the rear of the Goths", my aide said. "Needless to say, it turned into a slaughter. I came to enquire whether you may know anything about their presence in the area."

"Maybe", I said, and I craned my neck to look behind him. "You seem to have misplaced the Illyrians and my legions", I jested.

My aide's expression turned serious. "I have ordered the legions to march south through the Iron Gates Pass at double pace", he said, his lips pursed. "The few Illyrians that Legate Marcellinus did not take with him are scouting their advance and protecting their flanks."

I must have frowned.

"You have not heard?" Diocles asked.

"For the sake of the gods, spit it out", Hostilius snapped.

"Legate Marcellinus and the Illyrians have engaged with the barbarian horsemen ravishing Moesia Inferior", Diocles said. "But he was forced to fall back to the old fort at Ratiaria to regroup."

"Do you know which tribe the invaders belong to?" I asked.

"Other than the fact that they crossed over from Oltenia and decorate their arrows with strange markings, we know very little", my aide said.

I shared a look with Gordas, who mirrored my concerned expression.

There was no doubt in my mind that the feared Taifali had come to the lands of Rome.

Chapter 16 – Taifali

The legions that had defended the rampart against the onslaught of the Crow had emerged victorious, but not unscathed. Many legionaries had lost their lives and even more had been wounded. I knew that to force them to march south at double pace would serve to undo the hard-won morale that they had gained.

We left the cohorts of the five legions that fought in the Battle of the Devil's Dyke under the command of a trusted tribune to take them south of the Danube at a pace that would not overtax the wounded. Gordas, Hostilius, Cai, Diocles and I rode to catch up with the vexillations of the other legions that were making their way south through the Iron Gates.

Mid-afternoon, while riding east along the valley of the Tibiscus towards the Gates, we came across the Roxolani and the Yazyges who were returning to the flatlands west of the mountains, the plains that they called home.

"Where are your legions, Father?" Aritê asked when her scouts brought us into her and Naulobates's presence.

The Roxolani needed to return home to safeguard the tribe and for that reason I decided to keep the invasion of the Taifali from her.

I gestured to the west. "We have left them to lick their wounds while we go south", I said. "Were you successful in your hunt?"

"Following Cannabaudes's defeat, the remnants of his army scattered into clans and tribal groupings", Naulobates said. "It made it easier for us to ride them down and kill them. Some must have escaped our blades and arrows, but they will either perish in the coming winter or be taken as slaves by the Carpiani", he added with a shrug.

When I bade my daughter farewell she embraced me and whispered into my ear. "You would not be hurrying south if Rome is not in need of your blade, Father", she said. "I know and appreciate that you do not wish to weaken us further. May Arash guide you on your path."

I blessed her, issued a nod of confirmation and turned Intikam's head towards the Empire.

* * *

Three days later, less than a watch after passing through Ad Aquas Herculis, the derelict town that had once been the playground of senators and emperors, we finally caught up with the Illyrians and the vexillations under Diocles's command.

Come evening, we congregated around a cooking fire outside my aide's tent.

"Twenty-five thousand mounted savages are a lot for ten thousand Illyrians to take on", Hostilius said while he sipped from his cup.

"Vibius did well by retreating from the Taifali", I said. "I never intended for the Illyrians to be effective against mounted archers, especially when they are outnumbered three to one."

"Riders born to the plains will always be able to outrun and outmanoeuvre Roman horsemen", Gordas confirmed. "Although the Illyrians are well-armoured, horse archers will whittle down their numbers by targeting their horses and then withdrawing."

"Which means that we will face the same challenges as Legate Marcellinus", Diocles said. "We have more infantry at our disposal, but legionaries are even less mobile than the Illyrians."

"You are almost correct", I replied, my words drawing a frown from Diocles and a grin from Hostilius. "We have something that Vibius does not possess."

"Which is?" my aide asked.

"The element of surprise", I replied, and took another swig from my cup.

"Tomorrow, Gordas, Hostilius and I will go south with a small escort of mounted guards", I continued. "We will not cross the river at Drobeta but ride south and east along the northern bank towards Desa, the Roman fort on the northern bank of the Danube, opposite Ratiaria." I turned to face Diocles. "Tell me, do we still have a presence at the fort?"

Diocles's head was akin to the Great Library, and after a few moments he replied, "A vexillation of the *XIII Gemina* garrison the fort at Desa, although it is only two centuries."

I nodded.

"Where must I take the legions?" Diocles asked.

"Continue the march south at double pace", I said. "Once you reach Drobeta, do not cross the Mother River, but divert the legions towards Desa. Make camp no closer than two miles inland of the fort."

"I understand, Lord Emperor", Diocles said. "And I will obey."

* * *

Two days later, we stood on the deck of a barge that ferried us and our horses from the northern bank of the Danube to Ratiaria, the fort on the Roman side of the river into which Vibius and his forces had retreated.

Earlier, I had sent two legionaries from the garrison at Desa to the southern bank with a missive for my friend. They had crossed the river in a little skiff that Gordas had been kind enough to requisition, as he preferred to phrase it, from a local fisher.

Vibius was waiting for us at the river port when we arrived. "I have let you down, Lucius", he said after we embraced, his countenance dark.

We made our way uphill, through the streets of Ratiaria, to the fort which was situated on the high ground overlooking the river. None of the citizens were aware of their emperor's presence. Apart from a few curious glances from passers-by, we were largely ignored by the people as they went about their business.

"You are not to blame", I said to Vibius as we passed through the gates of the fort. "You had not the means at your disposal to defeat more than twenty thousand horse warriors."

"Had?" Vibius asked, raising an eyebrow.

"Let's just say that I plan on providing our barbarian friends with a little surprise", I replied, and I was glad to see that my words brought a grin to my friend's face.

On the morrow, half a watch before sunrise, Hostilius, Gordas, Vibius and I left the fort through a sally gate bordering the river. The invaders had made their camp sixteen miles east of Ratiaria and I was keen to see it for myself. Vibius had chosen a scout to accompany us - one of the elite *speculators*, who knew the surrounding lands like the back of his hand. At first glance, Statius Alexander did not seem to carry himself like a highly trained soldier, being a small, rat-faced individual with close-cropped hair, but it soon became evident that, despite his appearance, he possessed a high level of skill and was intelligent to boot.

"The savages are watching us all the time, lord", he said as we led our mounts out the gate. "As soon as they see a patrol leaving, a messenger gallops off to their camp like Hades himself is giving chase."

He directed us around the base of the wall and then along the water's edge, our movements screened by the riverbank, until we reached the cover provided by the trees.

"Where do you wish to go, Lord Emperor?" he asked once he had made sure we were not watched.

"Take us east, to the camp of the enemy", I said. "Make sure we remain in the shadows. I do not wish to end up under the blade of a barbarian flayer."

Statius issued half a grin. "I understand and will obey, Lord Emperor", he replied, and turned his horse about to do my bidding.

The *speculator* proved his worth, guiding us along overgrown ravines and heavily forested slopes until eventually, just before midday, we arrived on the banks of a minor river. We forded the shallows and followed its waters towards the Danube, keeping to the eastern bank. A mile downstream, the flow of the river increased as it made its way to lower ground. At that point, Statius turned away from the bank and led us farther east to a steep wooded hill overlooking the floodplain of the Danube at the mouth of the Ciabrus.

From behind the cover provided by a rocky outcrop, we studied the triangular camp of the Taifali far below. The northern extremity was bordered by the Danube, the western by the Ciabrus and the southern by the steep slope we found ourselves on. The camp's layout was typically Scythian, with the tents arranged in accordance with clan and tribal affiliations. Judging by the number of horses grazing along the banks, I estimated Vibius's assessment of their numbers to be accurate.

"Can we not fall upon their camp in the night and slaughter them all?" Hostilius asked.

"Statius and his men have reconnoitred the enemy's camp", Vibius replied. "During the hours of darkness, the Taifali have more than three hundred men patrolling the perimeter. We will not get within a mile of the tents before the alarm is raised."

We were still watching when a warband trotted into camp. They escorted a train of about twenty wagons, all made in the Roman style. Behind the carts followed a long line of prisoners, no doubt locals captured as slaves.

"I have scouted the countryside in all directions, lord", Statius whispered, his lips pursed and his demeanour grim. "The savages are systematically ravaging the land and stripping it bare of anything of value."

It was clear that the invaders did not fear us. They relied on their superior weapons and mobility to keep the Romans at bay, a strategy that was clearly paying off.

After eyeballing the camp for nearly a sixth of a watch, Hostilius stood to leave. "I've seen enough", he said. "Besides, all these barbarian camps are nothing more than a disorganised bunch of tents."

"We will wait until a third of a watch past noon", I said.

Hostilius scowled and stole a glance at the sun. "Why?" he asked.

"I have left orders for the tribune of the fort at Ratiaria to send a thousand horsemen out on patrol exactly at noon", I said. "They will canter east for no farther than five miles and then return to the fort."

Hostilius's scowl morphed into a grin. "Because you wish to see how quickly the Scythians get word of an approaching threat and how quickly they react."

I nodded, unclipped a skin from my saddle and reclined with my back against a boulder.

A sixth of a watch later, two barbarian riders thundered into the sprawling camp. They weaved through the sea of tents and swung from their saddles somewhere near the centre, presumably to report to their chieftain or king. Not long after, a war horn echoed and at least three thousand ululating warriors streamed from the camp, forded the Ciabrus, and galloped off towards the west.

"Now we can leave", I said, and swung up into the saddle.

On our way back I rode abreast of Statius, while Gordas scouted the now familiar route. "Do not be concerned", I said when I noticed the *speculator's* apprehension. "My barbarian friend will warn us if there is danger ahead."

For a span of heartbeats he studied Gordas, who sniffed the air like a wolf on the prowl. Convinced, Statius issued a nod.

"Tell me about the terrain between the Taifali camp and Ratiaria", I said.

He contemplated my question for a few moments.

"Lord", he said. "A dry floodplain borders the southern bank of the Danube. It is a strip of ground about two hundred paces wide that the farmers use as pastureland for cattle and goats. The soil is fertile and some use it to grow cabbages and leeks."

I nodded.

"To the south, the floodplain is bordered by a steep, forested ridge", he said. "Just like the one we watched the enemy from today."

Suddenly an idea came to me, or mayhap it was Arash who whispered into my ear. "Apart from the barbarian's camp, is there another place between here and the fort where the flat ground bordering the river is broader?"

"There is, lord", he said.

"Show me", I replied.

* * *

The place which Statius had described was ten miles east of Ratiaria - a five-mile-long stretch of open pastureland, seven hundred paces across. To the north flowed the Danube, and to the south lay a steep forested incline that bordered on higher ground.

"The flat ground that abuts the river is ideal for horsemen", Gordas said from where we watched from the edge of the trees. He twisted in the saddle and regarded the steep incline covered with shrubby undergrowth. "Maybe a small warband will be able to make it to the top, but not the numbers we saw in the camp of the Taifali."

"Good", I replied. "Then this is where we will crush the invaders."

Chapter 17 – Bear

The two days we waited for Diocles's legions to arrive at Desa was amongst the longest of my life. Almost every watch of the day reports arrived detailing the devastation that the Taifali visited upon the surrounding countryside. The barbarian horsemen raided farms and villages, butchered the men, took the women and children as slaves and torched that which they failed to carry away.

No matter how much I longed to lead the Illyrians through the gates, I knew better than most that it would only result in the destruction of the forces I needed to march on Palmyra.

On the afternoon of the second day after scouting the Taifali camp, Hostilius barged into my quarters, waving a scroll. "The Greek has arrived", he said.

"And the barges?" I asked.

"All twenty of them are anchored at Desa", he confirmed. "Concealed amongst the reeds on the northern bank."

"We need to visit Diocles without drawing attention to ourselves", I said.

"Gordas has already requisitioned a skiff", Hostilius replied, and bade me to follow.

* * *

Hostilius, Gordas, Vibius and I borrowed horses at Desa and rode north to meet my aide.

Most of the army was still strung out along the road when we arrived at the camp, two miles north of the river. The engineers had already marked out the boundaries and the soldiers were about to start digging the ditches and packing the ramparts that would become the marching camp.

"Tell them to cease their work", I commanded.

A frown appeared on Diocles's face. "Lord Emperor?" he objected. "Surely we are required to uphold the rules of the legions."

"The emperor makes the rules, doesn't he, Greek?" Hostilius growled.

Diocles conceded with a nod.

"Make camp, but do not fortify it", I said. "Tell the men to fill their stomachs before retiring for the night. I want them to be rested because they march a watch before daybreak."

"Where will the legions be marching to?" Diocles asked.

"Come", I said. "I will show you."

A third of a watch later, I reined in and walked my borrowed horse through the thicket that lined the bank of the Danube and pointed across the grey water to the pastureland that Statius had shown us three days earlier. "Tomorrow before dawn, the first five cohorts of each of the four legions at Desa are to march here and conceal themselves amongst the trees. Allow the men to rest and take repast during the hours of daylight", I said. "As soon as it is dark, the barges will depart from Desa so you should be able to commence the crossing at the start of the second watch of the evening, just after they arrive."

"A barge can accommodate one century at a time", Diocles said, "and is able to complete two trips in a watch. It means that four thousand legionaries can be transported across the river every watch."

"You should be able to get at least ten thousand soldiers to the southern bank", I confirmed. "Do not light fires and keep the men as quiet as possible. Legate Marcellinus will be waiting for you."

"I will see to it", Diocles said, his lips pursed with determination. "Where will you be, Lord Emperor?"

"Poking the bear", I replied.

* * *

The following morning, Statius Alexander, the *speculator*, reported to me. Earlier, I had asked him to watch the watchers.

"There are two sets of barbarian scouts keeping an eye on Ratiaria", Statius said. "Two of them are positioned in the woods just south of the fort, and two more about a hundred paces farther west."

I gestured for him to continue.

"They know their business", he said. "One conceals himself up in the branches while the other keeps watch from the forest floor. That way it is almost impossible to kill one without alerting the other."

"We could use bows", I suggested.

Statius's face fell. "We have a few men amongst us who hunt with the bow, lord", he said. "But none good enough to kill silently."

I noticed a grin appear on Gordas's lips.

"What do the men in the ranks call me?" I asked Statius.

"The Scythian", he replied. "Although I do not know the reason, lord."

"Report to my quarters at the start of the third watch of the night, *speculator*", I said. "And I will show you why."

Statius held up an open palm in protest. "With respect, lord", he said. "The forest at night is not the place for the Roman Emperor."

"Don't you worry", Hostilius opined from the far side of the room. "Take them with you and you may end up learning a thing or two."

* * *

When the scout arrived at my quarters at the appointed hour, Gordas was helping me to strap on the last of my Scythian armour. Unlike Roman armour, the scales were fashioned from the hooves of horses. It was as strong as iron but much lighter, and unlike metal scales, did not emit a sound when the segments rubbed against one another or bumped against the hilt of a blade.

"Take us to the scouts", I said, extracted my bow from its pouch, slipped the loop of a string into the horn nock, and took two armour-piercing arrows into my fist.

Gordas did likewise.

"You have only four arrows", Statius said.

"You told us there were four scouts", I replied.

"But what if you miss?" he asked.

Gordas issued a feral grin. "Men born to the Sea of Grass do no miss", he sneered, pushed past Statius, and melted into the darkness beyond.

A third of a watch later, the *speculator* led us through the same sally gate that we had used a few days earlier. This time we did not go east, but circled around the base of the wall in the other direction.

Gordas and I were no strangers to moving silently in the night. I noticed that, at least initially, Statius glanced over his shoulder almost continuously because he failed to hear us.

We moved through the undergrowth, guided by the dim light of a waning crescent moon, advancing no more than a dozen paces at a time to ensure that we did not frighten the creatures of the night, whose silence would surely betray our presence. Thirty paces into the shadows, Statius came to a halt and raised two fingers. We edged in beside him, and he first indicated something in the canopy above and then another shape reclining against a trunk, both about fifty paces distant.

He gestured that we should move closer, but I shook my head and waved away his protests.

For a span of forty heartbeats, I kept my gaze on the shape in the canopy until I saw the shadow shift.

I nodded to Gordas.

We both fitted shafts, drew back past our ears, and released almost simultaneously. The fletching of my arrow brushed my left thumb as it left the string and streaked into the canopy. At fifty paces, the three-bladed iron tips effortlessly punched through the bones of their skulls and lodged deep into the wood, pinning the corpses to the trunk.

Statius looked over his shoulder and for the first time that evening I noticed not concern in his eyes, but fear mixed with respect.

A third of a watch later, after dispatching the last of the barbarian watchmen, we made our way back to the fort. Statius said little, no doubt trying to come to terms with the happenings of the night.

* * *

Riding a horse in the night with only the light of Mani as a beacon is difficult enough. Mounting a large-scale cavalry attack during the hours of darkness is not only impractical but outright foolish.

It was for this reason that, when the Illyrians trotted out the gates, they were not riding to war, but were on their way to rendezvous with the Roman infantry that was crossing the river. My plan hinged on the element of surprise, so Statius led us on a circular route to negate the possibility of being discovered by other barbarian scouts that the enemy may have posted between Ratiaria and their camp.

When we eventually arrived on the open ground bordering the river, the barges were unloading the last tranche of legionaries crossing over from the northern bank.

"Are your men deployed?" I asked Diocles.

"They are, Lord Emperor", my aide confirmed.

"Good", I replied. "I will go to provoke the enemy. Do not show yourselves until I give the signal."

* * *

At the grey hour of the wolf, Hostilius and I waited at the head of a thousand Illyrians on the western bank of the Ciabrus River, just opposite the camp of the invaders.

"What's keeping Gordas?" the Primus Pilus asked, no doubt keen to get stuck in.

Just then the Hun seemed to materialise from the mist resting on the dark water. He walked his horse closer, the mare's sides stained by blood dripping from three fresh scalps. He gestured to the trophies. "Three warriors were watching the river", he said, grinning like a wolf. "At least five dozen guard the perimeter of the camp."

I nodded my approval. "If we are able to cross without being seen it will buy us at least three hundred heartbeats."

"That is the difference between life and death", Hostilius pointed out.

"Come", I said, and led the thousand Illyrians across the shallow river.

We had hardly emerged from the trees on the riverbank when a ram's horn blared. I took four arrows into my draw hand and nudged Intikam to a canter.

The bows of the Taifali were no doubt powerful, but they were no match for the lopsided horn and sinew bows of the Urugundi, the elongated top limb endowing them with superior power and range. I drew the string of my Hun bow to my ear, and a heartbeat later the arrow slammed into the torso of a sentry. Gordas and I released again and again, and as we closed with the sea of tents there were none left to oppose us.

But we had kicked the proverbial hornets' nest, and within the span of twenty heartbeats, the sleeping camp morphed into a hive of activity with warriors scrambling about to fit armour and saddle mounts.

I turned Intikam's head to the left, spurred him to a gallop and thundered along the edge of the sprawling camp, heading back to the river. On my command, the signifer raised the standard and an eerie wail left the iron maw of the wolf head. As one, the Illyrians unclipped war darts from the insides of their shields and cast the deadly missiles in amongst the tents. Once the fifth volley of *plumbatae* had risen into the sky, I turned Intikam west, back towards the Ciabrus River.

Hostilius, Gordas and I crossed first, but we waited until the last of the Illyrian warband had powered up onto dry ground, my eyes never leaving the enemy camp.

"When do we start riding for our lives?" Hostilius asked as we watched thousands of Scythian horsemen spilling from the camp, all heading our way.

"Now will be a good time", I replied.

Chapter 18 – Lambs

Although the Illyrians wore body armour, I had commanded that their horses remain unencumbered by the boiled leather and scale that they usually donned when riding into battle. It would exhaust the large warhorses and do little good in return. Most of it protected the front quarters of the mounts, the vulnerable areas when charging an enemy, and would serve no purpose when fleeing.

We must have put almost a mile between us and the camp when I stole a quick glance over my shoulder and noticed the first of the Taifali riders emerge from the treeline on the banks of the river.

"Will we make it?" I asked Gordas.

"If we maintain this pace, Intikam and my mare might escape", he replied casually. "But the others will all die."

"Slow to a canter", I commanded, and the signifer relayed the command.

The Taifali's mounts were not of the same quality as those of the Huns or the Roxolani, but still, the blood of the hardy horses of the Sea of Grass coursed through their veins and slowly but surely they closed the gap.

We thundered west along the two hundred-pace-wide flat ground bordering the river, alternating between a canter and a gallop to preserve our horses. By the time we were three miles from where Diocles was waiting with the legions, I knew that the Taifali would catch us before we reached safety. Intikam was the best of the best and even he, who had the blood of Simsek, was struggling to keep up the pace.

I shared a look with Gordas, whose expression served to confirm my suspicions.

"We must slow to a trot", the Hun said.

I twisted in the saddle and noticed that the Scythians, who were less than four hundred paces behind, were already stringing their bows and reaching for their quivers.

"No", I replied. "We will continue at a gallop."

"You will kill the horses", Gordas said, stating the obvious.

"But it will give me more time to beseech Arash", I replied, which silenced the Hun.

A short while later, the first of our warband's horses collapsed, the unfortunate soldier crushed by the weight of his mount.

"We should rein in, turn around and charge the enemy", Gordas suggested. "It will be glorious."

I was contemplating his suggestion when a cheer rose from the faltering ranks ahead of us.

Three hundred paces in front of the leading riders, a line of fully armoured Illyrians approached at a gallop, led by none other than Vibius. I thanked Arash for heeding my prayers and silently cursed my friend for disregarding the plan. But as they came closer I noticed that he led fewer than three hundred men, a paltry force that would surely be swept aside by the horde of Taifali.

He and his men were sacrificing themselves to save us.

I was about to intervene when Gordas spoke. "Your friend is reclaiming his tainted honour", the Hun growled. "You will be doing him no favours if you interfere. Leave him to choose his own fate."

Vibius and his fully armoured black riders surged around us, skilfully closed their ranks, and thundered down on the approaching horde, their lances levelled.

In reply, the Taifali's arrows darkened the early morning sky as thousands of shafts plummeted down on our saviours.

I pulled on the leathers and twisted in the saddle.

Unlike when they had encountered the full might of the Illyrians days before, the Taifali did not wish to feign retreat from a warband they outnumbered more than ten to one. Their broad-tipped arrows rained down on the well-armoured riders, but, save for a handful who succumbed to the storm, the iron tips failed to penetrate the thick leather and scale of the black riders.

In quick succession the Illyrians launched three volleys of war darts. Before the vicious barbs found their targets, the line of Roman horsemen split into two and wheeled about to gallop back the way they had come.

Many of the light-armoured Taifali leading the pursuit fell prey to the lead-weighted, barbed missiles. Horses stumbled into each other and scores of riders went down in a tumble of limbs and hooves. For a moment I believed that their charge would falter, but the Scythians surged around their fallen brethren, their ululating war cries silencing the screams of their dying.

The Romans' desperate charge had not halted the Taifali pursuit, but it allowed us to widen the gap to almost half a mile, enough to give the command to slow down to a trot. Gordas, Hostilius and I hung back, waiting for our saviour and his men to catch up.

When Vibius was close enough so that I could see the mischievous grin on his face, he raised a hand in greeting. His arm was still high when a black rider called out a warning, and moments later another volley of Taifali shafts slammed into the fleeing warband. With horror I watched Vibius's horse jerk its head to the side, three arrows embedded in its rump. The animal groaned in pain, stumbled, and went to ground. My friend was hurled from the saddle, coming to a rolling halt fewer than forty paces away.

Before Gordas or Hostilius could stop me, Intikam was at a gallop. Clinging onto my stallion with only my legs, one hand on the reins, I leaned down and grabbed Vibius by his harness. Arash strengthened the sinews in my arm and I swung him onto the back of my horse while Taifali arrows rained down on us. I felt the impacts as three, mayhap four, shafts slammed into the scales of my horse-hoof vest. The armour had been a gift from Bradakos, my mentor and king of the Roxolani, and the well-crafted scales turned the iron. When I glanced over my shoulder the Taifali were less than a hundred paces away. I said a prayer to the god of war and fire and dug my heels into my stallion's sides.

Arash heard my pleas.

Despite carrying the weight of two armoured men, I felt Intikam surge ahead and I knew that the Taifali's horses would never match my stallion's power. His lungs worked like bellows, the muscles bulging in his powerful neck, his ears drawn flat against his massive head.

And then Gordas and Hostilius were beside me. The Hun reached out, somehow transferred Vibius onto his mare, and together we thundered onto the green pastureland where twelve thousand legionaries and ten thousand Illyrians were waiting.

Like lambs to the slaughter the Taifali followed in our wake.

* * *

A Roman *buccina* heralded our arrival, and from the western edge of the pastureland, ten thousand black riders bore down on us. The left flank of the Illyrians was anchored against the Danube and the right against the steep forested slope, their ranks at least fifteen deep. I glanced over my shoulder and noticed that the Scythians were wisely reining in as they were not fool enough to meet the heavily armoured lancers' charge.

A ramshorn blared and the Scythians turned their horses around to head back the way they had come.

The shrill note of a *buccina* echoed off the slope, and in response five cohorts of heavy infantry jogged from the cover of the trees and formed up across the gap that served as an entrance to the pastureland that was fast becoming a death trap for the Scythians.

The Taifali commander roared, and once again the sky darkened with more than twenty thousand arrows.

With a sound resembling a clap of thunder, the front ranks of battle-hardened veterans slammed the bottom edges of their *scuta* onto the ground and went down into a crouch. The legionaries in the rear ranks raised their shields above their heads and slid them into place, their formation resembling the clay tiles of a Roman roof.

Arrows rained down like hail, but the iron-clad men of Rome weathered the storm.

Realising they were trapped, the Taifali thundered towards the perceived safety of the forested ridge.

The front ranks of the Illyrians came to a halt a few paces in front of us. The tribune commanding the black riders detached from the ranks and bowed his head. "Lord Emperor", he said. "What are your orders?"

"Signal to the legions in the forest to advance into the open and deploy in testudo formation", I said.

The *buccina* relayed my orders, and it seemed as if the trees themselves came to life as nine thousand soldiers stepped from the shadows into the light and morphed into a wall of plywood and iron no Scythian arrow could breach.

"Just give the command", Hostilius growled from beside me. "It is going to be a pleasure to watch these vermin being exterminated."

Suddenly I felt the undeniable presence of Arash, and I held up an open palm. "Wait", I said.

A frown split Hostilius's brow and he issued a deep sigh. "You want me to get you a branch, don't you, Domitius?"

* * *

Hostilius, Gordas, Diocles and I walked our horses towards the milling horde of Taifali, coming to a halt just outside of the range of their arrows. Although his right fist rested on his sword, Hostilius carried a leafy-green olive branch in his left hand and a scowl on his face.

A lone rider detached from the Scythian horsemen and trotted towards us, coming to a halt five paces away.

The man was no coward as he faced us without any of his oathsworn. Unlike most Scythians, the Taifali's hair was dark brown. His hair and beard were neatly plaited and adorned with the knuckle bones of vanquished enemies, and rings of silver and gold. Underneath his fur-trimmed kaftan he wore a scale vest of iron. A curved longsword, battle-axe and dagger were strapped to his leather belt, and a strung horn bow slung across his broad shoulders. Swirling blue-green tattoos covered the exposed skin on his face, hands and forearms.

"I am Senoch, king of the Taifali", he said in the language of the Sea of Grass.

"I am Eochar of the Roxolani", I replied, "but some call me the king of Rome."

"You are the one called Eochar the Merciless", he said. "I have heard your name whispered around the fires of the warriors of my sworn lord."

"Why do you come into my lands uninvited?" I asked.

"I am oath-bound to the Crow", he said. "The Taifali owe fealty to Cannabaudes, who has tasked us with raiding the lands of Rome south of the Mother River."

"Then you serve a corpse, Senoch of the Taifali", Gordas growled. "Eochar slew him with his own hand and scattered the bones of his warriors across the field of blood."

The Taifali stared at us in disbelief, but he could find no treachery in our eyes. Eventually he nodded and his shoulders slumped. "The horde of the Crow drove us from our ancestral lands", he said. "Those lands have now been settled by others and we have not the numbers to reclaim it."

"I will give you land so that you may resettle your people", I said. "But there are conditions."

He met my gaze and nodded, indicating that he was willing to negotiate.

"I will arrange for you and your men to be ferried across the Mother River", I said. "You may keep your loot, but the Romans you have captured as slaves must be released unharmed."

Again, he nodded.

"Ten thousand of your best warriors will fight under my banner for a year", I said. "They will receive food and fodder and a share of the spoils we capture. We will seal the arrangement with a blood oath before the gods."

He nodded, but replied with a question. "Which lands do you speak of?" he asked.

"The plains north of the Mother River bordering the Alutus", I replied.

"We travelled across those plains", he said. "It will suit us, but I have heard that to the west dwell the formidable Roxolani. They are ruled by a warrior queen who favours Argimpasa, the dark one. She is said to show no mercy towards her foes. I do not wish to occupy lands that will pit me against such a ruthless enemy."

"Do not concern yourself with her", I said. "She will not interfere."

"Who are you that you speak for a Scythian queen, King Eochar?" he asked.

"I am her father", I replied.

Chapter 19 – The East (January 272 AD)

Byzantium in Thrace, three months later.

Hostilius, Gordas and I reclined on couches that were arrayed on the balcony of the imperial palace. The colonnaded portico afforded a view of the exquisite gardens and the natural harbour beyond. We had travelled ahead to Byzantium accompanied by the Illyrian cavalry and Taifali horsemen. The six Roman legions and Berber cavalry were yet to arrive. In addition, we had decided to send two legions across the Middle Sea to Alexandria in Aegypt to force Zenobia to split her forces, while at the same time attempting to restore the grain shipments to Rome.

The Primus Pilus popped a handful of walnut-filled dates into his mouth and used his chin to gesture to an imperial galley gliding into the harbour. "Looks like they're back", he said, and swallowed the sweetmeats down with a gulp of white.

"Who will command the fleet sailing to Aegypt?" I asked, changing the subject.

"Vibius has to stay", Hostilius asserted. "He knows the East better than all of us put together. And for the love of the gods, don't send the Greek. He looks and speaks just like the provincials across the strait. We need him as well."

"Are you volunteering to go?" I asked the Primus Pilus.

"I've got better things to do than to scamper about the Aegyptian desert", he muttered. "Besides, you need me to watch your back."

My gaze drifted to Gordas who occupied a couch all by himself, slowly drawing a whetstone along the blade of his battle-axe.

"If you send the Hun, he'll probably put the whole of Aegypt to the sword, never mind the Palmyrene garrison at Alexandria", Hostilius said.

We were yet to come to a decision when Vibius and Diocles strolled into the room. I gestured for them to take seats, and a pouring slave rushed to fill their cups. Two days earlier, the two had travelled across the strait to Chalcedon in Bithynia in an effort to gauge the sentiment.

Vibius took a long draught of wine and reclined on the couch beside Diocles. "The governor of Bithynia is a good man", he said. "He has remained loyal to you amidst the advance of Zenobia's forces. Galatia, the province that lies directly east, has submitted to the queen of Palmyra."

"Or", Hostilius said. "The governor noticed the hundreds of Roman warships arriving in the harbour over the last weeks."

"The reason why he has remained loyal is not important", Diocles said. "It means that we will be able to cross the strait and use Chalcedon as a base from which to launch the campaign against the usurper. For that reason I have ordered the governor to bring supplies into the warehouses of the city. To ensure his continued support I have committed to pay for it with gold."

"Seeing that you've got all the answers", Hostilius said. "Who should we place in command of the fleet sailing to Aegypt?"

"Legate Bonosus, who commands the fleet stationed on the Rhine, is a contender for sure", Diocles said.

"He's as hard as they come", Vibius confirmed. "That's why it's a pity that he's hardly ever sober."

"In Bonosus's defence", Hostilius added, "the only way to deal with the Germani is to negotiate while everyone's drunk."

"What about Legate Probus?" the Primus Pilus asked.
"Marcus once told me that he is a distant relation. Maybe he's blessed with some of our late friend's virtues."

"I've heard only good things about him", Vibius said, and I noticed Diocles nod his agreement.

"Summon him", I said. "We have time. It will take weeks to ferry the army across the strait. Only then will the ships be available to sail south to Alexandria."

* * *

It was two days after the Ides of March when Diocles and I watched as *foederati* cavalry led their blindfolded horses across the gangplank of the transport vessel onto the concrete quayside of Chalcedon.

"I believe that this ship is the last one, Lord Emperor", my aide sighed, and issued a tired smile.

I slapped him on the back. "Wars are won or lost long before the day of the battle", I said. "And by the looks of it, you have already set us up for victory."

The ring of praetorian guards parted to let Hostilius pass. Over the preceding days I had seen my friend's frustration grow until it seemed as if his lip was curled into a permanent scowl.

"I had to oversee the daily punishment", he growled. "Almost half a dozen legionaries had to be put under the scourge."

"We will need those soldiers in the days to come", I said.

"I made sure that the ones who wielded the whips went easy on the bastards. Still, it'll be weeks until they're fit enough to strap on armour", he replied. "But you know what happens if we turn a blind eye, eh?"

I issued a curt nod as I knew better than most that iron discipline was required when more than seventy-five thousand killers succumbed to boredom. "We march in two days' time", I said to Diocles. "Issue orders to the commanders immediately."

For the first time in almost three months, I saw both of them grin.

* * *

From Chalcedon we marched east to Nicomedia. Mid-afternoon on the third day on the road, an outrider came to report. "There are many people on the road, lord", he said. "They are slowly moving towards the city and, er…"

It was clear that the scout had seen something that baffled him, so I untied a wineskin from my saddle and offered it to him.

"I cannot, lord", he said, averting his eyes.

"Drink", I said. "It is an order."

When he had taken a few large gulps I asked him to continue. "Describe what you saw", I said.

"Fifty men were carrying the freshly felled trunk of a large pine", he said. "And they were followed by a group of townsfolk, maybe four hundred men and women. The only thing I could think of was that they had cut themselves a ram and were marching to the gates of Nicomedia to batter it down. But they wore no armour and it seemed that they were, er…, crying."

I glanced at Diocles who had a grin plastered on his face, so I ordered the scout to keep the wine and dismissed him.

"It is the time of the annual festivities to honour Cybele", he said. "On the twenty-second day of March, the Greeks commemorate the death of the goddess's lover, Attis. The bearers of the tree are carrying the trunk to the temple in the city."

He had hardly finished when a small group of elders approached on horseback from the direction of the south, and I signalled for my guards to allow them through.

"Lord Emperor", their leader said after introducing himself and his companions. "We come to welcome you to Nicomedia. The day of your arrival is auspicious. It will be a great honour if you could preside over the sacrifices to Cybele that are performed at sundown."

Diocles leaned in closer so that our guests would not hear his words. "I suggest that you accept, lord", he said. "But emphasise to them that you are departing tomorrow."

I must have raised an eyebrow.

"Because the day after tomorrow is the Day of Blood", he clarified.

"What does that mean?" Hostilius asked from behind us.

"It will suffice to say that none of us would wish to be involved", Diocles replied.

Later that evening, once I had placated Cybele and the city fathers with my presence, Hostilius, Diocles, Cai, Vibius and I gathered in the villa that was made available to us.

"Our spies confirm that Zenobia has a strong cavalry force stationed at Ancyra", Diocles said, pressing the tip of his stylus onto the vellum map. "The capital of Galatia lies just more than two hundred miles to the east."

"Let me guess", Hostilius said. "She's been using this army to cower the provinces into changing their allegiance."

Diocles nodded. "It is the army that has been systematically moving west through the Eastern Provinces to claim them for the Palmyrene Empire."

"I wouldn't be surprised if her horsemen hadn't even had to draw their blades once", the Primus Pilus said, took a swig from his cup and reclined against the backrest of the embroidered divan. "The eastern cities are filled with spineless Greek merchants. They don't give a rotten fig who they pay taxes to as long as they are allowed to keep on hoarding more gold."

Diocles raised an eyebrow but did not gainsay the Primus Pilus. "Which means that we will be able to take back the cities without much effort, I suppose", my aide said.

"Exactly", Hostilius replied. "Assuming that Zenobia had not left a garrison to ensure that her newly conquered subjects remain loyal."

"Zenobia cares little for the provinces west of the Taurus Mountains", I said. "But she will wish to keep us from crossing the passes into Syria." I leaned in closer and pressed a finger onto the map, indicating the city at the mouth of the Orontes River. "The queen of Palmyra knows that Antioch is the gateway to her realm. She will do all in her power to keep us from taking the city."

"Then why didn't we just sail to Antioch?" Hostilius asked. "We could have saved ourselves a lot of trouble."

"We wanted to", Diocles admitted. "But it would have been almost impossible to land enough men simultaneously to breach the walls."

"We don't have enough ships, do we?" Hostilius surmised.

"To build them would have taken a year, mayhap two", I confirmed. "By that stage Rome's grain stores would have been empty and the people in open revolt."

"Suits me just fine", Hostilius said. "Marching toughens up the men nicely. Besides, it gives us the opportunity to chase Zenobia's vermin out of Anatolia."

"I agree", I said. "Anatolia is rich and fertile enough to supply our army for months."

"Great", Hostilius said, and stood to refill his cup. "We will push on towards Antioch, then."

"There is one problem, though", Vibius said, and pressed a finger onto the vellum. "To get to Antioch we will need to march our army through the Cilician Gates.

Hostilius shrugged. "What of it?"

I looked to Vibius to enlighten us as few knew the Eastern Provinces better.

"The pass is infamous in the East", he confirmed. "They say that *the man who fears not the Throat of the Mountain, fears not the gods.*"

"Old wives' tales", the Primus Pilus said, scoffing at Vibius's words.

"The Cilician Gates are treacherous", Vibius replied, "but potentially we have a bigger problem - a heavily fortified city that guards the entrance to the pass."

"What is it called?" I asked.

"Tyana", Vibius replied.

Chapter 20 – Merchant

Tyana, the fortress city guarding the approach to the Cilician Gates.

Six months earlier, a nobleman had arrived before the gates.

Were it not for the scroll that he presented to the head of the *collegium* of cloth merchants, the newcomer would not have been so readily accepted by the guild. But the sealed letter penned by the hand of the governor of Antioch carried much weight. Due to his extensive trade contacts in the East, the handsome stranger was able to supply the best quality silk at prices never before seen in the markets of Tyana, or for that matter, in the whole of Asia Minor. He was hated by competitors, but soon became the darling of the rich and powerful men and women of the city. Eager to be in his good graces, he became a fixture at dinner feasts and functions, where he recited works of Homer and Euripides and lavished gifts upon his friends and clients.

At a social event hosted by a wealthy trader, he was introduced to the man's wife, Irene. She was the daughter of the magistrate, a man called Hypatos, while her brother, Lyander, commanded the city watch. As fate would have it, Irene's husband fell ill soon after the dinner party and succumbed to dysentery. The silk trader visited the grieving widow to extend his condolences and to offer his support, but soon they were the talk of the city as her grief was vanquished by a blossoming romance.

The two lovers did not waste time, and risking the ire of the more conservative citizens, wed within a month. This selfless act of taking pity on a widow further ingratiated him with not only her immediate family, but also with the city elites.

Although Gaius Hairan liked to think that he had concocted the scheme, the truth was that Zenobia had planted the idea in his mind when he approached her after his brother had been taken as a hostage by Lady Vitruvia, the real power behind the breakaway Gallic Empire.

He sat in the study of his large villa in Tyana, sipping on Roman wine while in his mind's eye reliving the audience with the queen months before.

"The Cilician Gates are formidable, but not so easy to defend", she had said. "The truth is there are many paths across the mountainside suited to men on foot. This will not take the half-breed emperor and his legions long to discover. I will gladly sacrifice Tyana and its people in return for Aurelian's demise. Even if the Romans put every man, woman and child in the city to the sword, it will be worth it. Not only will we save your brother, but also Palmyra itself."

Gaius Hairan, or rather Heraclammon, as he was known in Tyana, took another sip of *falernian*, a smile playing around the corners of his mouth as he revelled in how easily he had managed to deceive not only Irene, but also the people of the city.

He was brought back to the present by a knock at the door. "Clammon, my dear", his comely wife cooed. "I am sorry to disturb you, but my father and Lyander are here to see you."

Heraclammon broke into a broad smile that even his own mother would have struggled to label as insincere. "I much prefer to share a glass of wine with you and your family than toil in my study, my love."

Irene led her husband by the hand into the spacious *atrium* of the villa where her father and brother were waiting. Heraclammon welcomed his guests, embraced them in turn, and honoured them by ushering the two into the *tablinum*, the private study reserved for only the closest acquaintances of the *paterfamilias* of the household.

Hypatos produced a scroll from a pouch and placed it on the ivory-inlaid table. "For weeks we have heard rumours, brought to the city by merchants travelling from the north", he said. "But now the rumours have become reality."

Heraclammon glanced at the scroll bearing the intricate seal of the Roman Emperor. "It is a missive from Aurelian himself", he surmised.

Lyander nodded. "The Roman army is on its way to the city", he said. "And the emperor wants us to open the gates to him."

Gaius Hairan knew that the moment of truth had arrived. Although he was almost overwhelmed by nervous tension, he managed to suppress his emotions. Rather than respond to the words, Heraclammon calmly picked up his glass goblet and took a long, slow sip to show that he had little interest in his visitors' revelation.

"Apart from his reputation as a merciless conqueror, we know little of the man in whose name the scroll was dispatched", Hypatos said. "We realise that you are a learned man who has extensive trade contacts all across the breadth of the Empire, and came to see whether you could shed light on the emperor's character, while offering us words of advice."

"You overestimate my talents, my dear friends", he said, his demeanour humble.

"Please give us your opinion", Lyander begged. "If we open the gates to Aurelian he may have my father executed for treason for shifting his loyalties to the queen of the East. Maybe if we keep the gates closed we might be able to negotiate a full pardon."

Gaius Hairan nodded conspiratorially. "Have you had any news from Ancyra?" he asked.

His guests shook their heads in reply.

"I heard that the council of Ancyra was condemned to death for allowing the city to bend the knee to Zenobia", Gaius Hairan lied. "They chose to open the gates. I suggest that we beseech Fortuna to calm Aurelian's ire before he arrives at Tyana."

And then came the question that Gaius Hairan had been waiting for.

"What would you do if you were in my place?" Hypatos asked.

Gaius Hairan had an answer at the ready, but he failed to speak for a hundred heartbeats to add credibility to his words.

"I would close the gates of the city to the army of the emperor", he said. "He will not advance to the Cilician Gates with an enemy at his back that could possibly disrupt his supplies."

The two visitors nodded.

"Once he has made camp outside the walls, I would send a trusted envoy to negotiate on behalf of the council", he continued. "You occupy a strong defensive position and Aurelian will be reluctant to weaken his forces by throwing his men against the mighty walls of Tyana."

Hypatos and his son were merchants who had never wielded a blade in anger. "Who would be willing to risk his life by riding out to speak with such a merciless tyrant?" Lyander asked, no doubt concerned that the task might fall onto his shoulders.

"I will do it, of course", Gaius Hairan replied. And for the first time that day his smile was truthful.

Chapter 21 – Envoy

Almost two weeks after marching from Nicomedia, we arrived at Ancyra.

Days before, the Palmyrene cavalry that numbered about ten thousand riders had departed for the East, withdrawing beyond the Taurus Mountains. It was a wise decision. Apart from being outnumbered, the hilly terrain of Galatia did not favour horsemen.

Although the city elders hailed us as their saviours and welcomed us with open arms, we did not remain for longer than the time that it took to install two third-line cohorts into the empty barracks. The Roman soldiers would act as a garrison to secure the army's line of supply in case Zenobia had a change of heart.

Ancyra was situated about halfway between Chalcedon and Tyana, the city that guarded the pass to the East. The following day, we continued our march south towards the Cilician Gates. All along the way, the people of the smaller towns and villages cheered us as we passed, no doubt unwilling to provoke the great war machine of Rome.

Nine days later, after crossing from Galatia into Cappadocia, we arrived at Salaberina, a small settlement with a low wall about three days' march north of Tyana. The town lay in the shadow of a towering white peak that rose high above the plain. Small rivulets of sparkling meltwater trickled down the mountainside and seeped into the green pastures farther down the slope.

While we waited for our tent to be erected, Gordas glanced up at the abundant grazing blanketing the hills. "We should stay here for two or three days", he said. "The grass is of good quality and the horses need rest, especially those of the Taifali. There are many ways to lose a battle - one of them is to be mounted on tired horses."

The Hun had a point.

"Make the arrangements", I said to Diocles. "The army will remain for two nights."

"By the way", Hostilius asked. "What is the wine supply looking like?"

"If we pass through the Cilician Gates without much delay we will be able to procure provisions at the harbour city of Tarsus", my aide said. "The wine should be sufficient to last until then."

The Primus Pilus turned to face me. "If the Greek says that we have enough, it means that tonight we can afford to issue double rations of wine", he said. "The boys have been marching under the hot sun for weeks. They need something to boost their morale. And it will lighten the load for the cart horses as well."

Later that evening as the sun set, we congregated around a fire in front of my tent in the centre of the legionary camp. Thousands of horses grazed on the lush grass on the slopes above, while the soldiers celebrated their extra wine rations with song and games of dice.

"What you expect at Tyana, Lucius of Da Qin?" Cai asked.

"I see no reason why the city should not open the gates to us", I replied. "Why would they risk our ire? Besides, Tyana is no different from the other cities in Galatia, apart from the fact that it has been under Palmyrene control for a few months longer."

"Send them a letter and ask them", Vibius suggested. "Then we do not have to speculate."

"I guess no harm can come of it", the Primus Pilus said. "It's not that they don't know that we are coming."

My aide rose to find his stylus but I waved him back to his seat. "You need rest", I said. "We will send a rider at sunrise."

* * *

Diocles was giving me the gist of the daily reports when Hostilius pushed open the flap and strolled into the praetorium. "The Hun's suggestion was sound", he said, and poured himself a cup of white wine, which he diluted with water. "I've mingled with the soldiers and there's no doubt that they were in need of a day of rest to mend their gear. It's been a tough march across difficult terrain."

The Primus Pilus had hardly gained a seat when Vibius arrived, a dusty rider trailing behind him.

The *speculator* saluted in the required manner and retrieved a scroll from a pouch slung over his shoulder. Diocles accepted it on my behalf.

"Tell me of Tyana", I commanded the scout.

"The defences are formidable, Lord Emperor", he said. "The walls are high and the approach to the gates is steep and guarded by many towers."

I gestured for the soldier to remain while Diocles enlightened us.

My aide scrutinised the message. He shook his head, his lips pursed.

"They're not going to open the gates to us, are they?" Hostilius said.

"No", Diocles confirmed.

The *speculator* rummaged in his pouch and produced a small piece of parchment. "Lord", he said, extending the scrap to Diocles. "The man who handed me the scroll pressed this into my palm."

Heraclammon of Tyana to Imperator Caesar Lucius Domitius Aurelianus Augustus.

Lord Emperor, the city council has decided to remain loyal to the queen of the East. When you are camped outside the walls, please refrain from unleashing your men before I have come to speak with you.

I will do anything in my power to ensure that you gain control of the city. I say this not because I wish to be rewarded, but because I value the lives of the people of Tyana.

I raised an eyebrow. "Although it is not clear, I suspect that this man might be offering to betray the city."

"They say that Greeks believe that one in three hundred of their countrymen would betray the rest at whim", Hostilius pointed out. "My guess is our man wants to be appointed magistrate of the city once the dust has settled."

"Or", Diocles said, "he is the only patriot amongst traitors. Heraclammon seems to be loyal to his emperor."

"We will soon find out", Hostilius said, and chugged the wine remaining in his cup.

* * *

Four days later, we made camp just north of Tyana, the city guarding the approach to the Cilician Gates. I ordered the cavalry to patrol the lands surrounding the city, but made no attempt to besiege it.

Late afternoon, we were interrupted by the arrival of an expected guest. "Lord Emperor", the guard said. "The emissary from the city has arrived."

"Show him in", I replied, and sat down on a purple couch with gold embroidery. Hostilius, Gordas, Vibius, Diocles and Cai were all seated on divans, eager to hear the words of the man who would give us Tyana on a plate.

Two imperial guardsmen escorted the man into our presence.

The emissary from the city bowed low, like a man used to paying respects to kings and emperors. "Lord", he said. "I am your humble servant, Heraclammon of Tyana."

"Do you speak for the city?" Hostilius asked.

"Although I do not serve on the council, tribune, they have asked me to come to you on their behalf", he replied. "The elders fear that you will have them killed."

"Do you not fear me?" I asked.

"I fear more for my family than for myself, lord", he replied.

I gestured for the man to continue.

"The city fathers will open the gates only if you guarantee their safety in writing", he said. "Also, all provisions that the city supplies to your army will have to be paid for in gold at market prices."

I felt the anger rise like bile.

"These lands have been part of the Empire for generations", I said. "Your city has betrayed the oath of loyalty to the emperor by choosing to side with a usurper. Tyana is in no position to make demands."

Heraclammon inclined his head. "I have no power over the council, Lord Emperor", he said. "All I can do is give them your words."

"Return to your council and say to them that if the gates are not opened by sunset on the overmorrow, I will take the city by force and leave not a single dog alive inside the walls."

"I will do as you say, Lord Emperor", he said, and backpedaled from the praetorium.

"There will be many fleeing the city tonight", I said. "They will do so because they know that once we have constructed fortifications around Tyana, their lot will be tied to that of the city."

All nodded as we were familiar with the realities of siege warfare.

"Get your *speculators* to catch one of them", I said. "And bring him to me when you do."

* * *

I was in conversation with Gordas when the duty tribune arrived at the door of my pavilion. "Lord Emperor", he said. "The prisoner you requested is ready to interrogate. Should I summon the torturers?"

I waved away the officer's suggestion. "Not yet", I said. "Bring him in."

Twenty counts later, a thin, gangly man was manhandled into the tent by two burly guards. The greybeard ceased his struggling when he laid eyes on me, regarding my fur-edged purple cloak with wide eyes. Judging by the quality of his clothes, he was not a peasant but a tradesman.

"I will order them to release you if you give me your word that your conduct will be civil", I said in Greek. I noticed the hesitation in his eyes and indicated Gordas, "Or I can ask my friend here to ensure that you behave."

The man bowed awkwardly. "I will do as you ask, lord", he said.

I gestured for a pouring slave to hand the man a cup of wine. "You are from Tyana?" I asked.

The man took a swig from the cup to wet his throat. "I was born in the city, lord", he said, his gaze drifting to Gordas. "I am called Neilos, and I am a fuller like my father and grandfather before me."

"Do you know a man called Heraclammon, Neilos?" I asked.

"Yes, lord", he said. "He is well known in Tyana. He trades in silks and fine-woven wool from the East. I regularly treat garments supplied by him and can tell that his wares are of high quality."

"Does he have a family?" Hostilius asked.

"Yes, lord", Neilos replied. "He has a wife and two children."

I shared a look with Diocles, who offered a shrug to show that he had nothing further to ask of the fuller. "Why are you fleeing the city and where are you going?" I asked.

It was a chilly evening, but still the fuller wiped perspiration from his brow with a sleeve. "I am taking my family north, to

Caesaria", he said, "because I do not wish to be within the walls when you exact punishment on the city."

"Why do you believe I will destroy Tyana?" I asked.

Again, he wiped perspiration from his brow. "Because, lord, that was the fate of Ancyra."

"Where did you hear that?" I asked.

"From Heraclammon", Neilos replied.

Chapter 22 – Gates

Late afternoon the following day, Heraclammon arrived at the praetorium where my friends and I reclined on couches. I invited the emissary from Tyana to join us.

"The city fathers do not wish to listen to reason", he said, averting his eyes in shame. "They believe that you do not have the time nor the men to waste against the mighty walls."

"I will do what I have to", I replied, and took a sip from my cup, my eyes never leaving the Greek.

"I do not wish the people of the city to pay the price for the foolishness of the council", he said.

I nodded to show that I agreed. "What course of action do you suggest?"

The Greek leaned forward and lowered his voice. "To the east of the city, where apple orchards abut the wall, the ground slopes upwards, almost like a siege mount. There, the wall walk can be easily reached by a ladder the height of two men. When the sun rises tomorrow, I will make sure that no guards patrol the ramparts along that section."

"And what do you wish to receive as a reward for giving us the city?" Hostilius asked.

"I wish only for the people of the city to be spared and for the gratitude of my emperor", Heraclammon replied piously.

"Come to my tent once we have taken the city and you will receive your just reward", I said.

A brief smile of triumph flashed across Heraclammon's face before he inclined his head. "I will do as you command, Lord Emperor."

"What will you do with the city?" Hostilius asked once the traitor had departed.

"Is it not clear that this creature has deceived the city council?" Diocles said. "We should be merciful."

"Make an example of Tyana and give the city to the soldiers to loot", Gordas growled. "It will show other cities along the route what happens to anyone who dares to defy the emperor. If they fear your wrath, they will throw open the gates."

"Best to give mercy only to those willing to extend it, Lucius of Da Qin", Cai said, and I knew in my heart that the Easterner was right.

"I believe that Heraclammon is telling the truth about the way into the city", I said, changing the subject. "He needs to gain our trust to do whatever evil he is planning."

"Send Vibius and me", Hostilius suggested. "There's no reason for you to put yourself in harm's way."

"There is little risk", I replied. "We will take a first-line cohort. If we are able to gain the rampart, the city guard will be no match for trained legionaries."

"In the meantime, I'll have the carpenters cobble together half a dozen ladders", the Primus said, and stood to leave. "That's if the sappers can find a proper tree in these barren hills."

* * *

I extended my arms to the side so that Diocles could strap on my muscle cuirass over my bloodred wool tunic. The blackened steel was embossed with silver, depicting a magnificent winged stallion trampling the enemies of Rome, while each strip of my boiled leather skirt was finished with a silver cap sculpted in the image of a god. Once I had adjusted my greaves and attached my blades to my arming belt, I fitted my riveted black helmet, which was adorned with silver brow ridges and a matching nose guard.

I disdained from draping my cumbersome *paludamentum* over my shoulders, rather fitting a purple cloak edged with black fur.

"You look like Ares come to the world of men, lord", Diocles said.

"Good", I replied, and walked out into the darkness where Hostilius and Gordas were waiting.

* * *

"Giving the boys double wine rations turned out to be an excellent decision", Hostilius whispered while the first centurion of the *Third Augustan Legion* arranged his six centuries within the cover provided by the apple orchard. "The sappers couldn't lay their hands on a proper tree so instead they dismantled two empty wagons that were used to transport amphorae."

The grizzled primus pilus of the *Third Augustan* approached once his men were in position. "The boys are keen to get stuck in, Lord Emperor", he said. "Are you going to give the city as a reward to my men?"

"You are to gain the rampart with as little bloodshed as possible", I said. "Once you and your men have taken control of the wall and the gatehouses, you will await my orders."

The officer saluted in the required way.

"I will personally lead the assault upon the wall", I announced.

For a moment I believed that the officer wished to object, so I added, "Do you understand your orders, centurion?"

The years of iron discipline took over. He clamped his jaws and saluted again. "I understand, Lord Emperor, and I will obey."

"Have you lost your mind, Domitius?" Hostilius growled once the centurion was out of earshot. "That slimy Greek has set a trap for you, and you are strolling into it like a fool."

"I will have you and Gordas by my side if things go wrong, won't I?" I replied.

Hostilius issued a scowl and glared at me. Then he sighed in resignation and drew his *gladius*. "Very well, I know you won't change your mind", he said. "But don't say I didn't warn you."

I walked through the gap between two centuries and halted at the edge of the orchard, twenty paces from the foundations of the wall. Tyana had not had an enemy at the gates since the days of Hadrianus, so the city fathers paid little heed to the soil that the prevailing wind had slowly deposited against the base of the eastern wall. Heraclammon was right - the top of the rampart was less than twelve feet above the level of the ground.

I glanced over my shoulder at the orange and red eastern horizon that heralded the imminent sunrise. Then I looked up at the wall and noticed that the watchmen who usually patrolled the rampart were absent.

"Come", I said. "It is time."

Three legionaries from each of the six centuries rushed towards the wall. With a level of skill perfected by repetition, they planted the feet of the ladders two paces from the base of the wall and tipped them over so that the ends came to rest just below the stone crenelations. Two legionaries gripped the sides of each ladder while a third man held it stable from underneath by gripping a rung.

I took a deep breath and sprinted towards the nearest ladder. Taking care not to step on the fingers of the soldier stabilising it, I clambered up the rungs. When I was three feet from the battlements, I drew my *gladius*, expecting a hidden enemy to show himself at any moment. But I gained the wall walk without so much as laying eyes on a defender. Gordas and Hostilius climbed onto the rampart a heartbeat later.

"Looks like you were wrong about the Greek", I said, and sheathed my sword.

Hostilius kept his blade at the ready while slowly moving his gaze from side to side, unwilling to concede. "Don't let your guard down, Domitius", he said as more and more legionaries filed onto the wall. Soon, small groups of soldiers started to trot off towards the left and right to secure the towers and gatehouses, the clinking of hobnails on stone announcing their presence to the townsfolk.

Hearing a raucous from inside the city, I took two paces forward. I placed my palms on the rough stone of the low wall facing the streets and leaned forward to get a better view. Fifteen feet below on a large open area, probably a market of sorts, city dwellers were gathering. Soon, a large crowd had assembled with more and more streaming into the square. They stared and pointed at the files of legionaries jogging along the wall walk, none noticing the presence of their emperor.

Shouts of, "Arm yourselves, the emperor's men will visit his wrath upon us", and , "the city guard has abandoned the walls, we will have to defend our homes and our families", rose from the crowd.

I realised that I had only moments to avert bloodshed, so I hopped onto the low wall. Still, few paid me any heed. Hostilius must have read the situation and he boomed in his primus pilus voice, "Citizens of Tyana! Hear the words of your emperor!"

The gods aided me because the moment that the sun rose above the peaks of the Taurus mountains, a westerly breeze spread my purple cloak. Garbed in my splendid armour, I like to believe that to the townsfolk I must have appeared like Mars himself come to earth. "Men and women of Tyana, my legions have taken control of the city. Return to your homes so that I may consider your fate with a mind unburdened by anger."

My words silenced the voices of dissent and the mob dispersed until the market square was deserted.

Hostilius rammed his blade back into its sheath. "Looks like you were right after all", he said, and shrugged. "Maybe this Heraclammon is not the backstabber I made him out to be."

Chapter 23 – Reward

"We have secured the gates, Lord Emperor", the Primus Pilus of the *Third Augustan* reported.

I could see in the centurion's eyes that he was itching to unleash his cohorts on the city, but I stared him down until he averted his gaze. As much as he wished to appease his men, he must have been aware of my reputation as a man devoid of mercy. Although he was old enough to know that rumours were often exaggerations, he was obviously not keen to gamble his life on it.

"Take a full cohort and secure the forum and the administrative centre", I said. "Summon the elders and a man named Heraclammon. I will meet them there within a third of a watch."

* * *

"You have to be careful", Hostilius cautioned as we strolled along the main street towards the forum. "Denying the legions plunder is dangerous business."

"Then it is better to let the gods decide the fate of the city, is it not?" I asked. "They, unlike me, are infallible."

The Primus Pilus fixed me with a sidelong glance. "It depends on which god you're referring to."

"Let Arash the Avenger decide their fate", Gordas suggested, the Hun as keen as always to shed blood. "We can burn the city afterwards to expunge the mens' dark deeds."

When we arrived at the forum I asked to be taken to the office of the magistrate. As the most senior functionary in the city, his workplace proved to be spacious, and it flowed onto a large covered porch. The colonnaded portico was cool and airy, offered comfortable seating on couches, and afforded a view across the grander part of the city.

Hostilius and Gordas were about to follow me inside, but I shook my head. "I wish to speak with Heraclammon in private", I said. "Although I do not trust him, he has delivered the city into our hands. He might be reluctant to tell me that which I wish to know if you are present."

"I guess you can handle a cloth merchant", Hostilius shrugged. "Just shout if you need help."

As soon as the Greek was ushered into my presence I dismissed my guards and servants, and gestured for him to take a seat on one of the embroidered couches arranged on the portico. I filled two silver goblets with dark red wine and handed one to my guest.

"You were true to your word", I said, and raised my chalice in a toast.

Heraclammon reciprocated and we each took a gulp of wine.

"I am honoured to serve you, lord", he said. "All I wished to do was to save the city from being given over to plunder."

"It may yet happen", I said, and emptied my goblet.

A frown settled on Heraclammon's brow. "Lord?" he asked, clearly confused.

"Why did you spread the rumour that I razed Ancyra to the ground?" I asked.

My question stunned the Greek into silence. Rather than to press the issue, I turned away from him to refill my chalice, allowing him ample time to stew in his own proverbial juices.

While pouring the wine I noticed movement reflecting off the polished silver of the goblet. I spun around, just in time to block the long, thin blade that Heraclammon was about to plunge into the back of my neck. Rotating my wrist, I wrapped my right hand around his elbow and struck a powerful blow to his chest with the heel of my left hand, which made him stagger backwards.

I could have called out for help then, but I had been raised by Scythians, and it was not my way. Heraclammon ripped off his cumbersome overgarment, his short-sleeved tunic revealing sinewy, muscular arms and legs that were clearly not a result of vending silk.

The time for subterfuge had passed. "What is your name, warrior?" I asked.

"My name is Gaius Hairan of the Attar", the Greek snarled. "I am the blade of Queen Bat-Zabbai of Palmyra, the true ruler of the East."

I raised an eyebrow. "That explains why you attacked me from behind."

The assassin lunged in reply.

I stepped back, out of range of the blade, but it was a feigned blow lacking power. His left hand came around as if he wished to hit my upper arm with a fist - a strange tactic when fighting a man in armour. I twisted my torso, took the blow on my breastplate instead, and heard something sharp and metallic scrape along the embossed iron.

The Greek jumped back out of reach. He balled his fist to display the spiked ring adorning the index finger of his left hand, "There is no antidote", he said, no doubt wishing to instil fear, and focus my attention on it.

I slipped my Hun dagger from its sheath and flipped it to my left hand.

Zenobia's man came at me again. He led with his left hand, swiping the poisoned ring in an arc to cut my forearm.

I swatted aside the weak blow with my left vambrace, blocked the thrust of the thin-bladed dagger with my right, stepped in, and smashed my forehead down onto the bridge of his nose - a blow that Hostilius had taught me.

Heraclammon staggered under the power of my strike and his hand went to his face in an attempt to clear the blood from his eyes. When he had restored his vision he rushed forward, sweeping his blade from side to side.

I blocked the blow with my left hand, and using his own momentum against him, turned his wrist and heard the bones snap. His dagger fell from his ruined hand, but I did not relent and flung him over my hip onto the white marble, his head hitting the edge of the low table. Before he regained his wits, my blade moved like lighting and pinned his good hand to the wood.

"Tell me what awaits me in Antioch", I said. "And your death will be quick."

"I can see that you are favoured by the god of war, Scythian", he said. "When you reclaim Augusta Treverorum for the Empire, promise that you will free a man named Rahim. Then I will tell you."

"Who is he?" I asked.

"He is my brother", the Greek replied

I nodded, and he told me that which I wanted to know.

* * *

Hostilius stared at the corpse lying in a pool of blood before prodding it with his boot. "He looks dead to me", he said.

I bent over at the waist, picked up the severed finger adorned with the spiked ring smeared with poison, and dropped it into the glowing coals smouldering in one of the cast iron braziers. "He was in the employ of Zenobia", I said.

"Have you decided the fate of the city?" the Primus Pilus asked.

I gestured for Hostilius to follow me. "Come, we will speak with the elders. They will decide their own fate."

"Lord Emperor", the magistrate said, and inclined his head when we walked into the meeting room where he and his fellow elders were being held under guard by legionaries of the *Third Augustan*.

I gestured for the leading men of Tyana to take seats, and flopped down onto a couch as well.

"Why did you defy your emperor?" I asked.

"Lord", he said. "We heard that you set your soldiers loose in Ancyra and hoped that if we closed our gates, you and your army would pass us by."

"Who told you of Ancyra's destruction?" I asked.

"A trusted merchant", Hypatos replied. "The husband of my daughter."

"Is he the one called Heraclammon?" I asked.

"Yes, lord", the magistrate replied, a frown of confusion furrowing his brow.

"Heraclammon, your envoy, betrayed the city by showing us the way onto the ramparts", Hostilius said.

Hypatos's shoulders slumped. He averted his gaze and shook his head in disbelief.

"What would you want me to do with the traitor?" I asked. "What do you wish his fate to be?"

For long the magistrate failed to reply, but then he raised his eyes. "The fault is mine", he said. "I wish you to pardon the traitor."

"Because you are merciful towards Heraclammon, I will spare you from my wrath", I replied. "But I will not allow a traitor to live, so Heraclammon's life is forfeit."

I raised an open palm to stall any response. "Your emperor has spoken", I said, and dismissed them with a gesture.

While making our way from the forum we crossed paths with the first centurion of the *Third Augustan Legion*. He saluted, and within earshot of his men, he asked, "Have you decided the fate of the city, Lord Emperor?"

"We will rather claim loot from our enemies than from our own people", I said. "The city will not be touched."

But the centurion somehow drew courage from the presence of his men. "But lord", he said, "I heard a rumour that you gave an oath that not a single dog would be left alive if Tyana defies you?"

"That is correct, centurion. And I am a man of my word", I replied. "If you wish it, you have my consent to enter the slums of the city and kill all the dogs."

Under cover of the raucous laughter of the men of the legions I leaned closer and growled, "Question my orders again in front of your men, centurion, and you will not be as fortunate as the people of Tyana."

"I understand and I will obey, Lord Emperor" he said, and this time he made sure to avert his eyes.

Chapter 24 – Tarsus (May 272 AD)

"The Cilician Gates are undefended, Lord Emperor", the commander of the scouts said. "We followed the Cydnus River downstream until we glimpsed the walls of Tarsus in the distance. Not once did we come across any sign of the enemy."

Once I had dismissed him, I turned to face my companions. "It rhymes with what Heraclammon told me", I said. "He claimed that Zenobia and Zabdas, the commander of her forces, are waiting for us to come to them. Somewhere in the region of Antioch they plan to meet us in the field."

"I wouldn't trust that bastard's words", the Primus Pilus cautioned.

"It makes sense that the Palmyrene army is camped near Antioch", Gordas said. "Why would Zenobia tire out her warhorses if she can let them graze on the lush grass of the pastures bordering the Orontes?"

I stole a glance at the bone-dry hills surrounding us. "And while the queen's mounts are getting fat, we are straining our horses by traversing this arid land", I sighed.

"After dispatching legions to Aegypt and garrisoning most of the cities along the supply route, we should reach Antioch with the equivalent of two legions", Hostilius said.

"If we add the ten thousand Illyrians and ten thousand Taifali, we command a considerable force", Diocles added.

"Not if we will be facing twenty thousand iron-clad cataphracts", Gordas pointed out in his matter-of-fact way. "They will sweep the Taifali and the Illyrians from the field in a single charge."

"That is not all we will be facing", Vibius said. "Zenobia commands thousands of horse archers drawn from the desert tribes of Arabia."

"Talking about desert clans", Hostilius said. "When will Adherbal and his Numidians join us?"

"All things being equal, the Berbers will land at Tarsus within days", Diocles said. "The same ships that have transported the legions to Aegypt will carry Adherbal and his horsemen across the Middle Sea."

"Any news on how Legate Probus is getting along in Aegypt?" Vibius asked.

"We received a missive earlier today", my aide said. "Probus has retaken Alexandria, which was only defended by a small garrison. The good news is that if he keeps pressing on to the south he will soon have the grain supply to Rome restored."

"What's the bad news?" Hostilius asked.

"If Zenobia left only small garrisons in Aegypt, it means that she has amassed her forces in Syria and Arabia", I replied.

* * *

At the narrowest point of the Cilician Gates Pass, where the cliffs on each side of the gorge rose to the height of a thousand feet, the path that the ancients had carved into the side of the slope was only wide enough to allow a single wagon to pass at a time. This slowed the passage of the army, and despite planning on reaching Tarsus in five days, the journey ended up lasting almost a week.

Regardless of the challenges presented by the narrow road, following the flow of the river meant that we had access to plenty of water. In addition, the people of Tyana had generously supplied us with provisions for the soldiers and feed for the animals, so that by the time we reached Tarsus, the men were rested and the horses' condition much improved.

From Tarsus to Antioch was less than a hundred miles as the crow flies, but the two cities were separated by the Gulf of Issus, or the Marandynian Bay as the Greeks called it. It meant that it would take the army almost seven days to march to what most considered the capital of the East.

On Gordas's recommendation, we decided to remain at Tarsus for ten days to allow the horses to recover fully. It also provided us with the opportunity to scout the position of the enemy and to prepare a strategy to take on the army of Zenobia, that was almost certainly superior in numbers.

Although I did not harp on it publicly, when I was alone I beseeched Arash at every opportunity to grant the Numidians a favourable wind so that they may reach us in time.

On the morning of the sixth day at Tarsus, my prayers were answered.

"You have a visitor, Lord Emperor", a grinning Diocles said when he entered the praetorium of the camp outside of the city.

A heartbeat later, Prefect Adherbal stepped into my quarters. Before he could go down on one knee, I gripped his forearm in the way of the warrior. "It is good to lay eyes on you, my friend", I said. "I have sacrificed to the gods for your safe arrival."

"I would ask a boon of you, Lord Emperor" he replied, his expression serious.

I gestured for him to do so.

"I would rather cross the Styx than journey across the waves of the Middle Sea again, lord", he said. "I have no wife or children, and no reason to return to Africa. If the gods will it and I live to see the end of this campaign, I wish to be granted an estate in Italia where the climes are agreeable to a man of the desert. There, I wish to live out the rest of my days."

"I have heard that the winters in Brundisium are tolerable even to a camel", I said, which brought a smile to his face. "Diocles will find you a vineyard cooled by the breezes that blow in from the Aegean."

"You have unburdened my shade, Lord Emperor", he said. "I will now go to tend to my men."

The Numidian commander had hardly left the tent when Hostilius and Gordas arrived, accompanied by an officer of the *speculators*. His clothes were dusty, his hair matted, and he smelled of horse, which showed that he had ridden far and hard.

Before I granted him leave to speak, I gestured for a pouring slave to pass the soldier a cup of diluted white wine, and waited until he had gulped down the contents.

"Speak, centurion", I said once his throat had been wetted.

"We reconnoitred all the way to Antioch, lord", he said. "Apart from a handful of small groups of Palmyrene mounted scouts we found none of the enemy between here and the great city to the east. The army of the usurper is encamped north of the city on the plain bordered by the great lake to the east and the Black Mountains to the west. They draw their water from the Orontes that flows through the city."

"Tell us who we will be fighting and how many there are", Hostilius said.

"When I scouted the area around the lake, I saw the cataphracts practicing manoeuvres on the flatland bordering the camp", the elite scout replied. "There must have been twenty thousand of them at the least. When the iron-clad horsemen thundered across the plain I could feel the ground shaking through the soles of my boots." I noticed that the *speculator* averted his gaze and knew from experience that he did not wish for me to see the fear in his eyes.

"What else did you see?" I asked.

"Mounted archers", he said. "I estimate forty thousand. We spied many banners decorated with strange symbols and creatures of myth."

"Did you notice any standards belonging to Rome's Eastern legions?" Hostilius asked.

"We did not see any, tribune", the scout replied. "Nor were there any tents in the Palmyrene camp resembling the legions'."

"You have done well", I said, and gestured for Diocles to hand the man a small purse on his way out.

"Zenobia trusts the Roman soldiers as much as they trust her", Hostilius surmised. "She no doubt sent the legions to the remote borders of her domain because she knows that as soon as the legionaries lay eyes on their legitimate emperor they'll turn on her and stick their iron in her back."

Hostilius was right about the queen's reasons, I believe, but of more importance was the fact that we would not have to put our own to the sword.

While Hostilius and I were discussing the absence of the Eastern legions, Diocles unrolled a scroll depicting the area around the city of Antioch. He flattened it out on a low table in the centre of the couches and weighted it down with the gold goblets we hardly ever used.

"The approach to Antioch along the main road is from the north", my aide said, tracing his stylus along a line marked on the map. The path winds its way through hill country, but thirty miles north of the city, the mountains fall away to the east and west. Here, nestled between the Black Mountains of Amanos to the west and the hill country of Cyrrhestica to the east, lies a great plain, thirty miles long and twenty miles across.

"What's this?" Hostilius asked, indicating blue markings on the velum.

"More than half of the flatland is covered by the waters of a great lake", Diocles said. "The road leading to Antioch runs along the western shore where the open ground is suitable for cavalry warfare."

Gordas issued a grunt that I assumed to be an indication of his agreement with the Greek. "The Palmyrenians will not allow us to cross the flatland", he said. "That is where their heavy horses will be most effective."

Vibius pressed a finger on the large body of water just east of the Roman road on the approach to Antioch. "If Zenobia blocks our advance, can we not bypass her forces by marching around the lake and attacking them from the rear?"

Diocles nodded and ran his stylus along a lesser road that followed the eastern shores of the lake. "We can travel along this road that leads to the town of Immae. From there we can use the main road that approaches the capital from the east."

"The Palmyrenians are not to be underestimated", Vibius cautioned. "I have heard much of Zabdas, the general who commands Zenobia's army. He is the one who gave the Sasanians a bloody nose in the time of Odaenathus. He will surely expect us to get up to mischief and send a cavalry force to keep us from attacking his forces from the rear."

"Call back the *speculator* who reconnoitred the lake", I said.

Not long after, the scout arrived.

"Tell us about the back way around the lake", I said.

"The road follows the northern shore for a few miles, lord", he said. "Where the road passes between the main lake to the south and a smaller one situated to the north, there is a choke point."

For a moment the scout lowered his gaze while he searched his mind for the words to describe what he had seen.

"The smaller lake sits like a head on a body, lord", he continued. "A shallow creek connects the two bodies of water like a neck joins the torso to the head."

"Zabdas will block our passage where the road is at its narrowest", Diocles said. "It seems like circumnavigating the lake is not an option after all."

"Are you suggesting that we meet the cataphracts head-on, Greek?" Hostilius asked. "Don't forget that the Parthians destroyed six of Crassus's legions with ten thousand horse archers and only a thousand cataphracts. Zenobia has twenty thousand of those shining iron bastards."

"Zabdas will try and neutralise our horse archers and Illyrians with his cataphracts", I said. "Only the legions can stand against his heavy horsemen. But if we lead the attack with the legions, the mounted archers will whittle down our numbers while their iron-clad horsemen wait for the opportunity to crush our exhausted men."

I stared at the map for what felt like an eternity.

Then I felt the presence of the Arash the Destroyer and I knew what had to be done.

Chapter 25 – Lake

"Only one legion!" Hostilius exclaimed, and eyed me for at least twenty heartbeats, his expression incredulous.

Then he lowered his voice, and asked, "Are you jesting, Domitius?"

"I'm as serious as I've ever been", I replied, and took a sip from my cup.

"The mounted archers of the Palmyrenians will shoot the Romans to pieces", Gordas stated, throwing his weight in with Hostilius.

"I suggest you do not dismiss my words before you have heard me out", I said. "It is part of a grander plan."

"Let's hear it, then", the Primus Pilus said, refilled his cup, and reclined on the couch.

Once I had told all, I was rewarded by nods all around.

"How do you know that Zabdas will swallow the hook?" Vibius asked.

"I am confident that he will", I replied. "Because I will be the bait."

* * *

Ten days later, a third of a watch after the sun appeared above the hills of Western Syria, the Roman army marched from the gates of the camp situated on the northern edge of the great plain north of Antioch.

Hostilius, Gordas, Vibius, Diocles and I rode at the head of the Illyrians, who were drawn up to the left of the Roman legion. The Numidians were deployed to the rear of the black riders, while a mob of ten thousand Taifali *foederati* milled about behind the neat ranks of the single legion.

The Orontes Plain, as it was known, lay north of the capital of the East, nestled between arid hills. The plain itself was green and fertile, fed by the Orontes River that brought abundant water from the mountains of Phoenicia to the south. Despite it being early in the morning, it was hot and humid and I was already perspiring underneath my Illyrian armour. The cloudless sky was a good indication that the day would be scorching, and I thanked Fortuna for her goodwill.

Vibius gestured at the enemy scouts visible on the crests of the distant hills. "I wonder what they will report to Zenobia and Zabdas", he said.

Hostilius glanced over his shoulder at the peculiar formation of the Roman army. "They will be saying that the emperor of Rome has lost his mind", he said.

None gainsaid my friend.

Before I could offer a retort, a shimmering line of silver appeared on the southern horizon.

We continued our advance in silence, overawed by what we knew was the might of Palmyra, the riders and mounts clad in iron from head to toe, or hoof, in the case of the large warhorses.

When we drew level with the northerly shore of the sprawling lake to our left, I nodded to my signifer and the *buccina* called a halt.

Just then, a dusty rider on a lathered horse was escorted into my presence. The *speculator* saluted in the required way and I gestured for him to report. "You were right, Lord Emperor", he said. "A force of at least a thousand cataphracts are making their way around the lake from the east."

I dismissed the outrider and twisted in the saddle. "Unleash the Taifali", I said, and again a series of notes from the Roman war trumpet echoed across the plain.

After a hundred heartbeats, the first of the Scythian riders trotted through the gap between the legion and the Illyrians. While his men made their way to the front of the army, Senoch steered his horse closer and reined in three paces away.

The Taifali king inclined his head and I reciprocated. "Lord Eochar", he said. "You of all people should know that my warriors are less than content to follow your plan."

"They will share in the loot", I replied, and could not help but notice that the cataphracts were less than a mile away. A Palmyrene war horn blared, and the heavy horses went to a trot.

Although Senoch's complaints were warranted, time was of the essence, so I gestured to the wall of armoured horses approaching from the south. "Tell your men that each warrior who survives the day will receive a horse from the spoils of war."

The Taifali king's bearded face was split by a grin as he knew that such a tangible reward would appease and motivate his men. He nodded, jerked on the reins and cantered away.

Moments later, having received the tidings, a war cry rose from the Scythian ranks and ten thousand ululating riders surged towards the approaching foe.

Zabdas was an accomplished commander who had defeated Roman and Sasanian generals alike. He wasted no time and dispatched contingents of his own mounted archers to repel the Scythians. At least twenty thousand riders flowed around the flanks of the advancing heavy cavalry and bore down on the Taifali.

The Palmyrene light archers, that were modelled on their Sasanian equivalents, were mostly drawn from the clans of the desert. Like the Scythians, they wielded the horn and sinew recurve bow, but unlike their counterparts from the steppes, whose scale vests could turn the tips of hunting arrows, they wore little armour other than padded leather.

The Taifali were the first to release their arrows and I saw the shafts rise high. Before the missiles struck, the Palmyrenians' first volley was in the air. Hundreds of enemy saddles were emptied by the Scythians' first strike, and moments later, when the foes' arrows bit, scores of Taifali tumbled from the backs of their mounts.

Senoch's warriors and the enemy riders thundered towards one another, releasing arrows as they did. When a hundred paces separated the two forces, the Taifali wheeled about and galloped back to the Roman lines. The fleeing Scythians, who were spread out across the width of the battlefield, twisted in their saddles and released their arrows across the rumps of their horses while the foe gave chase.

"It is time", I said, fitted my cavalry helmet and fastened the strap before the Illyrian *draconarius* raised the wolf head standard high in the air. In response, ten thousand black riders charged straight at the Taifali.

I nudged Intikam to a canter, clamped my thighs against his sides, raised myself from the saddle, hefted my oval cavalry shield, and lowered my long, thin lance until it was parallel to the ground. Moments earlier, it had seemed unavoidable that we would slice into our own *foederati*, but the Scythians demonstrated their supreme horsemanship and flowed around and through the Illyrian formation. When we emerged from the dust, fifty paces from the front ranks of the enemy's light archers, I kicked Intikam to a gallop.

In a desperate attempt to save themselves, the enemy archers turned their bows on the onrushing Roman horsemen. But the Illyrian riders were well armoured and the heads and chests of their horses clad in iron and boiled leather, rendering them almost impervious to everything but an arrow guided by Fortuna herself.

I raised my shield, slapped away an errant shaft and braced myself. My lance sliced into the torso of a foe, lifting him from the saddle and throwing the corpse underneath the hooves, ripping the spear from my fist. Intikam did not falter and crashed into the enemy rider behind. The smaller desert horse succumbed to the strength and weight of my enormous stallion and stumbled to the ground, crushing its rider.

Having lost my lance, I faced a third foe with my blade in my hand. He failed to match my speed and I sent him across the Styx.

"Enough!" I boomed, and the signifer relayed my orders. In response the Illyrians wheeled about, leaving thousands of enemy corpses littering the ground. The black riders did not retreat at a gallop, but at a trot, enticing the approaching cataphracts. But their general possessed the experience and self-control not to be tempted into rash action that would turn a minor setback into a full-blown disaster. The heavy horsemen ignored the Illyrians, their eyes fixed on the lightly armoured Taifali who were milling about in front of the Roman infantry.

The heavy horsemen of Palmyra were clad in iron scale and chain that were thick enough to turn arrows, spears and swords. Their main weapon was a ten-foot-long lance that was so heavy that it had to be wielded with two hands. The *kontus* was tipped with a thin, armour-piercing blade that could cut through almost any armour the Romans possessed.

When the advancing cataphracts were five hundred paces from the Scythians, I gave the order for the legion to change their formation - a manoeuvre they had repeatedly practised before the walls of Tarsus under Hostilius's supervision. I watched as they transformed into a hollow square with sides two hundred paces long and six ranks deep. The *buccina* issued a note and the legionaries opened a gap in the side of the square facing the enemy. The Taifali galloped through the opening, which was immediately sealed once all the horsemen were inside, to present an unbroken wall of plywood and *pila* to the enemy.

Gordas gestured at the hollow square where the Taifali were dismounting. A handful of warriors were herding the horses into the centre of the formation while the majority lined up behind the legionaries, their recurve bows swung across their shoulders and their quivers tied to their belts. "Senoch rules with a fist of iron", the Hun said, respect thick in his voice. "Men born to the Sea of Grass will refuse to fight on foot unless they fear their commander more than death itself."

The Palmyrene general proved that he was no stranger to war. He must have realised that it was pointless to throw the heavy cavalry against the legion as no horse would charge into a solid wall of shields. It was however a proven strategy to weaken Roman infantry formations by an onslaught from mounted archers. Once the inevitable gaps appeared in the exhausted ranks of the defenders, the cataphract would attack and crush the foe.

A war horn blared and the armoured men and horses of Palmyra halted to allow mounted archers to flow around their flanks.

With the attention of the enemy focused on the infantry square, they paid the Illyrians little heed as we continued our retreat, only coming to a halt four hundred paces distant, on the shore of the lake. I hoped that Zenobia and her advisors would view it as another blunder by the Roman Emperor.

As the enemy bowmen bore down on the stationary square, the front rank of the legion kneeled and slammed their *scuta* onto the ground. The soldiers in the second rank raised their shields over their heads and slid the bottom rims across the top edges of the *scuta* of the men in front. The ranks behind followed suit to create a formation that was almost impervious to missiles.

The sky darkened as the desert tribes unleashed a storm of arrows at the Roman square. They circled the formation, just beyond the reach of *pila,* and emptied their quivers in an effort to break the Romans' cohesion. For once the legionaries were not sitting ducks, and the Taifali, who were protected by the iron-clad legionaries, began to launch their shafts at the enemy. The Scythians were excellent archers from the saddle, but with both feet planted on the ground they hardly ever missed their targets.

While the battle raged around the legion, the Illyrians were all but idle, the *turmae* taking turns to water their horses in the freshwater lake. Meanwhile the Palmyrene cataphracts sat in their saddles a mere seven hundred paces distant, waiting in the scorching sun to be called upon to finish the toil that their bowmen had started.

For nearly a sixth of a watch, the enemy's mounted archers continued the onslaught. The legion not only prevailed, but won the war of attrition with the ground bordering the square heaped with enemy dead.

Zabdas must have realised that although his forces were still superior in numbers, he ran the risk of the army's morale being destroyed. He needed a minor victory, no matter how small, to bolster the confidence of his men, so he gave the command.

"Here they come", Hostilius said, as about half of the cataphracts pivoted to face us square on. There was no doubt that they were heading straight for the Illyrians and their Numidian allies.

"Remember", Gordas said to us. "They are faster than you may think. Give the order sooner than later."

I nodded to the signifer, who relayed my command for the Illyrians to order their ranks to face the foe head-on. Twenty heartbeats later, I nudged Intikam to a trot when the gap between the two cavalry forces had shrunk to four hundred paces. At three hundred paces I kicked my stallion to a gallop, the wail from the maw of the *draconarius's* wolf head standard ordering the men to follow suit.

Thousands of cataphracts lowered their lances as the heavy horses went to a gallop. The earth shook under the onslaught of forty thousand hooves as the wall of iron and horseflesh approached at a blistering pace.

"Now!" I boomed, and the wail escaping from the wolf head morphed into a shrill screech.

The companies of Illyrians and Numidians wheeled about, turning their horses away from the steel-encased riders thundering down upon us. I feared that I had left it too late, but disdained from glancing over my shoulder despite imagining that the tip of an enemy *kontus* was only feet away from my back.

We galloped away at full speed until, after two hundred heartbeats, Gordas spoke from where he rode abreast of me. "You can give the order to slow down to a trot", he said. "Before you have us kill the horses."

I twisted in the saddle and saw that the cataphracts had gone to a walk.

"Looks like they've given up the chase", Hostilius muttered.

"Nothing to be concerned about", I replied. "The Palmyrenians have trained on the shores of the lake for months and they know that we are working ourselves into a corner."

Chapter 26 – Antioch

It was almost noon and the unrelenting Syrian sun was slowly roasting me alive inside my dark armour. I removed my helmet, wiped the sweat from my brow and glanced at the heavy cavalry of Palmyra who were still advancing, albeit at a trot.

Soon, we noticed that there was not only a body of water to the south, but we were traversing the high ground separating two sections of the lake. Both shores were overgrown with reeds and waterside shrubs. Every so often there were stretches of shoreline that had been cleared of vegetation, presumably by the local population harvesting reeds or wishing for open ground to fish from, or water their flocks.

I was still studying the landscape when the heavy riders charged a second time. We did not feign an attack but simply outpaced them, fleeing east along the road hugging the northern shore of the lake.

When I noticed the reed beds on both sides converge on the road, I turned to the scout who was guiding us. "How far to the choke point?" I asked.

"Just more than a mile, lord", he replied.

I kept my eyes on the dense foliage lining the shores until Hostilius scolded me. "Stop staring, Domitius", he whispered. "You're going to give away the plan."

"I don't see them", I said, making sure to keep my eyes to the front.

"Of course you won't", the Primus Pilus said. "Your orders were for the legionaries to conceal themselves, not stand about waving their standards."

I offered a scowl in reply.

"If they wish to destroy us with another charge, the Palmyrenians will have to water their horses soon", Gordas interjected, his eyes fixed on the approaching riders. "Then we will see whether the legion followed your orders or not."

Gordas had hardly spoken when the cataphracts changed their formation. A thousand riders fanned out to block the open ground between the two shores, while the rest guided their mounts closer to where cool water lapped against the lakeside.

I waited patiently until the Palmyrenians were clustered around the beaches, their exhausted horses competing to reach the water first.

"Sound the attack", I said to the signifer, who pressed the *buccina* to his lips.

The reed beds seemed to come to life as five thousand legionaries issued a battle cry. They charged from cover and fell upon the press of heavy cavalry.

Employed correctly, cataphracts can be devasting, but pitted against heavy infantry in a tight press, the ambush soon turned into a slaughter.

The Romans hemmed in the riders with a wall of shields and forced them deeper into the muddy waters. Working in pairs, the legionaries pulled the iron-clad warriors from their saddles. The ones that did not drown in the shallows were butchered by a dagger in the base of the neck or a blade through the eye-slit.

Hostilius used his chin to gesture to two thousand or so riders who had managed to evade or break free from the Roman ambush. They were slowly riding back the way they had come. "Are we going to allow those bastards to get away?" he asked.

I looked to Gordas for his opinion. "The Illyrians' horses will not overhaul the enemy before they reach the rest of their army", the Hun said. "But the Numidians will easily catch them."

While the legion completed the slaughter, my companions and I cantered west, trailing behind Adherbal and his men who I had given free rein to ride down the foes. We were still two miles from the battlefield when the first of the enemy's warhorses staggered from the loose formation, collapsing under the weight of their heavy armour.

"They are ripe for the slaughter", Gordas growled from beside me just as Adherbal signalled for his men to attack.

We caught up with the Numidians who were stalking the cataphracts like vultures approaching injured prey. The agile riders from Africa easily avoided the exhausted warhorses and cumbersome lances of the Palmyrenians and used the blades of their short stabbing spears to cut tack before pulling the iron-clad monsters from their mounts, all in full view of the commanders of the army of Palmyra.

Seeing the disaster unfold, Zabdas dispatched mounted archers to chase away the Numidians, but before the remaining cataphracts could be saved, a wave of black riders rode in from the east. The Palmyrene commanders had no way of knowing that the Illyrians' horses were also close to collapse. The war horns of the foe echoed across the field and the enemy host started to retreat.

It was by no means a rout. Zenobia still possessed twelve thousand heavy riders and more than thirty thousand mounted archers - a powerful force for sure. But we had broken the morale of the Palmyrenians. What is more, we filled the hearts of our own men with iron confidence and lined their pockets with loot.

* * *

While the army plundered the abandoned camp of the Palmyrenians, Hostilius, Vibius, Diocles and I retired to the pavilion that must have belonged to Zenobia.

Hostilius poured himself a cup of purple *basarangian* and reclined on one of the gold embroidered silk couches. "The men are too exhausted to march back to their own tents", he said. "I suggest we set a watch and spend the night inside the enemy's camp."

I raised an eyebrow because Hostilius was usually a stickler when it came to army regulations, which made it compulsory to construct a fortified camp while traversing enemy territory.

"What if the enemy falls upon us during the hours of darkness?" Diocles asked, his voice carrying an accusatory tone.

"If Zenobia orders her men to attack they'll probably slit her and Zabdas's throats instead", the Primus Pilus scowled. "Besides, I've been on the losing side, and I'll wager that the Palmyrenians won't even have the heart to take the evening meal, never mind attack the army that's just given their arses a good and proper kicking."

Vibius reached for another down-stuffed pillow, which he used to prop himself up. "If they're half as tired as I am they're already sleeping", he croaked. "I agree with the Primus Pilus."

"I doubt whether Zenobia will defend Antioch", I said. "If she does, there is a good chance that the people will turn against her and trade her to us in exchange for their freedom."

"She still commands twelve thousand cataphracts", Vibius said. "They, alone, are enough to turn the tide in any battle."

Diocles was poring over the daily reports, seated at an ornate desk I imagined had belonged to Zabdas. "The Taifali sustained heavy losses", my aide said. "But the casualties amongst the legions and the cavalry were light." He perused a few wax tablets before he continued. "Injuries, however, is another story altogether. At least three in ten of the soldiers will be unfit to march or ride without two or three weeks of rest."

Gordas strolled into the tent, having earlier gone to make sure our horses were properly taken care of. "The battle and the heat have taken a heavy toll on the horses", the Hun said, accepting a cup from Vibius. "They are in bad shape and will take many days to recover."

"Tomorrow we will find out whether we will be besieging Antioch", I said. "If the capital and its harbour are defended, we will have one more battle to fight before we can allow the men and the horses a brief respite."

* * *

I was in exactly the same position I had been when I had fallen asleep when Hostilius shook my ankle. "Domitius", he said. "You need to hear this."

Every sinew in my body ached and I was forced to extend a hand so that Hostilius could pull me to my feet.

"It is still a watch before daybreak", the Primus Pilus said while I splashed my face with the water in the wash basin. I was accosted by a pleasant smell and assumed that the queen of Palmyra was partial to using rose water for her ablutions.

Hostilius sniffed the air. "Just don't get too close to the scout", he said. "You reek of flowers like a Parthian whore. Soon there will be rumours that you've taken to using perfume and before you know it the boys in the legions will be laughing behind your back and saying that the young pouring slave is your catamite." He picked up my purple cloak that reeked of sweat and horse and wrapped it around my shoulders. "There you go", he said, and gestured for the guards to usher in the *speculator*.

"Lord Emperor", the scout said, and saluted in the required manner.

I acknowledged him with a nod and indicated for him to report.

"The Palmyrene forces are abandoning Antioch", he said. "Thousands are streaming east along the road to Emesa."

Once the outrider had gone, I sat down on a couch. "A thin line separates boldness from foolishness", I said. "I am tempted to order an assault on the Palmyrene column, but there is a good chance that we could fall prey to their heavy cavalry. We are in a strong position and I believe it will suit us to allow them to retreat so that we may restore Antioch to Roman rule."

"I agree", Hostilius said. "Only fools and drunkards stumble about in the dark to attack an enemy of unknown strength on unfamiliar terrain. Besides, we need to allow the men a few days to enjoy the spoils of war."

Once the Primus Pilus had departed, I removed the dirty cloak, wrapped myself in a soft fur, stretched out on the couch, and fell into a dreamless sleep.

Chapter 27 – Daphne

The following morning, while Diocles and I were reviewing the reports of the previous day's battle, the duty tribune entered the tent. "There is a priest who wishes an audience with you, Lord Emperor", he said. "The man claims that he is the leader of the Christian sect within the city."

"Send him home", my aide snapped, irritated at the interruption.

"What is his name?" I asked.

"Domnus", the tribune replied.

Diocles and I exchanged a look. Almost twenty years before, a follower of Jesus had guided us through a gorge abutting the city walls to escape the clutches of the Sasanian invaders. The young man's name was Domnus.

"Send him in", I said.

Although many years had passed since I last laid eyes on him, I immediately recognised the man who wore the black robes associated with the office of a high priest.

"It is good to see you, my friend", I said, breaking into a smile as I gripped his arm.

"It has been so many years, I doubted that you would still recognise me, Lord Emperor", he said, reciprocating my grin.

"How could I forget the man who saved me and my friends from the Sasanians", I replied, and gestured for the priest to take a seat.

"Are you here in your official capacity as Bishop of Antioch?" Diocles asked.

"No", he replied. "I used the Gorge of Parmenius to escape the city so that I may warn you. I know that we do not serve the same god, but you treated me and my fellow Christians with respect. For that reason, I do not wish harm to come to you."

I must have frowned. "Warn me about what?" I asked. "My scouts informed me that the Palmyrenians fled the city during the hours of darkness."

Our guest leaned in and lowered his voice. "It is true that Zenobia and her army have taken leave of the city", Domnus replied, his tone conspiratorial. "But I heard from a reliable source that the queen of the East has hatched a plot against the emperor."

Just then Hostilius strolled through the door of the tent, whistling a marching tune. The Primus Pilus halted mid-stride when he noticed our guest. He stared at the black-robed man for a span of heartbeats before taking a step closer and slapping the priest's shoulder in a brotherly way, but still hard enough to make him wince. "Domnus", he said. "I didn't think that you'd still be crawling around the catacombs of Antioch."

"Christians are not being persecuted by the Empire like in the days of Philip the Arab and Decius", Domnus replied with pride. "We no longer need to worship in the shadows."

"Good for you", Hostilius replied absentmindedly, and poured himself a cup of wine.

"Talking about worshipping", the Primus Pilus continued. "Later today, Gordas, Vibius and I are planning on riding to the temple of Apollo in Daphne to give sacrifice to the gods for our victory. It's in the laurel groves near the Springs of Castalia and Pallas, less than five miles south of Antioch. Why don't you join us?"

Domnus stared at Hostilius in bewilderment.

"I mean", Hostilius corrected himself, "why don't you join us, Domitius?"

I gestured for the Primus Pilus to take a seat. "Domnus has slipped out of the city to warn his old friends of danger", I said, and indicated for the priest to continue.

"Brother John, who is a member of our congregation, oversees the maintenance of the aqueduct that brings fresh water from the Daphne Springs to the city", Domnus said. "Yesterday, late afternoon, he was walking the watercourse when he noticed a group of Palmyrene soldiers ascending the hill through the cypress woods. He said that there were at least five hundred of them and they wore the armour of Zenobia's elite guard."

"Nothing is sacred anymore", Hostilius sighed. "The bitch must have divined that we would go to Daphne to sacrifice and she knows that it is the one place where the emperor will be vulnerable. I guess that means our trip is cancelled."

"No. We are still going to Daphne", I said, appalled at Zenobia's lack of respect for the gods. "But not to sacrifice to Apollo, but rather to Arash."

Not wishing to have any part in the planning of violence, our priest friend made to leave, but Diocles stalled him with a raised palm. "Bishop", my aide asked while scrutinising a scroll. "Why do my records tell me that Paul of Samosata is Bishop of Antioch?"

Domnus sighed, and slumped down again. "That", he said, "is a long story."

Hostilius slapped his knees with his palms and stood to leave. "Well, priest, you can tell the emperor and the Greek while I go and arrange a welcoming party for the men who are planning on ambushing us."

"Enlighten us", I commanded Domnus, and gestured for a pouring slave to fill our cups.

* * *

The sun was high in the sky when a mounted Hostilius and I led two cohorts of legionaries along the path that winded up the hill of Daphne, the sanctuary four miles south of Antioch. Although the day was as hot and humid as the one before, it was bearable because we marched in the shade cast by lush olive- and laurel groves, planted on broad terraces that the ancient Greeks had carved into the hillside.

As we rounded a turn, Hostilius raised an open palm and the cohorts came to a halt.

Above the treetops higher up the hill, I noticed a triangular pediment supported by ornate capitals topping enormous marble pillars. "That'll be the temple of Apollo", the Primus Pilus said. "How do you want to do this, Domitius? I'm sure that the Palmyrene soldiers will be watching the approach."

I dismounted and gestured to the dozen guards who had accompanied me. "The praetorians and I will continue to the temple, to draw Zenobia's killers into the open. While the enemy's eyes are on us, you and your men can move through the groves."

I noticed a scowl forming on Hostilius's scarred visage. "Do not be concerned", I said. "We will find sanctuary inside the inner chamber and defend the narrow entrance while your men encircle and trap the assassins in a ring of iron."

He was about to object, but I raised a palm. "It is the only way", I said.

Under normal circumstances the complex would have been bustling with pilgrims, merchants and priests, but given the major battle that had taken place just a few miles to the north, the grounds of the temple would have been deserted were it not for the handful of priests and acolytes going about their daily chores.

I strolled to the marble steps leading up to the grand entrance of the antechamber, where a white-robed priest attended the doorway.

He bowed low. "Please lord", he said, averting his eyes. "Apollo is a god of healing, not of war. We do not allow weapons of death inside the sacred walls."

I was not in the mood for explaining myself and felt the rage of Arash rise like bile. "Am I not the *pontifex maximus*, the supreme priest in all the lands of Rome?" I asked. "I have come to worship far-shooting Apollo for delivering the Palmyrenians into our hands. Do you think that we wielded no weapons in the great battle on the plain, priest?"

It was my hubris that made me believe that I was the one who had put the fear of the gods into the man, who, by then, was shivering uncontrollably. "Step aside", I commanded, and pushed past the priest, leading the way through the reception area into the inner chamber that was adorned with a bronze statue of Appollo wielding a magnificent silver bow, polished to a bright shine. My gaze was drawn to the quiver attached to the god's belt. It was crafted from pure silver, etched with exquisite detail and filled with a dozen shining arrows. Although I had other things on my mind, I felt the presence of the god and immediately regretted my arrogance. I strolled toward the statue of the heavily muscled archer, bowed my head, placed my hands at the feet of the lord of horses and archery, and asked for his forgiveness.

Because it was a place of worship and meditation, only one flickering oil lamp provided illumination in the *cella*. It was strategically placed in a recess within the stone wall to enhance the larger-than-life statue. I blame my preoccupation with Apollo's bow, as well as the low light, for my failure to notice the dark shapes crouched behind the table intended for the votive offerings of the faithful.

Before my guards could follow me into the chamber, the killers struck. Some believe that Apollo is the Roman Arash. I, for one, am willing to provide witness of it being so.

In the polished surface of his recurve bow the god alerted me to a shadow rising from behind, the orange light of the lamp reflecting off the curved blade of a Persian *shamshir*.

I swung around, simultaneously striking out with my left hand. The inside edge of my open palm slammed into the side of the assassin's neck, just below the ear. The blow was unexpected and the force sufficient to crush the sinews in the man's neck. I snatched the falling sword from the corpse's hand and used the borrowed blade to block a downward strike from a second attacker. Having diverted the killing blow, I stepped in and slammed my forehead into the bridge of his nose, which caused him to stagger backwards. Moving with the attacker, I hit him in the face a second time, the base of my palm ramming the bones of his ruined nose into his brain.

From the direction of the doorway, I heard a clash of blades and noticed three of Zenobia's men preventing the praetorians from entering the *cella* before their comrades' bloody toil had been completed.

"You will die today, Roman", the nearest of the three remaining attackers facing me growled in Greek. "And what remains of your army will be wiped from the face of the earth at Emesa."

The fool's ranting provided me with the opportunity to take my Seric iron blade into my fist.

Zenobia's men fanned out to surround me. I retreated until I felt the statue at my back.

"Your time is up, Roman", the warrior on the right hissed.

In response I lunged at him, my blade flashing as fast as lightning. The tip of my iron slid into the flesh of his neck, just above his armour, the razor edge severing sinews and arteries before piercing his spine.

The foe beside him roared in rage and used the opportunity to slash with his curved sword, a powerful strike intended to sever my outstretched arm. I stepped from the path of his weapon, jerking my sword from the neck of the corpse, but felt the familiar sting as his blade scored a line across my unprotected upper arm. The assassin stepped in to finish me, but I moved to the left to place him between me and the last remaining man.

The warrior lunged, his sword aimed at my chest.

I twisted my torso to the side and used my own blade to push his sword from its path, the honed edge scraping across the scales of my amour. In the same movement, I slid my left foot back and rammed the captured *shamshir* into the warrior's upper leg.

He was my enemy, but a brave man nonetheless. Knowing that his fate was sealed, he came at me, leaving me little other choice but to bury my Eastern blade in his groin. Before I could extract it, he grabbed it with both hands, forced it deeper into his body and collapsed to the side, ridding me of both blades.

The lips of the last assassin split into a leer when he realised that I was without a weapon.

I backpedaled as he advanced, only coming to a halt when my back foot hit the base of the statue of the god. I stole a glance over my shoulder and my eye caught the glint of the silver arrows.

The Palmyrene warrior issued a roar and swung his curved blade across his shoulder, a blow intended to cut deep into the vulnerable part where the shoulder meets the neck.

Without thinking, I grabbed one of the oversized arrows and used the haft to block the downward strike, deflecting the attacker's blade to the side. For a moment it left him unbalanced, and rather than wait for him to recover, I lunged, almost blindly in the murky darkness. I know not if the arrow was guided by Fortuna, Arash or Apollo, but at least ten inches entered the man's eye and he collapsed facedown onto the mosaics.

Moments later, my guards dispatched the last of Zenobia's men who were blocking the doorway leading into the inner chamber. The centurion of the praetorians stepped over the dead and stood beside me, studying the grisly scene. The officer walked over to the last man I had killed and turned the body over with a boot. "How did this one meet his end, lord?" he asked. "There's no wound."

My first thought was to point out to the guard that the corpse had an arrow lodged in the eye, but I thought better of it. I stepped in closer and saw that there was no sign of the shaft I had only moments before thrust into his skull. Then I glanced over at Apollo and could not help but notice that rather than a bow, the god gripped a lyre in his fist and there was no sign of a quiver whatsoever.

"He must have smashed his skull against the edge of the marble", I replied with a shrug.

Chapter 28 – Dispute

The Palmyrene soldiers managed to evade encirclement and retreated to the summit of the Daphne Hill. Zenobia's men all wielded horn bows, which necessitated the legionaries to storm the hill in testudo formation.

It took the greater part of the afternoon to clear the area, with the majority of the foes not meeting their fate at the sharp end of a Roman blade, but rather tumbling to their deaths in their effort to flee the inevitable.

Later that day I led the army to Antioch. The rulers of the city welcomed us with open arms, while the people lined the streets and cast palm branches onto the cobbles as we made our way along the main thoroughfare towards the palace complex situated on the island in the Orontes.

Just before sunset, Hostilius, Gordas, Cai, Vibius, Diocles and I congregated on a colonnaded portico that afforded spectacular views across the circus maximus and the Orontes River. While sipping chilled white wine from a silver goblet, I brought my friends up to speed with the happenings of the day.

"Arash favours you", Gordas said once I was through. "Your work on this earth is not finished."

"I'm not so sure if it was Arash's handiwork", Hostilius said. "I'm inclined to say that it was Apollo himself who intervened. The only thing that baffles me is why he traded his bow for a lyre."

"Hermes, Apollo's brother, created the lyre", Diocles said. "After Hermes was caught stealing Apollo's cattle, he gave Apollo his lyre so that his brother would forgive him his transgression. I believe that the god wants you to be merciful, Lord Emperor. Why else would he have first shown you a bow that symbolises war and thereafter a lyre that indicates forgiveness?"

"Please don't forgive Zenobia", the Primus Pilus said, suddenly concerned that I would take my aide's words to heart. "Looking at the tricks that the queen of Palmyra has gotten up to, even Clementia herself won't absolve her."

"I am told that many of the important men of Antioch have fled the city because they fear Aurelian's wrath", Diocles said. "Mayhap the god wants you to forgive the citizens and allow them to return in peace?"

"If you forgive the bear for stealing your sheep, he will take your cattle", Gordas growled.

"Absolving the unrepentant like drawing pictures on water", Cai said.

"Maybe these men could be forgiven for offering support to Zenobia", I said.

My words were met by frowns from all around.

"On condition that they repent, of course", I added.

"And how will you know if they regret their actions?" Hostilius asked.

"Well", I replied. "If they were to make a substantial contribution towards our campaign against Palmyra, I believe we can safely assume that they have seen the error of their ways."

Diocles was the first to break into a grin. "Apollo is also the god of wisdom", he said, no doubt eager to bolster the war chest.

* * *

Antioch was a large city with many wealthy and powerful men within its walls. And where such men reside, disputes are rife.

Soon, I started receiving requests to hold court. It was not something that I enjoyed, but I needed to repay an old friend for his loyalty and reckoned that I might as well adjudicate on a few matters.

Come the second watch of the morning, I was already sick and tired of dealing with petty squabbles between merchants when the functionary who had made the arrangements approached.

I gestured for the quaestor to proceed.

"Lord Emperor, the Christians of the city have requested that you assist them in settling an internal dispute." The man leaned in closer and lowered his voice. "These religious fanatics can be quite tiresome, lord", he sighed. "I counsel that you send them home to bicker amongst themselves rather than waste your precious time."

"Give me the names of the men who are representing the factions", I said.

"The Bishop of Antioch, Paul of Samosata, and another priest who is known as Domnus", the functionary replied, reading from a document.

I raised an eyebrow and exchanged a glance with Diocles.

"Send them in", I commanded, and moments later two priests were ushered into the audience chamber.

Paul of Samosata was a large man. Not tall, even by Roman standards, but thick set with heavy, sagging jowls. His black hair, cut short in the Christian style, contrasted with his corpse-pale complexion. An embroidered cassock was draped around his robed shoulders, rings adorned his fingers and a heavy gold cross inlaid with precious stones hung at his chest.

"Lord Emperor", Paul said, bowing low. "I thank you on behalf of the Christian church for granting us our request." His voice was as smooth as honey, and despite his appearance he spoke with confidence born of authority. It was easy to understand how he had attained the position of head of the church of Antioch in the first place, and also why he was able to retain it.

My friend Domnus, on the other hand, appeared rather small and insignificant beside the imposing man.

"State your case", I commanded.

For long, Paul ranted on about the reasons why the church wished to replace him. When I could take it no longer I raised a palm and gestured for Domnus to speak. When he was done,

I stood from my throne and approached the two men, my hands folded behind my back.

"I care little whether or not you are preaching heresy", I said to Paul. "But I do know that the one you call the Great Shepherd preached humility. I wonder, bishop, why do your followers sing hymns in your honour rather than praises to your God?"

Paul opened his mouth, no doubt to offer a reasonable explanation, but I raised a palm to silence him and came to a halt a pace away. "I know that you were kept in your position through the patronage of Queen Zenobia", I whispered, and allowed my hand to find the hilt of my blade. "If you are still within the walls of Antioch when the sun sets, you will meet your God sooner than you have planned."

I retook my seat, wet my throat with a swallow of wine, and delivered my formal judgement. "Let it be written", I said. "After careful consideration I have decided to uphold the judgement of the Bishop of Italia. Domnus will replace Paul of Samosata as bishop of the city. My decision is final."

I had hardly dismissed them when Paul hurried out the door, no doubt to pack the gold that he had stolen from his flock.

* * *

Our plan was to advance to Emesa where Zenobia and her generals were waiting. For the best part of two weeks, we were kept busy by the challenges that arose in resupplying the army. Eventually I was forced to requisition shipments of grain from the newly reconquered province of Aegypt to supplement the food and fodder we received from Asia Minor, west of the Taurus Mountains.

The stronghold we were about to march on was situated in arid flatlands a hundred and thirty miles south of Antioch. Our saving grace was the fact that the Roman road followed the Orontes, so the river would provide us with an almost endless supply of fresh water.

Hostilius, Vibius and I were sharing the evening meal when we were interrupted by Diocles. My aide was accompanied by a centurion of the *speculators*, who, judging by his smell and disheveled appearance, had just returned from a scouting mission.

"I have not yet compiled a written report, Lord Emperor", he said. "But I will do so and submit it once I have answered your questions."

"Tell me what we will be facing on the plains of Emesa", I said, and gestured for a pouring slave to give the man a cup of wine.

"My men and I reconnoitred the enemy camp for two full days", the centurion said. "We counted ten thousand heavy horsemen executing their manoeuvres, lord. The cataphracts were supported by at least twenty-five thousand mounted archers - the same men we fought on the plain near Antioch", he added, and paused to wet his throat with a swallow of wine.

"Sounds like good news to me", Hostilius said, raising his cup. "There's only thirty-five thousand of them left. On the plain north of Antioch we fought almost double that number and managed to kick their arses good and proper."

The *speculator* cleared his throat. "There is more, lord", he said, clearly embarrassed that his pause had caused the Primus Pilus to draw the wrong conclusion.

Hostilius issued a scowl. "For the sake of the gods, get on with it, then", he snapped.

"Groupings of infantry were training on the plain as well", he said.

"Infantry?" Hostilius asked. "Since when does Palmyra have foot soldiers?"

"They do employ a few hundred skirmishers", I replied, recalling my conversations with Odaenathus. "Mostly slingers and unarmoured foot archers that irritate the enemy with missiles before they flee to the safety of the heavy cavalry."

"The warriors we saw are no skirmishers, lord", the centurion replied. "They are well-trained men who wield iron spears and carry large round shields reinforced with boiled buffalo hide. Their appearance is much like that of the Numidians, but they are taller and their skill with the lance is impressive. Their banners display depictions of the sun, moon and evening star."

I looked to Vibius for an answer. "My father owned a Parthian slave", my friend replied. "He was a warrior taken in the time when Emperor Caracalla raided deep into the eastern lands."

"Never trust a Parthian", the Primus Pilus warned.

Vibius raised an eyebrow but continued nonetheless. "Frahat told us stories of the Parthian Empire's wars", he said. "He spoke of a powerful kingdom that lies to the south of the Land of Kush. In those days, spearmen from the Kingdom of Axum crossed the Red Sea and took the southern lands of Arabia by strength of arms. They are a warlike people who march under the banner of the sun, moon and evening star."

"How many Axumites did you see?" I asked.

"Their numbers were very similar to that of two legions", the scout replied, which made my throat constrict.

"It seems that Zenobia has recruited far and wide", Diocles remarked drily. "I did not realise she had that much gold in the treasury."

"The Axumites need the favour of Palmyra so that their wares can reach the markets of Rome", Vibius said. "Not only does Zenobia have the gold to buy mercenaries, but also the influence to bend powerful men to her will."

I was watching the *speculator*, who was clearly becoming anxious due to the interruptions. "Allow the centurion to finish his report", I said, and gestured for the officer to continue.

"On the morning that we departed, more mercenaries arrived from the east, lord", he said. "They marched in neat ranks, like legionaries, and carried large wicker shields covered with thick rawhide that were painted bright yellow and adorned with tribal markings. The warriors all wore riveted plate helmets and scale vests that extend to their knees. There were many, I estimate five thousand."

"Describe their weapons", I said.

"Apart from spears, they carried two-pronged javelins and I saw curved swords and battle-axes strapped to their arming belts."

I shared a look with my friends, as many years before our paths had crossed with the brutal Dailamites, the heavy spearmen of the Sasanians.

"So the Sasanians are involved", Hostilius concluded.

"Not necessarily", Vibius said. "The Dailamites live in the heavily forested mountains of Persia. Although the king of kings has tried, he has never been able to subjugate the hill tribes. I heard that the shahanshah lets them be, as long as the spearmen are willing to fight as mercenaries when war comes to the land."

Diocles had been keeping count. "It appears that we will be facing fifteen thousand heavy Palmyrene infantry", my aide pointed out. "Which means that the legions will be outnumbered two to one. Our cavalry, that numbers twenty-five thousand riders, will be facing thirty-five thousand Palmyrene riders."

"We need more infantry", Hostilius said. "If the Dailamites and the mercenaries from Axum know their business, the legions are going to be hard-pressed."

"Where are our allies from the desert, the *Tanukh*?" Gordas asked, his voice carrying an accusatory tone. "Did Amr not boast of contributing ten thousand horse archers and five thousand camel-mounted spearmen?"

I have had no tidings from Amr, who had promised to bring his warriors across the desert to Antioch. "I believe that the *Tanukh* will honour their word", I said. "I will not be surprised if Zenobia's forces are responsible for the fact that Amr's riders have not joined us."

"We will have to make do with what we have", Diocles said.

Vibius cleared his throat. "I recall that the hills of Lebanon are infested with clans that are rumoured to have been at odds with Palmyra for generations", he said. "Mayhap we will be able to lure the wild men to our banner with gold and the promise of revenge."

"Are you suggesting that we get a mob of wild savages to go up against the iron-clad horsemen of Palmyra?" Hostilius asked.

"Desperate times call for desperate measures", I sighed.

The Primus Pilus rolled his eyes. "May the gods help us", he said, and chugged the wine remaining in his cup.

Chapter 29 – Antilibanus

We ended up spending another two weeks in Antioch while we waited for supplies to arrive, injured soldiers to recover and horses to regain condition.

On the Nones of August, I led the army from the marching camp on the banks of the Orontes.

Five days later, we arrived before the wide open gates of Apamea. While the army made camp outside the walls, the city elders escorted me and my entourage along the mile-long colonnaded main street. They spoke of how they had suffered under the tyranny of Zenobia, and I watched while they sacrificed at the Temple of Zeus Belos, beseeching the god to grant victory to the armies of their beloved emperor.

Once the god had been appeased, we continued to the massive open-air theatre near the western gate where we were forced to attend one of Sophocles's Greek tragedies. Amid an oration by Aegisthus, Hostilius tapped me on the shoulder from behind. "I've been thinking", he said, drawing frowns of disapproval from the white-robed men seated around us. "Although sitting through this Greek poppycock is pure torture, sacrificing a watch of our time is better than having to fight our way to Emesa, eh?"

Diocles, who was engrossed in the play, offered Hostilius a thin scowl. "The magistrate tells me that he has spoken to the councils of Larissa and Arethusa, the towns on the road to Emesa", he whispered. "Both cities are arranging performances in the theatre to entertain us", he said, a cruel grin splitting his lips. "And", my aide added, "the duration is closer to two watches than one."

* * *

The following morning before the camp was struck, Vibius arrived at the praetorium. "I am riding to Laodicea on the coast, and from there I will make my way to the hill country", he said. "The clubmen I wish to recruit reside in the Antilibanus Mountains."

"I will be going with you", Hostilius said. "Since you are recruiting infantry, I need to eyeball them to make sure they'll fit in."

I harboured a suspicion that the Primus Pilus feared sitting through another evening of Greek tragedy.

He was not the only one.

"I believe that only the emperor is fit to evaluate the suitability of foreign mercenaries", I said. "Which is why I will be joining you."

I noticed a worried look flash across Diocles's clean-shaven face, no doubt concerned that he would be deprived of a favourite pastime. "Well", he said. "Diplomacy demands that at least one of us attend the festivities."

"We appreciate your sacrifice", Hostilius said, and slapped the Greek on the back.

"Likewise", my aide replied.

* * *

While Diocles and Cai happily took care of Greek tragedies and diplomacy on the road to Emesa, Hostilius, Gordas, Vibius and I rode west towards Laodicea, accompanied by an escort of mounted praetorians. It took two days of hard riding to reach the coastal city, where we left the guards behind and rode west towards the foothills of the Antilibanus Mountains.

It was late morning on the second day on the road when Hostilius reined in at the crest of a hill. He raised a palm to shield his eyes from the glare of the sun, studying the hills dotted with giant cedars. "How in hades are we going to find these men?" he asked. "If they even exist."

"Before we departed from Apamea, I sent three scouts ahead to arrange a meeting with one of their chieftains", Vibius said, retrieved a folded itinerarium from a saddle bag, and pointed up the path. "According to the map, the village should be less than three miles into the hills over yonder."

The track snaked down the decline and levelled out at the bottom as it entered a narrow ravine where ancient cedars blocked out the sun. Hostilius rode ahead of me, his hand on the hilt of his blade. "Real nice place for an ambush, eh?" he said, just as Intikam's ears pricked up.

"Have a care", I warned, slid my blade from the scabbard and pulled on the reins.

Twenty paces in front of Hostilius, a man stepped from the shadows. The olive-skinned warrior's hair was tied at the back and he sported a thick, matching black beard. In his left hand he held a small, round bronze shield adorned with intricate patterns, and in his right a two-foot-long club that appeared to be forged from iron. He wore a loose, ankle-length brown robe over an undyed tunic that was held in place by a broad leather belt.

I pushed past Hostilius and reined in six paces in front of the warrior. "We seek the chieftain who commands the loyalty of the warriors who reside in the Antilibanus", I said, and used my sword to indicate the hills surrounding us.

"Who is asking?" the warrior growled in peasant Greek.

"The man who commands the legions of Rome", I replied.

Not wishing to draw unnecessary attention to ourselves, neither of us had dressed in the garb of Roman officers, never mind the splendid armour and purple cloak one would expect to adorn the body of the emperor.

"And I am Heracles on my way to steal the Mares of Diomedes", the warrior replied.

"North of the mountains", I said, indicating with my sword, "Zenobia of Palmyra has assembled a mighty host. At Antioch we dealt them a crushing blow, but Rome wishes to buy your sword arms so that we may vanquish the usurper once and for all."

For long the man regarded me without issuing a reply.

"They say that the emperor is a warrior who knows no equal", he said. "Prove your worth, Roman, and we may share a cup of wine and speak of gold and warriors."

I sheathed my blade and swung down from the saddle. As my boots hit the ground, the warrior issued a feral roar and attacked.

* * *

"I command a formidable force, Lord Emperor", Abdel said, and leaned forward to hand out cups brimming with dark mead. The chieftain groaned as he righted himself, his lower back no doubt still painful from going to ground during our brief encounter earlier in the day.

The clansman raised his cup and winced as the mead stung his split lip, but he set his tender jaw and took a long swallow of the strong fermented honey. "My lip hurts like hades", he said, issuing a sheepish smile, "but compared to my wrist and back, it is nothing."

I acknowledged him with a grin. "How many men?" I asked.

"Five thousand men, all able to wield clubs of iron or bronze", Abdel replied. "And I wish for five gold coins for each warrior."

Hostilius shook his head and spoke to me in Latin. "I think we're wasting our coin, Domitius", he said. "We'd be better off without them. The Palmyrene infantry will gut these savages in heartbeats. For the love of the gods, they fight with sticks."

"What is he saying?" Abdel asked.

"He says that your men do not wear enough armour to be able to hold back the allied infantry of Zenobia", I said. "And that your price is too high."

"For generations, we have fought the armies of the Parthians, Sasanians and Palmyrenians", Abdel boasted. "We do not wear armour because iron slows us down."

"Three gold coins for every warrior you provide", I suggested.

Abdel waved away my counteroffer. "I tell you what, lord", he said. "We will fight for free, but we wish to have ten gold coins for every one of the iron-clad monsters we kill."

"Take it", Hostilius whispered. "If these savages manage to kill more than five cataphracts I'll pay the gold myself. I just hope that they don't do more damage than good."

* * *

By the time we reunited with the Roman army they were camped outside of Arethusa on the banks of the Orontes, twelve miles north of Emesa.

"None of the towns or cities along the way resisted us, Lord Emperor", Diocles confirmed. "They have all assured us of their enduring loyalty."

"Good to know", I said, sat down on a couch, and gestured for my friends to join me.

"When do you believe we will be joining battle with the army of Zabdas and Zenobia?" I asked.

"It could be as early as tomorrow", Hostilius said. "But I would prefer it if we made camp closer to Emesa to avoid the boys having to fight after a hard march."

I nodded my agreement. "The battle will be fought on ground of the enemy's choosing", I said. "The plain around Emesa suits their cavalry, especially their cataphracts. They will also get to choose the time of the battle. It would be foolish of us to offer battle before the walls of the city. Zenobia will let us stew in the sun for hours before she accepts the challenge."

"How do you think the enemy will deploy?" Vibius asked.

"Their infantry will be the backbone of their formation", Hostilius said. "Five thousand heavy Dailamite spearmen in the centre flanked by the lighter Axumite regiments."

"That means that our infantry will match theirs in number", Diocles said.

Hostilius offered a scowl. "We will be facing ten thousand Axumites and five thousand Dailamites with two legions", the Primus Pilus said. "How is that equal, Greek?"

"You forget about the five thousand clubmen from the Antilibanus Mountains", Diocles said.

"Discount those savages", Hostilius snapped. "The best we can do is use them as a reserve stationed at the rear of the legions."

"And the cavalry?" Vibius asked.

"The Palmyrene horsemen will be equally divided between the two flanks", Gordas said. "Five thousand cataphracts and twelve thousand horse archers on each side of their infantry."

"I suggest we station five thousand Illyrians on each flank", I said. "The remaining five thousand Taifali will bolster the Illyrians on the left, and the Berbers will support the contingent on the right."

"Should we employ the same tactics as we did on the plain north of Antioch?" Diocles asked.

I shook my head. "This time we are facing an army who is superior in both infantry and cavalry", I said. "And I am certain that the enemy will not be twice-tricked by the same ruse."

"We will have to break their infantry with the legions", Hostilius growled. "That is the only way."

"I agree", I said. "The battle on the plains of Emesa will be decided by the foot soldiers. But if the cataphracts are allowed to smash into the flanks of the legions, we will not prevail. Our cavalry will have to keep the enemy horsemen occupied until we are able to rout the Palmyrene footmen."

"Easier said than done", Vibius sighed, and took a long draught from his cup.

Chapter 30 – Emesa (July 272 AD)

Four days later, on a pleasantly cool and overcast morning, I rode at the head of the army as it advanced across the plain north of Emesa.

Gordas glanced up at the grey clouds that were threatening rain. "The queen has learnt her lesson", he said. "Her warhorses will fare better today."

There was no doubt in my mind that the Hun was right, so I grunted in agreement.

I was flanked by two Roman legions that was supported by an unruly mob of clubmen trailing behind the neat, but thin ranks of legionaries who presented a frontage of almost a mile.

Vibius guarded the left flank with five thousand Illyrians, supported by an equal number of Taifali horse archers. On the right flank, Adherbal's Berbers provided missile support to the remaining five thousand black riders commanded by Diocles.

As we had expected, five thousand heavily armoured Dailamite spearmen with large shields and two-pronged spears were drawn up in the centre, their ranks more than ten warriors deep. They were supported by ten thousand Axumite footmen, five thousand on each side of the Persian mercenaries.

It was not the Palmyrene infantry that concerned me the most, but the massive wings of cavalry flanking the enemy centre. In the Western lands there was almost always a river, a forest or a boulder-strewn hill to anchor the flank, but on the wide open plain of Emesa there were no obstacles to prevent the enemy cavalry from circling around the flanks to strike the foot soldiers in the rear.

"Whoever wins the battle on the wings will carry the day", Gordas said, regarding the enemy formation from his dark eyes, set deep within his elongated skull.

"If Zenobia manages to scatter our horsemen, she will unleash her cataphracts and they will strike the legions in the flanks and rear", Hostilius confirmed.

I studied the cavalry of the foe that outnumbered us almost two to one, and was forced to swallow back the yellow bile rising in my throat.

"Looks like the bitch and her henchman wants to have a word", the Primus Pilus said as a small group of riders pushed through the ranks of enemy infantry and started towards us. They came to a halt roughly midway between the armies, well out of arrow range.

I gestured for the praetorians to remain. Hostilius, Gordas and I approached the enemy delegation, reining in ten paces from Zenobia and Zabdas, who were guarded by two cataphracts mounted on enormous warhorses. My eyes were drawn to the heavy horsemen, and I noticed that even their reins were of iron chain to prevent an enemy blade from severing them. My actions did not go unnoticed.

"They are impressive, are they not?" Zenobia said from atop her white Nisean.

The queen of Palmyra sat straight in the saddle, dressed in gilded scale armour befitting a warrior queen. Her dark, henna-blackened locks contrasted with the silver diadem set with a large opal, and matched the jewels that dangled from her lobes and adorned her long, slender neck. A generous application of kohl accentuated her dark eyes, and her olive skin was brushed with gold powder, endowing her with a shimmering, godlike appearance.

But I knew better than most that beneath her outward beauty lurked an intelligent but cold-hearted killer who did not hesitate to shed blood to advance her own interest.

Beside the queen rode Zabdas, Palmyra's chief general. It was the first time I had laid eyes on him and it was clear why he was rumoured to be the rock upon which Odaenathus had built the army of Palmyra. Although most of his body was encased in gilded scale, the veins on his heavily muscled forearms, protruding from underneath his vambraces, hinted that he was a warrior of renown. His conical iron helmet was polished to a shine and sported a nose guard and an apron of thick chain to protect his neck. A plume of black horsehair matched the fur-edged cloak that was draped over his broad shoulders, marking him as a man of consequence. By the looks of it he was firmly under the spell of the queen.

"You have come a long way since I first met you, Roman", Zenobia said in Greek, the venom in her voice threatening to pierce the veil of beauty and expose the darkness lurking beneath.

"You have sworn fealty to Rome, but you have tasted power and wish for more", I replied. "Reaffirm your oath and you may remain in the palace and rule Palmyra with my blessing."

Zabdas issued a snicker of amusement. "Your words is that of a king who knows that his fate is sealed", the big Palmyrenian growled. "You know that your riders cannot prevail against the horsemen of the desert", he added, indicating the flatland with a sweeping gesture. "Bel, the lord of the plain will guide their blades. The gods of the Romans have no power in these lands."

"Then it is good that I do not serve the Roman gods", I said, as a light drizzle started to fall.

"Who do you serve?" Zabdas asked.

"Arash the Destroyer, the lord of the field of blood", I said, and turned my horse's head around, back to the thin ranks of the Roman army.

* * *

We had hardly rejoined the ranks when the blast of a Palmyrene war horn echoed across the plain.

The infantry of the enemy remained as they were, but like a great bird of prey wishing to take to the sky, the wings of the army of Palmyra started to stir. The foe's assault was led by the heavy cataphracts, with the horse archers trailing behind.

Vibius and Diocles knew their orders, so my signifer remained silent. Instead, I mouthed a prayer to Arash, beseeching the god to render his assistance. A heartbeat later, the Roman cavalry responded and surged forward to meet the enemy's charge.

Gordas studied the cataphracts with an expert eye. "They are holding back their mounts", he said. "They are sly, like the wolf."

I felt a stab in the pit of my stomach, but the die was cast and it was up to Vibius and Diocles to respond to whatever tricks the horsemen of Palmyra had up their sleeve. As the two giant waves of riders thundered towards one another, I could not help holding my breath in anticipation. There was no way that the Romans and their allies could meet the charge of the heavy cataphracts head-on, so when the forces were a hundred paces apart, the Taifali released a wave of arrows, the Illyrians cast a volley of war darts and the light javelins of the Berbers rose high into the air. After releasing their missiles, the Romans and their allies skilfully wheeled about, their tight formation fanning out and splintering into smaller units of five hundred riders to enhance their manoeuvrability.

Another Palmyrene horn blared.

In response, a great cheer rose from the enemy infantry, and twenty thousand spearmen surged forward at a jog. The way they kept their cohesion was nothing less than impressive.

I nodded to the signifer and the Roman infantry responded in kind. Once the ranks had flowed around us, my retinue and I advanced, but our eyes remained glued to the charge of the cavalry where we knew the battle would be decided.

Zabdas had learned from our earlier encounter near Antioch, and the response of the heavy riders was timed to perfection. What their Nisean mounts lacked in endurance they made up for by their immense power and speed. Unlike at Antioch, the warhorses of Palmyra were well rested and no doubt in peak condition. The iron-encased monsters surged forward at a pace that surprised even Gordas. I heard the Hun gasp in astonishment as the solid wall of iron and horseflesh accelerated at a staggering pace and ploughed into the ranks of the retreating Roman riders, who had underestimated the swiftness of the foe. Hundreds of Illyrians, Taifali and Berbers met their demise at the sharp end of a heavy *kontus*. The cries of dying men and the pitiful whinnies of injured horses drifted across the plain just as the two opposing blocks of infantry came together, the sound of thousands of clashing blades drowning out the noise of the perishing Roman cavalry.

Hostilius's full attention was focused on the infantry, but Gordas and I were still enthralled by the battle of the horsemen. Not only did I dread the defeat of the Roman mounted troops, but feared that Vibius and Diocles had perished in the initial clash. The Roman cavalry had received a crippling blow from the heavy riders of Palmyra, but to their credit they did not scatter. The survivors remained in their squadrons, fanning out across the plain, limping away in what I would like to call an orderly retreat, but which, from the enemy's perspective, must have appeared to be a rout.

To best pursue and eliminate the Romans, the enemy cavalry followed suit and split into smaller units. I watched in dread fascination as a fleeing unit of Illyrians were caught between the hammer and anvil of two squadrons of cataphracts. The jaws of iron-clad warriors closed around the panicked Roman riders, annihilating them to the last man. Soon, both wings turned into a hunting ground with the hunters being the Palmyrenians and the Romans the prey.

But any huntsman will tell you that an injured beast can be dangerous.

On the right flank I noticed an *ala* of Berbers turn the tide on their pursuers. With great skill they wheeled about, struck the desert horsemen of Palmyra with a wave of javelins, and penetrated deep into their ranks, their flashing swords soon cutting down the last of the foe.

On the left, a squadron of Illyrians all but annihilated a company of mounted Palmyrene archers, but they were in turn scattered by a charge from heavy cataphracts.

I felt a hand take my arm in a grip of iron. "The legions are driving back the spearmen, Domitius", Hostilius said, his gaze fixed on the infantry battle. "They're winning, but it's no rout. It's slow, gruelling work."

I turned my attention to the infantry battle and saw the Dailamites retreat another step, giving way to the relentless pressure of the legions as the superior training and armour of the Romans were starting to tell. The Axumites flanking the Persian mercenaries were skilful warriors, but never had they faced a military machine perfected over the span of a thousand years, and the legionaries ground away their resistance, one spearman at a time.

Dreading to accept the disaster playing out on the flanks, I tore my gaze away from the infantry and beheld the flanks where the battle could best be described as a melee. Enemy horse archers were being slaughtered in droves by the well-armoured Illyrians but they, in turn, had no answer to the thick armour of the cataphracts that were laying into their ranks with flanged maces and swords. It would take a while, but I realised that there was only one outcome, and that outcome did not favour Rome.

I was still trying to come up with a solution when a messenger on a lathered horse arrived from the right flank. "Lord

Emperor", he said, and saluted. "Legate Marcellinus reports that although they have slaughtered thousands of the enemy's light horsemen, they are losing the battle on the right wing. Their swords and lances are proving useless against the armour of the heavy cavalry."

Then Arash whispered into my ear and I heard the words of Abdel echo inside my mind, *'For generations, we have fought the armies of the Parthians, Sasanians and Palmyrenians.'*

"Bring me the leader of the men from the Antilibanus", I commanded a praetorian, and twisted in the saddle to face Hostilius. "Tribune", I said. "Give the order for six third-line infantry cohorts to detach from the battle formation. Three cohorts are to attack the enemy cavalry on the left flank and the same number on the right."

"If doubt whether we can hold off the mercenary spearmen with the remaining legionaries", the Primus Pilus said, and stared at me as if I had taken leave of my senses. But after a heartbeat had passed, he set his jaw, saluted, and said, "I understand, Lord Emperor, and I will obey."

While Hostilius relayed my commands, Abdel sauntered over, a slight scowl on his face. "You called for me, lord?" he asked, his tone casual.

"You know your way around the iron-clad monsters?" I asked, and gestured to where our horsemen were being bested by the cataphracts.

A feral sneer split his bearded face. "I beg you, lord, unleash us", he hissed through gritted teeth. "And we will show you."

"Make it so", I said, and the chieftain spun around to do my bidding, no doubt eager to earn the coin we had agreed upon.

Once the two rear ranks of the legions had trotted off towards the flanks, the advance of the infantry ground to a slow halt. "The tide is turning against us", Hostilius said, indicating the Romans, who, deprived of almost a third of their number, were starting to give ground.

I swung down from the saddle, handed the leathers to a praetorian, and accepted his black *scutum* in return. "Come. It is time for the emperor to put iron into to the sword arms of the soldiers of Rome", I said, drew my *gladius*, hefted my shield, and pushed through the ranks of legionaries to reach the heart of the battle where the fighting was at its fiercest.

I had hardly taken my place in the line when a Dailamite spear snaked out from behind the wall of shields, the vicious two-pronged blade aimed at my exposed sword arm. I twisted my hips, pulled my *scutum* in tight against my shoulder and took the hit on the iron boss. With the same swiftness as the strike, the spearman jerked the blade back, once again presenting his large, oval shield.

Although many seasons had passed, I had fought the Dailamites before and was familiar with their favoured tactic where they trapped an enemy sword between the blades of their two-pronged spear. Typically, they would grip their weapon a handspan behind the business end, catch the blade of the enemy, and use leverage to twist the weapon from the grip of their opponent. Once disarmed, they moved in for the kill.

I lunged at the one-inch-wide gap between the two shields facing me, the flat of my *gladius's* blade held vertical to pass through the narrow slit. The tip of my sword did not taste flesh, but I felt the impact as the Dailamite adroitly caught the blade between the prongs of his spear. He twisted his wrist to securely trap the iron, making it almost impossible to wrench the blade free - which would be most men's instinctive reaction.

Unlike me, most men had not been trained by a master of the sword.

Knowing that my adversary's weapon was engaged with mine, I stepped in. Before the Dailamite could rotate his spear to relieve me of my *gladius*, I used my momentum and superior leverage to thrust my blade to the side, slamming my shoulder into the lower part of his shield as I did so. The spear flew from the mercenary's grip, and the top rim of his shield tilted forward, exposing his torso.

But I had not the time to aim my blade at his neck.

I allowed him a fraction of a heartbeat to overcorrect, and as he jerked his shield upwards to cover his face from the strike he believed imminent, I dropped to a crouch and cut deep into the side of his knee.

He moaned in pain and dropped the shield a handspan.

This time I was in position, my blade drawn back and my hips loaded. I moved forward and the flat of my *gladius* scraped the edge of his shield and pierced his neck.

The enemy to the left used the opportunity and thrust with his spear, the blade aimed at my face. Hostilius issued a roar and the Primus Pilus's *gladius* flashed, severing the haft of the spear just behind the iron.

I dropped my shield and slashed my blade across the Dailamite's throat.

A shout of triumph rose from the praetorians behind me. "The emperor has breached their line!" they boomed, and surged into the gap.

Exhausted, I stepped from the fray and allowed my elite guards to exploit the gap in the enemy ranks. The infantry battle was far from over, but the legions' morale had been restored, and suddenly the Palmyrenians were the ones shuffling backwards and looking over their shoulders.

Dreading that the Palmyrene cavalry had routed the Roman horse, I gained the saddle and turned my gaze to the wings.

What I witnessed was hard to comprehend.

While the armour-piercing lances and swords of the Illyrians had proven ineffective against the heavily armoured cataphracts, the simple weapons of the Antilibanus mercenaries were something to behold. With great skill they sidestepped the swipes of the iron-encased monsters and lashed out with their iron and bronze clubs. The heavy weapons failed to inflict visible damage on the plate and scale of the cataphracts, but it was soon apparent that the blows were powerful enough to shatter the flesh and bone encased inside the armour. The hillmen moved amongst the ranks of the cataphracts, dodging blows and counterattacking at a speed which beggared belief.

We watched a hundred of Abdel's men overpower a group of fifty cataphracts. They slid in underneath the scale aprons of the Niseans, cut the girths and wrested the impervious monsters from their saddles, ending the struggle with a single strike to the thick iron helms.

"Not badly done for base savages, eh?" I said, turning to the Primus Pilus. "It seems that you will have a substantial bill to foot."

Hostilius narrowed his eyes. "I suggest you stop gloating, Domitius, and get the Illyrians to attack the enemy infantry's flanks. That way we'll all be alive to figure out how we will pay Abdel's bill."

I grinned, and did as my friend suggested.

Chapter 31 – Tanukh

"Three thousand cataphracts at ten gold pieces each comes to thirty thousand aurei", Diocles said. "Which is substantially more than Abdel's original demand."

"Please, spare me the details, Greek", Hostilius said. "There's more to life than counting coin."

Diocles rolled his eyes.

"How much of Zenobia's gold was in Emesa's vaults?" I asked.

"Enough to pay Abdel fifty times over", my aide replied.

"What are you whining about, then?" Hostilius said, raised his cup, and reclined on the couch. "Pay the man and get on with it."

"It is about the principle", Diocles countered, but got no further as he was interrupted by Gordas and Vibius strolling into the praetorium.

"The queen and her general have escaped", the Hun sighed, and took a seat beside Hostilius. "I believe that they, and what remained of their army, have gone east to seek refuge behind the walls of Palmyra."

"Those fortifications are formidable", Hostilius said.

"The walls of Zenobia's city is nothing compared to what lies between here and Palmyra", Gordas said. "The road runs through a sea of sand and rocks, a wasteland infested by vipers, scorpions and bandits. And the scouts report that Zenobia's army has poisoned the wells along the way."

"So what do we need to do to be able to cross the desert?" I asked, and took a swallow of iced wine.

"I suggest that we visit the temple of Elagabal and sacrifice to the lord of the mountains", Vibius replied. "Because we will need a miracle of the gods to get an army across that wasteland."

* * *

Four days later, a third of a watch before sunset, the gods answered our pleas.

I had tasked Diocles with calculating the supplies the army would require to cross the wasteland to Palmyra in order to maintain a possible protracted siege. This had resulted in my aide's disposition becoming increasingly dour, up to a point where even I avoided his company. In a moment of inattentiveness, I walked into the praetorium and failed to notice him sitting at a desk partly hidden by a weapons stand.

"Every foot soldier needs at least an *urna* of water a day", Diocles said, and bade me to take a seat while he remained at the desk. "A horse and rider require about three times the quantity if they do not overexert themselves. If the army wishes to travel as a unit, it will take seven days to journey across the desert."

I could not help but feel like a boy being instructed by a tutor, but kept my composure and nodded in reply. "Eight thousand legionaries, seven thousand Illyrians, four thousand Berbers and three thousand Taifali are fit to go east", I said.

Diocles frantically scribbled on the wax tablet until he arrived at a figure. "That comes to sixty thousand *urnae* of water for the legionaries and close to three hundred times a thousand *urnae* for the horsemen. If we assume that the riders will be able to carry two days' worth of supply and the foot soldiers one day, it still leaves three hundred and ten thousand units of water. Our ox-wagons can carry four hundred and fifty, so we will need almost seven hundred wagons just to transport the water."

Just then Hostilius strolled in. The Primus Pilus took a seat and listened to the tail-end of my aide's calculations.

"What about the fodder for the horses, the mules and the oxen?" Hostilius asked.

"I am coming to that", Diocles snapped.

"Let me help you out here, Greek", Hostilius replied, his tone dismissive. "Even if you could lay your hands on a thousand wagons and sixteen thousand oxen we would still not have enough water and food to cross the wasteland. Besides", he added, "we don't need any of that anymore."

A frown of annoyance slowly furrowed Diocles's brow and I contemplated fabricating an excuse to leave my two friends to their bickering, but before I was able to come up with something viable, Vibius strolled in, deep in discussion with a turban-wearing man.

Amr of the *Tanukh* grinned and went down on one knee. "I apologise for my tardiness, Lord Emperor", he said. "We had no choice but to defend our families from the onslaught of the queen."

I waved Amr to his feet and gripped his arm in the way of the warrior. "How come you are here when Palmyra threatens to attack the ones you hold dear?"

"After her defeat at Emesa, Queen Bat-Zabbai has withdrawn her warriors from the countryside", the desert lord replied. "They now guard the walls of Palmyra."

"How many troops have you brought with you?" Vibius asked.

"Almost a hundred riders", he replied. "Mostly goatherds and camel drovers."

I must have frowned in confusion.

"I know they are few", he said with half a smile, "but to you they are more valuable than ten thousand mounted warriors. They are all men who know the lay of the land along the road to Palmyra. They know the location of every hidden spring, well and pasture."

"Twenty thousand", Diocles replied, smiling for the first time in days. "I believe they are more valuable to us than twenty thousand riders."

* * *

Come the following morning, I sent a cohort of legionaries to set up a makeshift fort at the nearest waterhole along the road to Palmyra, which one of Amr's goatherds had assured us were less than a mile south of the Roman road, about twenty miles east of Emesa. A hundred Berbers accompanied the legionaries and guides, acting as outriders to ensure that they did not fall prey to an ambush by Zenobia's warriors while they were building fortifications.

Once the supply base had successfully been set up at the water source, we stocked the outpost with fodder for the horses and food for the men. It took almost two weeks to create a line of such bases, twenty miles apart, stretching from Emesa all the way to about thirty miles west of Palmyra.

Only once the supply line had been secured did we march east, the army still carrying as much additional water, food and fodder as our limited number of wagons allowed.

We broke camp early in the morning, two-thirds of a watch before sunrise. To our surprise the men did not complain, as it meant that we could afford to rest during the hottest part of the day and end the march a third of a watch earlier than was the norm.

The second evening on the road, a third of a watch after sunset, Amr and Adherbal arrived at the praetorium.

"No sign of Zenobia's warriors?" Hostilius asked.

"Nothing", Amr said. "I rode out with the prefect and his men today and we did not see so much as a single scout watching from a hill."

A pouring slave presented the men with cups filled with watered-down white wine, and I gestured for them to take seats.

"I think we crushed the will of Zenobia's men", Hostilius said. "Twice in a row we've kicked their arses. Maybe she and Zabdas have already fled across the Euphrates. I'm sure that King Bahram of the Sasanians would welcome enemies of Rome with open arms."

"I hope you are right", Amr said, and took a long swallow to wash the day's dust from his throat.

* * *

Mid-morning on the morrow, I shielded my eyes with an open palm to peek at the sky. There was not a cloud in sight, which meant that there would be no relief from the relentless onslaught of the sun. Behind me and my retinue followed a snaking column of legionaries, marching in full armour with their shields at the ready.

Hostilius wrapped his reins around a saddle horn and used both hands to pry his helmet from his sweat-soaked skull. "I know we are marching through hostile lands", he said. "But we should seriously consider allowing the boys to cover their shields and strap them to their packs. We don't want half the legionaries to go down with sunstroke, eh?"

I removed my own helmet as well, and took a long swig from my waterskin. "Zenobia is not done yet", I said. "She has the blood of the lords of the desert, who are a resilient people. How else are they able to survive in this wasteland?"

The words had hardly left my lips when a stream of ululating horsemen spilled from one of the countless ravines on the northern side of the Roman road. The sky darkened with shafts and throwing spears, and instinctively I grabbed my shield from the saddle and raised it at an angle above my head. I felt half a dozen iron tips strike the plywood, followed by a burning sensation just above my ear. The horsemen released another volley, then thundered back into another defile, disappearing in a matter of twenty heartbeats.

Down the column, I heard a *buccina* ordering our horsemen to pursue. "The cavalry is to remain as they were", I said to the signifer. "Zenobia wants us to pursue them."

"Signal for the column to halt", I heard Hostilius bark. The Primus Pilus swung down from the saddle and reached out a hand.

I ignored him and pressed a palm to my temple, which came away red. I struggled to focus on my bloodied hand and it felt as if I were on the deck of a liburnian in the midst of a storm.

"He's going to fall", I heard a voice shout.

Then everything went black and I felt myself tumble from the saddle into the abyss.

Chapter 32 – Palmyra

Hostilius gently, but firmly, pressed an open palm against my chest to prevent me from rising from the furs. "No", he said.

I looked towards Cai for assistance, but judging by the expression on the Easterner's face, I realised that he was of the same mind as the Primus Pilus. Defeated, I lay back. "Where are we?" I asked.

"Camped outside the walls of Palmyra", Gordas said from the other side of my bed.

"Did we take casualties?" I asked.

"Only fools who ignored your orders and removed their helmets", Hostilius replied, his tone accusatory.

I issued a scowl and was rewarded with a sharp pain in my temple. I reached out and probed the sinew that Cai had used to stitch the laceration.

"The wound was a bad one to start with", the Primus Pilus confirmed. "But you stuffed it up good and proper when you fell from the saddle."

An intense feeling of humiliation suddenly pushed the physical pain to the side. Thankfully it was the moment Diocles and

Vibius ducked into the praetorium, a scroll carrying the seal of the queen of Palmyra in my aide's fist.

"Welcome back, Lucius", Vibius said as he and Diocles joined the others seated around my bed.

Hostilius leaned over the bed and gently lifted my torso from the furs, allowing Cai to prop me up with a few down-stuffed pillows.

"What is that?" I asked.

"Zenobia's reply to your letter, Lord Emperor", he replied.

"My letter?" I asked.

"The last thing we wanted Zenobia to know is that you were walking the shadowlands between life and death", Vibius said. "It was actually Diocles who came up with the suggestion to quell the rumours by sending a letter to the queen in your name."

"What did my letter say?" I asked.

"Just the usual crap", Hostilius replied. "You ordered her to surrender and gave your oath that you would spare her and the citizens of Palmyra if she did."

"It seems that I am not needed anymore", I said, suddenly pitying myself.

"I agree", Vibius grinned. "Apart from the small matter that all but a handful of the soldiers in the camp are here because of their loyalty to you, Lucius. Were it not for that, we would not need you, of course."

I waved away my friend's words. "Let's hear her reply, then", I said.

Septimia Zenobia Augusta, queen of the East, to Lucius Domitius Augustus.

Matters of war are best accomplished by valour and not by the stylus. In my veins flows the blood of Queen Cleopatra of Aegypt, who preferred to die by the sword rather than bow to the enemy. Why do you believe I am any different?

I am told that you, who are not even able to defend yourself against the brigands of the desert, wish to lay siege to the mighty walls of my city. You will soon find that Palmyra has powerful allies. When they arrive, you will lay aside the arrogance with which you command my surrender.

"At least it is to the point and not open to interpretation", I said.

"Do you think that she is bluffing about her allies?" Vibius asked.

"Zenobia's cunning is not to be underestimated", I said. "It is not that difficult to imagine that she had a hand in Hormizd's demise and Bahram's ascension to the Sasanian throne. If that is true, a Sasanian army might be marching to Palmyra's relief as we speak."

It was a sobering thought for all.

"If that is the case we should not waste the lives of our men by assaulting the wall", Hostilius cautioned.

I nodded my agreement. "Thanks to Amr and the *Tanukh* we are well provisioned with food, fodder and water", I said. "We should rest the men and the horses. While we regain our strength we will starve Palmyra into submission."

"A siege it is, then", Hostilius sighed, and raised his cup.

* * *

"Tomorrow it will be a month since we arrived", Hostilius said, irritation thick in his voice. "And don't scratch", he scolded. "You know Cai told you not to."

I picked at a scab and flicked it away, which earned me a scowl from the Primus Pilus.

Before Hostilius could offer a retort, Diocles ushered Amr into the tent. "I have received word from my spies that a Sasanian army has left Ctesiphon and is on its way to cross the Euphrates at Dura", he said.

"So Zenobia wasn't bluffing after all", the Primus Pilus said.

"How many?" I asked.

"Five thousand", Amr replied, his expression grim.

Hostilius slapped him on the back. "That's good tidings", he said. "Five thousand men are too few to pose a threat to us."

"They are warriors of the immortal guard", Amr replied.

Hostilius and I exchanged glances as we were familiar with the elite royal guard of the Sasanians.

"I remember them. They are tough bastards", the Primus Pilus opined. "Combined with Zenobia's warriors, five thousand immortals may just turn the tide in her favour."

"Then we had better make sure they never reach Palmyra", I replied, and picked another scab from my scalp.

"Easier said than done", Hostilius said. "If we weaken the army that is besieging Palmyra, Zenobia will get wind of it and attack. If, on the other hand, we don't send a sufficiently strong force to turn back the Sasanians, the immortals will reach the city and lift the siege."

I turned to Amr. "You spoke of having ten thousand horse archers under your command", I said.

The *Tanukh* lord lowered his gaze. "Many of my warriors perished in the war with Queen Bat-Zabbai", he said. "And I have sent the remaining men home to care for their herds and protect their families from brigands."

I nodded, as I realised that the *Tanukh* had no standing army.

"But", he added. "Due to the war, the caravans coming in from the east have all but dried up. That means that I can call upon my camel-mounted spearmen."

"Gods help us", Hostilius muttered, and chugged the wine in his cup.

* * *

Five days later, Hostilius, Gordas, Vibius and I rode abreast of Amr, who led a force of four thousand camel riders. The desert lord, my friends and I, and the thirty praetorians escorting us were on horseback while the *Tanukh* were all lumbering along mounted on camels, heading east towards the river, the border between Rome and the Sasanian Empire.

The great fortress of Dura had been built on a hill overlooking a crossing point in the Euphrates. Although it stood on the western bank, it had always been under Parthian control until Emperor Traianus had wrested it from the Easterners, more than a hundred and fifty years before. When Shapur of the Sasanians invaded Roman lands almost twenty years earlier, he besieged the fortress, eventually breached the walls, ravaged the town, and sold the survivors into slavery. The shahanshah did not try to retain Dura, and likewise, the Romans were too busy trying to save their ailing Empire to waste resources in an attempt to recover it.

"Is Dura still deserted?" I asked Amr.

"Desperate goatherds used to use it for shelter", the *Tanukh* lord replied. "They are the ones who spread tales of the shades of restless dead walking the streets of Dura when darkness comes. Nowadays all avoid the ruins that is a tomb to thousands of Roman and Parthian soldiers."

"Where there's smoke, there's fire", Hostilius said.

"Maybe", I replied. "We will soon find out."

Because of the intense heat of the desert we were forced to rest and water the horses frequently. Unlike our mounts, the camels of the nomads seemed to be unaffected by the temperature and required very little water while being able to maintain a steady pace.

"The camels are impressive, eh?" I said to Gordas while we were watering our horses from a spring trickling from a rocky outcrop. Not far away, in a boulder-strewn ravine, the *Tanukh* warriors lounged in the thin shade of a grove of date palms while their camels foraged for fallen fruit.

Gordas regarded the camels for a span of heartbeats while he stroked the neck of his mare. "They are best suited to a man who has lost his eyes and had his nose cut off", the Hun said. "They are despicable, ugly creatures that reek like a Roman latrine ditch left untended in the summer sun."

"And that's on a good day", Hostilius said, throwing in his weight with Gordas. "You should smell them on a rainy day."

Chapter 33 – Euphrates

We spied the limestone walls of Dura long before we laid eyes on the Euphrates.

Rather than approach the crossing point along the main road, Amr led us off the cobles to a low ridge a few hundred paces to the south, where we crested the rise and descended into a defile with a small stream at the bottom. "Somehow the Euphrates makes its way into these ravines", the desert lord said. "We should remain here until the scouts have reconnoitred the ford in the river."

Once we had cared for the horses, we reclined in the shade of ancient ghafs and junipers that flourished on the banks of the brook. Having watered their camels, the *Tanukh* warriors divided into their clan groupings and soon they were slaughtering the sheep and goats that they had procured from herders earlier in the day.

Just before sunset, the outriders returned, reporting that the Sasanian force had arrived on the far bank of the river and that they were setting up camp.

"They outnumber us", I said, and leaned forward to stir the mutton stew simmering in the iron pot suspended above glowing dung cakes. "What do you suggest?"

"We wait for half of the Sasanian force to cross", Gordas replied. "While we overwhelm the warriors on the western bank, we send arrows into the ones trying to come to the aid of their comrades."

"I like it", Hostilius said. "It's simple and it'll work."

"The immortals will see us coming", Amr remarked. He reached out, took a handful of sand from beside the fire and allowed it to run through his fingers onto the ground. Even in the near dark, a fog of fine dust was discernible. "We will raise a dust cloud visible for miles."

"Why don't we hide inside the walls of Dura?" Vibius asked. "When the time is ripe we can spill from the south gate. The wadi abutting the walls will keep us from the eyes of the enemy until we are almost upon them."

"How in hades do you know the fortress on the Euphrates so well?" Hostilius asked.

"When I was a boy, I often travelled with my father when he visited Dura", Vibius said. "The city used to be quite magnificent - a melting pot of arts, culture and cuisine where the East met the West."

The Primus Pilus scoffed at Vibius's words. "Rome doesn't need other cultures, especially not the effeminate ways of the Persians", he said. "Maybe Shapur and his merry men did us a favour by destroying Dura. It's like chopping off a festering limb before the whole body gets infected."

Before Vibius could offer a retort, Amr raised his open palms. "My men will not enter the city", he said. "They believe that when darkness falls, the shades of the dead roam the deserted streets."

I did not ask Amr if he shared the beliefs of his warriors, but rather suggested an alternative. "When your men have slaked their thirst and filled their bellies, why do we not use the light of Mani to ride to Dura? We will spend the night on the flat ground in front of the western wall, out of sight of the river."

"As long as we do not go inside the city when it is dark", the *Tanukh* lord replied.

* * *

When the sun rose above the eastern horizon, Hostilius, Gordas, Vibius, Amr and I entered the city via the Palmyrene Gate in the western wall. Vibius led us through the broad streets to the temple of Zeus that abutted the eastern wall. From its elevated position at the edge of a sheer rise, it afforded a panoramic view across the ford in the great river.

From inside the temple, we watched as half a dozen Sasanian outriders made their way across the water. Once on the western bank, two riders cantered north and two south, while the remaining two trotted in the direction of the Roman road leading to Palmyra.

My gaze remained on the two riders approaching the base of the cliff, concerned that they would stumble upon the *Tanukh* force concealed in the ravine abutting the walls of the city. But they reined in to confer, and rather than ride up the wadi they cantered south, clearly intent on giving the cursed fortress a wide berth.

Hostilius reached beneath his tunic for his amulet. "It seems like Amr's men are not the only ones who have heard the tales about Dura", he said, eyeing the deserted corridors with suspicion. "I'm telling you now, I have a bad feeling about this place."

"The rumours work in our favour", Vibius said, indicating the two Sasanian scouts cantering away from the walls.

"I hope it stays that way", the Primus Pilus growled.

* * *

Dura was built on an escarpment overlooking a narrow floodplain bordering the Euphrates, which meant that the wall facing the river was unassailable for all intents and purposes. In addition, deep ravines protected both the northern and southern walls.

It took the best part of a watch for the enemy outriders to reconnoitre the area and return to the force of immortals arrayed on the eastern bank. Because we had left the Roman road a few miles west of the city and used the ravines to navigate our way to Dura, our passage was not discovered by the Sasanian scouts.

It did not take long for the first battalion of immortal guards to guide their mounts into the slow-flowing river.

I turned to face Amr. "It will take the enemy a third of a watch to get two thousand men to our side of the river. On my signal, two and a half thousand of your riders must spill from the wadi and fall upon them from the south", I said. "A thousand must circle around the western wall, make their way through the northern wadi, and fall upon the rear of the immortal guards."

Amr nodded. "It is a sound strategy", he said. "What about the remaining five hundred?"

"Take your best five hundred bowmen and station them on the riverbank. While your warriors are engaged with the immortals, task the archers with sending shafts into the men attempting to cross the river", I said. "If the remaining three thousand Sasanians join their comrades on the western bank, we will have to flee for our lives."

"I will make sure that they have three quivers each", Amr said. "We will not fail you, lord."

I knew that there was little we could do to influence the outcome of the confrontation. The *Tanukh* lord departed to give effect to my orders, while Hostilius, Gordas, Vibius and I remained in the temple to watch the battle unfold.

When about two thousand Sasanian riders were arrayed on the western bank, the nomads spilled from the southern ravine onto the three hundred-pace-wide floodplain bordering the river, catching the immortal guards by surprise.

But the Sasanian riders were elite warriors. Before the armoured spearmen of the *Tanukh* could get to grips with them, the immortals deployed into a near-straight line that matched the frontage of the ranks of the desert nomads.

Gordas pointed at the lumbering camels approaching the enemy riders, who were still dressing their line. "Were the *Tanukh* mounted on armoured horses, they would have struck the Sasanians while they were in disarray", the Hun said.

Only a fool would have waited for the camel lancers to strike the stationary Sasanian horsemen, and the enemy commander was no fool. When the two forces were two hundred paces apart, the immortal guards spurred their horses to a gallop, the way they dressed their line a testament to their excellent horsemanship. When a hundred paces separated them, the enemy lowered their lances, their formation as straight as a well-crafted arrow. In contrast with the near-perfect ranks of the Sasanians, the camel lancers appeared to be closer to an unruly mob than a disciplined force.

"It doesn't look all that good", Hostilius said, his palms clutched around the marble handrail of the temple's balcony.

I was about to agree with the Primus Pilus when, within the span of ten heartbeats, the Sasanian line became as ragged as the ranks of the *Tanukh*.

"It seems like the stench of camels comes with certain benefits", I said as the enemy horses baulked at the unfamiliar smell.

A heartbeat later, the two ragged forces collided with a clash that I could feel through the soles of my feet. Were it not for the reaction of the immortals' mounts, the consequences would have been dire for the *Tanukh*, but their horses' fear of camels served to even things out. Soon, the battle turned into a contest of attrition. The immortals were more skilled at war, but the *Tanukh's* camels were better armoured.

Then a thousand camel lancers spilled from the wadi north of the city, racing to strike the Sasanians in the rear.

The fight left the immortals as soon as they became aware of the second force. Many fought and died a warrior's death, but hundreds turned their horses' heads back to the ford in the Euphrates, only to fall to the storm of arrows that Amr's camel archers were unleashing on the Sasanians still on the eastern bank.

Gordas was the one who noticed it first. "Trouble", the Hun growled, and pointed at the eastern horizon.

I squinted into the distance and spied a dust cloud rising from behind a rise less than a mile east of the river. Moments later, a line of riders crested the hill and I felt a stab of panic in my gut.

"Cataphracts", Vibius concluded. "At least a thousand."

"We have to warn Amr", I said, and led the way to where we had left the horses.

We reached the *Tanukh* just as the last of the Sasanians fell to the spears of the nomads. Amr noticed our presence and pushed his mount through the mob of unruly camel lancers. Some were thrusting their spears in the air and cheering their victory while others were already looting the dead or gathering the mounts of vanquished enemies.

"We won a great victory", Amr said, grinning from ear to ear. "The armour and weapons of the immortal guards are highly prized in our lands."

I gestured to the far bank of the river where three thousand Sasanians were arrayed in neat ranks, just out of arrow range. "They are not going away", I said.

"We will slay the immortals with our arrows if they try to cross", Amr said, no doubt still beset by the daemon of battle.

"That is possible", I replied, and pointed at the metal-encased cataphracts mounting their warhorses across the Euphrates. "But your shafts will be useless against them."

Amr's eyes grew wide when he spied the cataphracts and he shouted for his men to withdraw from the field. His sub-commanders relayed his orders but the *Tanukh* were slow to respond.

I took the nomad lord by the arm. "Amr", I said. "Take your camels and flee into the wasteland where the cataphracts cannot follow."

"What about you, lord?" he asked.

"Give me a guide who knows where the water is", I said. "We have good horses and will ride for Palmyra."

From the corner of my eye I noticed the cataphracts advance through a hail of arrows, the missiles having no effect on the heavily armoured horsemen.

I clasped arms with Amr, who called out to a scruffy man on a mangy camel. "This is Waddah, lord", he said. "He is my best scout and knows of the wells."

"Can you ride a horse, Waddah?" I asked, just as the first cataphracts exited the river and ploughed into the *Tanukh* too slow or greedy to abandon the loot.

Waddah stared at me with a blank expression, confirming my suspicion that he spoke only his native tongue.

Amr barked an instruction to the scout, who passed the reins of his camel to another nomad, and swung up into the saddle of one of our spare horses.

The lord of the *Tanukh* hollered to his men, nodded in my direction, and led the mob of camel riders into the wasteland of Arabia.

"Come", I said. "It is time to return to Palmyra."

I led my friends and thirty mounted praetorians into the ravine south of the city and powered up the track. A short while later, we emerged from the wadi onto the flatlands bordering the western wall of Dura. I reined in my stallion and twisted in the saddle to determine whether the Sasanians were pursuing. I noticed that the heavy cataphracts were already dismounting and watering their horses, but the immortal guards were thundering after the nomads.

"They might catch them", Gordas opined. "Horses are much faster than camels."

Hostilius offered a shrug. "That's for the gods to decide", he said. "At least the bastards aren't coming after us."

The words had hardly left his tongue when a group of a hundred and fifty immortal riders appeared from around the edge of the cliff down on the floodplain, and urged their horses into the ravine.

"At least our ride to Palmyra won't be boring", Vibius said, and kicked his gelding to a canter.

Gordas was the only one who found his jest amusing.

Chapter 34 – Khamsin

"At least we have a guide who knows where the wells are and the Sasanians don't", I heard a praetorian say to a fellow guardsman while we were watering the horses.

"Don't be a fool, Sextus", his comrade responded. "They will just follow our tracks."

"We could poison the wells", Sextus replied. "A dead horse will quickly rot in this inferno."

"Why don't you suggest it and volunteer that they use your spare horse?" his comrade snickered.

Hostilius had also overheard the conversation and we exchanged glances as we swung back into our saddles. "I don't like poisoning wells", I said, and nudged Intikam to a canter. "It will be the last resort."

While it was true that we were well mounted, the same did not apply to the praetorians. Our animals had the blood of Scythian and Hun horses, while the imperial guards' mounts were sourced in the lands of Italia. In less than a watch, the Sasanian horsemen had reduced the gap to such an extent that I feared that they were close enough to pick us off with well-aimed arrows.

I shared my concern with Gordas, who glanced over his shoulder. "Their arrows might be able to reach us", he confirmed.

"Why don't you shoot back?" Hostilius asked.

"Their arrows are enhanced by the swiftness of their horses", Gordas said. "Their shafts will have fifty paces more reach than ours."

The Hun had hardly explained the principle when an arrow thudded into the ground ten paces behind the trailing praetorian.

"We have to pick up the pace", I said to Gordas, who nodded.

Before I could relay the order, disaster struck. A Sasanian arrow sprouted from the shoulder of Waddah. The *Tanukh* scout cried out in pain and tumbled from the saddle, falling heavily onto the stones of the Roman road.

"Ride on! It's an order!" I boomed, pulled on Intikam's leathers and galloped back to where the scout lay sprawled on the cobbles. I reached down, grabbed a fistful of soiled garments, and heaved the gangly man across the neck of my powerful stallion. At least three arrows slammed into my armour, but the thick scale turned the iron tips of the shafts. I dug my heels into Intikam's sides, and even with the weight of two men, my horse managed to catch up with my retinue, who must have slowed down in spite of my orders.

Arrows were still falling amongst us, and against our better judgement, we increased the pace to a gallop until we had stretched our lead to five hundred paces. I stole a glance over my shoulder and could not help but notice that the horses of the praetorians were tiring.

"They will last no more than a watch", Gordas growled. "When the time comes, we will have to leave them behind."

"What in hades is that?" I heard Hostilius say.

Turning my head away from our pursuers, I noticed a reddish-brown haze on the western horizon. I took the injured scout by the arm and gently but firmly gave him a shake. Apart from issuing a groan, the man failed to respond.

"Allow me", Hostilius said, grasped the severed shaft stuck in the man's shoulder, and gave it a twist.

Waddah issued a scream of pain and opened his eyes. For the span of a heartbeat I feared that he might throw himself from Intikam's neck, but he seemed to come to grips with the situation and slumped once more. I tapped him on his good arm and indicated the phenomena visible on the horizon.

The scout glanced in the direction I pointed and a deep frown creased his brow. "*Khamsin*", he whispered, fear thick in his voice.

I looked over my shoulder and noticed that the immortal riders were no longer following us, but galloping in the direction of the ravines that Amr had visited the previous day. I reined in and looked to Vibius to enlighten us. "It is the dark wind - the black hurricane of the desert", he said. "We must seek shelter."

The respite allowed the injured scout to hobble over to his mount and gain his own saddle.

I glanced around, but on the flatlands there was nowhere to hide. Then my eye caught the glint of the afternoon sun reflecting off the limestone walls of the great fortress and I felt the presence of the guiding hand of Arash. "We will return the way we had come, to find cover inside the walls of Dura", I said.

Hostilius followed, looking over his shoulder at the rolling wall of sand and dust that was approaching at an alarming rate. "We're not going to make it", he said.

"We will try", I replied, and nudged my horse to a canter.

The storm caught up with us half a mile outside the western wall. Waddah swung from the saddle and gestured for us follow his example. He pressed his head against the neck of his horse and covered his face with a forearm, urging his mount forward as best he could. By the grace of the gods we managed to keep to the Roman road and stumbled on through the swirling sand, blinded and suffocating on the fine dust. What must have been a sixth of a watch later, but felt more like an eternity, we spilled through the Palmyrene Gate.

Vibius immediately turned off the main street and led us to the right, the wind shadow of the great wall providing some relief from the burning sand. We picked our way past a dilapidated bath complex and the ruins of a sanctuary to Zeus, and arrived at a building surrounded by sixty-foot-tall marble columns that abutted one of the massive stone towers set in the city's defensive wall. Vibius ascended the steps and threw himself against the thick oak, but the gates refused to budge. Soon, the rusty hinges succumbed to our combined effort and the doors opened a crack, just wide enough for us, the scout and the praetorians to lead our horses inside. In the side wall of the inner chamber, a stout wooden door provided access to the ground floor of the tower, that was large enough to accommodate the horses. The praetorians occupied the inner chamber, which meant that my friends and I claimed the innermost sanctuary for ourselves. After barring the main gates, we used the water in our skins to rinse the sand from our eyes and shared most of what remained between us and our mounts.

"Who is this temple dedicated to?" Hostilius asked once Gordas and I had removed the arrow from the scout's shoulder and cauterised the wound with fire.

"Aphlad, the god of storms, who is venerated by the first people of these lands", Vibius replied. "Which explains why the locals have left the temple undisturbed. Look", he added, indicating an oil lamp in a recess in the wall. "Even the oil lamps are still here."

"Now that you mention storms, how long do these blows last?" the Primus Pilus asked when we had settled down for the night, the howling wind rattling the door in its frame as if a titan wished to break it down.

"Usually not longer than a watch or two", Vibius replied.

Hostilius sighed. "Which means that we will have to spend the night inside the walls", he said, his right fist clutching his amulet.

* * *

Come the following morning, the storm was still raging. The good news was that, contrary to the tales of horror told by the herders, we were not disturbed by the shades of the fallen.

Late afternoon, the gods answered our pleas and the storm finally abated. Once the wind had died down, Hostilius, Gordas, Vibius and I lifted the locking bar from its brackets and ventured out into the open. I ordered the praetorians to ready the horses while my friends and I made our way along the sand-covered streets, heading to the far wall to establish whether the Sasanian army that had marched to Zenobia's aid was still encamped by the river. We gained the battlements via a tower, from where we could see for many miles across the wasteland.

For long the Primus Pilus studied the wide expanse. "The enemy must have fled before the storm", he said, and pointed at the battlefield of the previous day. "Even the bodies are gone."

"Maybe the storm swallowed them", Vibius said. "I have heard tales of the *khamsin* burying entire armies beneath the sand."

The Primus Pilus shrugged noncommittally. "Let's hope for the best", he said.

"We need to water the horses and fill our skins before we ride west to Palmyra", Gordas said as we descended the steps of the tower. "We do not know if the wells suffered the same fate as the army of the Sasanians."

Just opposite the agora, halfway back to the temple of Zeus, Gordas suddenly raised a palm and came to a stop. The Hun sniffed the breeze like a feral creature, and gestured for us to duck into an alleyway. "Horsemen", he said, and turned to face Vibius. "Lead us back to the temple and be quick about it", he added, indicating the footprints we had left in the layer of sand. "They will come for us."

We were still a block away from the sanctuary when the first of the mounted immortal guards emerged from an alleyway and guided their horses into the street, two hundred paces behind us. The Sasanian commander issued orders and the riders thundered towards us, intent on riding us down.

"Time to run", I said, and broke into a sprint, my friends following close behind.

The praetorians had followed my orders and taken the horses outside to brush them down and saddle them. When they realised that their emperor was in danger, the guards gained their saddles to sacrifice themselves. "Leave the horses!" I boomed. "And get inside the temple."

As we filed through the crack, I caught a glimpse of our pursuers and noticed that they numbered at least a hundred and thirty warriors. The praetorians slammed the doors shut just as the first arrows thudded into the wood.

"I can't help but feel like a chicken trapped in a coup", Hostilius said as we lowered the locking bar into place. "A chicken without water."

"Pity about the horses", Gordas replied.

A frown creased the Primus Pilus's brow. "I'd rather not have the horses but have water", he said.

"Horses have blood", the Hun said, issuing a wolflike leer.

Hostilius scowled in reply.

Although the Primus Pilus scoffed at the idea, Scythians did not shy away from consuming the blood of their mounts when their survival depended upon it. The harsh reality was that we had no access to water and that the sanctuary was besieged by a force outnumbering us three to one.

"I am tired", I said. "I suggest we get some rest. Tomorrow we can beseech the gods to deliver us from this trap."

Hostilius sucked down the last mouthful of water from his skin and spread his cloak on the marble floor. "Maybe you should start tonight", he said, and was snoring before I could reply.

* * *

When I woke up in the middle hours of the night, it was deathly quiet. I was about to turn onto my other side when my eye caught movement at the doorway separating the inner and innermost chamber. Instinctively my fist tightened around the hilt of my dagger and I rose to a crouch. Concerned that the Sasanians had managed to gain access to the temple, I went to investigate and was just in time to spy a dark shape making its way into the tower. The form passed through a ray of moonlight that entered through an arrow slit, and I noticed that it was a man garbed in the uniform of a Roman centurion. For a moment I pondered whether the officer could be part of a search party sent by Diocles. I immediately discarded the thought, but followed the man nonetheless.

As I ducked through the door that gave access to the tower, the soldier lowered himself to the floor, leaning with his back against the far wall.

I closed the wooden door behind me and carefully made my way towards the officer.

"Care to join me for a cup, stranger?" the centurion offered, and I noticed that he cradled an amphora in his lap.

I sheathed my blade and joined him on the floor. He extended his hand and we gripped forearms in the way of the warrior. "Julius Terentius, Hastatus Prior of Legio XVI Flavia Firma", he said, and saluted.

I returned his salute. "Lucius Domitius", I said. "I, too, used to serve as a centurion in the legions of Rome."

The officer, who must have been of an age with me, grunted his approval. He filled two cups from the amphora, passed one to me, and took a long swallow. Then he lowered his head in shame, resting his forehead on his free hand. "I've lost all my men", he said. "Every single one of them perished in the tunnels."

"Have you ever fought in the tunnels, Lucius Domitius?" he asked while draining his cup.

"No", I replied.

"It's worse than you can imagine", he said. "There is hardly any air to fill one's lungs, and the first you know of a blade is when iron pierces your flesh."

"After we foiled their plans to undermine the walls, they raised a siege ramp", he said. "They came on the Nones of October but we beat back those bastards until their corpses littered the ramp. Just when we thought we had the better of them, the city guard raised the alarm. The enemy had dug another tunnel below the ramp, having used the noise of raising the slope to disguise the sounds of their pickaxes hammering through the rock underneath the wall."

"I rallied half a century of my men", he continued. "And although I feared venturing into the realms of the underworld, I led them into that dark hole. We were three hundred paces into the bowels of the earth when the Sasanian scum worked their dark magic. We were overcome by thick, yellow smoke that billowed from the tunnels, fanned by the bellows of those whoresons. I saw my men die, gasping for breath with their hands clasped around their own throats."

"How did you manage to survive?" I asked.

Julius Terentius raised his head and met my gaze. I shuddered when I stared into his cold, lifeless eyes.

"The ferryman refused me passage across the Styx", he said. "Charon said that I was cursed because I failed my emperor and I had no coin to change his mind. I have walked these streets for two decades and I am doomed to walk it for eternity."

I felt intense pity for the lot of the soldier and raised my right hand so that he could lay eyes upon my seal ring, which halted him in his tracks, his dead eyes wide.

"Your emperor absolves you, centurion", I said, and presented him with an aureus on an outstretched palm.

He reached out and accepted the coin, brushing my hand with corpse-cold fingers.

Chapter 35 – Lice

"Wake up, Domitius", Hostilius said. "The bastards outside are stirring. We've got to be ready when they come."

I wiped the sleep from my eyes, licked my chapped lips with a dry tongue and gained my feet, just in time to hear shouting in accented Greek from outside the gates. "I know that you are in there, Lord Emperor!" the voice boomed. "We have found your horse and your ivory baton of authority."

The man, whom I suspected to be the commander of the immortal guards who had pursued us, continued without waiting for a reply. "If you open the gates, I guarantee safe passage for your men. You, however, will have to accompany me to Shahanshah Bahram, who will release you once you have sworn fealty to him. I have dispatched a rider to Palmyra, requesting the presence of the queen. Should you refuse to give yourself up, I will have your men flayed alive once we have broken down the door, and then give you over into the hands of Zenobia as soon as she arrives."

As Hostilius listened to the words, his scowl seemed to grow. "Those Sasanians reek, eh?" he pointed out. "I can smell that bastard's breath even though he's standing on the other side of the gate. By the way, I'd rather be flayed alive than fall into the hands of that evil bitch."

The Primus Pilus's rant made the praetorians burst out in laughter, which did not escape the ears of the immortal commander. "Laugh all you like, Roman dogs", he spat, his tone suddenly hostile. "You are trapped and at my mercy. Not even your gods can save you now."

"Do you know anything about how Shapur took this fortress?" I asked Vibius, choosing to ignore the rant of the man on the other side of the oak.

"The Sasanians killed the garrison and deported the people of the city, leaving no witnesses", Vibius said. "But I heard that a slave who managed to escape told stories of how the enemy entered the city through tunnels while the garrison fought a second force on the wall walk."

Just then, the entire temple reverberated with the noise of a heavy axe or hammer repeatedly striking the thick oak of the gates. I led my friends into the inner chamber and examined the construction, immediately realising that the oak was reinforced with bands of iron. "Even if we do not bolster the wood, it will take them at least a day to breach the gates", I said, and could not help but notice the expressions of panic on the praetorians' faces.

Hostilius leaned in. "It's all fair and well, Domitius", he whispered. "But men need to feel that they're toiling to make a difference. Give them something to keep busy with or else they'll be at each other's throats long before the Sasanians breach he door."

"We need to bolster the gate with rubble", I ordered. "We will break down the lesser walls in the tower chamber and stack the stones on the inside of the gate."

While the praetorians toiled, we congregated in the innermost chamber.

"We can open the gates", Gordas suggested. "And fight our way through their ranks."

"Thirty against a hundred and twenty?" Hostilius asked. "We will all end up dead."

"It is possible", the Hun replied. "But it will be a glorious death, which will place us in the favour of Arash."

"I agree with the Hun", Vibius said. "But we need to surprise them."

"They are watching the gate like hawks", the Primus Pilus said. "How in hades are you going to surprise them?"

"The best we can do is open the gates and attack before we are weakened by thirst", I said. "At midnight, we will exit the temple and fight our way through to the horses. If anyone has a better idea, I am open to suggestions."

* * *

While the praetorians took a break from their labour, I wandered into the tower chamber, the vivid dream of the previous evening still haunting me. I walked over to the place where the centurion had rested against the wall and noticed that all was not as it should be. Crouching, I cleared away the sand with a palm, revealing an ill-fitting slab of rock inserted amongst smaller flagstones. With considerable effort I forced the tip of my dagger into the gap between the slabs. Using the blade as a lever, I lifted the edge, slipped the fingertips of my left hand beneath the stone and tipped it over, nearly falling into the dark hole beneath.

I removed an oil lamp from a recess, and the flickering light revealed that the hole was the access point to a crude tunnel that led towards the city wall. I lowered myself into the blackness, reached back for the lamp, bent down, and started shuffling along the underground passage where I stumbled across the remains of a legionary crumpled on the tunnel floor. The unfortunate soldier was still clad in full amour, his bony fingers clutched around his throat.

I shuffled on, taking care not to disturb the corpses. Fifty paces on, I noticed a skeleton encased in the garb of a centurion, his armour and *phalerae* identical to that of the man who I had shared a cup with the previous evening. The officer's body was draped over a small, half burnt-out wooden barrel. I imagined that Terentius had sacrificed himself in the hope of extinguishing the evil concoction that Shapur's men had used to generate the noxious fumes that exterminated the Romans. Farther down the tunnel I noticed a few unused barrels and small hemp bags leaking greenish-yellow powder that appeared to be sulphur.

Unsettled by the discovery of what seemed to be the body of a man I had spoken to in my dreams, I turned around and made my way back whence I came, a plan slowly taking shape in my mind as I did.

I found my friends in the tower chamber, staring down at me from above. Hostilius kneeled and reached down into the hole. The Primus Pilus offered me a hand and I gladly accepted.

"We leave you alone for a moment and you get up to funny business", he said as he pulled me from the tunnel.

I slapped the dust from my clothes and indicated the underground passage. "Send four volunteers from amongst the praetorians to establish where the tunnel leads", I said. "I suspect that it emerges on the far side of the wall."

"And tell them not to disturb the fallen", I added.

* * *

"Lord Emperor", the centurion of the praetorians said once he had helped the last of his men out of the hole. "The tunnel gently curves to the left, towards the wadi south of the city. We followed it for about three hundred paces and had to clear away much rubble, but we found an exit hidden in the ravine."

"Tonight we will surprise the enemy while they are sleeping", I said once the four of us had returned to the innermost chamber.

Gordas issued a grunt that I interpreted as agreement.

"We will be thirty against more than a hundred and twenty", Vibius said. "Even if we fall upon them while they are sleeping, we will be fortunate if we can put twenty to the blade before the others wake up."

"The praetorians are handy with their swords", Hostilius said, "but I tend to agree with Vibius. We will struggle to put down more than twenty or thirty before they overwhelm us. Remember, we will be facing elite immortal guards, the best fighters in all the lands across the Euphrates."

"I don't plan to put them to the blade", I replied.

* * *

Earlier, the praetorians had removed the stones that braced the door and stacked them to the side. The Sasanians, who had never ceased to batter the gates, had taken heart as cracks appeared and their efforts to force their way inside had intensified as the night progressed.

A third of a watch before the middle hour of the night, Hostilius and I dropped down into the tunnel. Behind us followed twenty-five praetorians. Gordas, Vibius, the injured scout and five of my guards remained inside the temple.

By the light provided by two small oil lamps we navigated the low, narrow tunnel, careful not to trample the bones of the brave legionaries who had lost their lives almost two decades earlier. Hostilius paused when we reached the remains of Julius Terentius. "Poor bastard", he said, studying the bones for a span of heartbeats. Then he bent down and removed a grimy gold coin still clenched between the teeth of the skull. He rubbed a thumb across the dirty gold and issued a gasp as my image was revealed on the newly-minted coin.

The Primus Pilus narrowed his eyes. "What are you not telling me?"

"Put it back and don't ask questions", I said, and he did as I asked.

Once out of the tunnel, we moved north in the shadow of the wall towards the Palmyrene Gate. I heard the low murmur of conversing men, and noticed the outline of two sentries watching from the battlements. I unslung my strung bow from my shoulder and took two armour-piercing arrows into my draw hand. When my thumb touched my ear I exhaled and released. Before the first arrow reached its target, the second missile was already on its path. Almost simultaneously the two heavy tamarisk shafts slammed into the necks of the immortals. For a moment the corpses swayed on their feet before tumbling over the battlements, coming to rest at our feet. "Not so immortal now, are you?" Hostilius growled as he stepped over the bodies and followed me into the dark streets.

We did not go to the Temple of Aphlad, but made our way along the main thoroughfare towards the agora, which was the only space large enough to accommodate the horses with ease. Two sentries guarded the mounts of the Sasanians, and they met the same fate as the watchers on the wall.

After we slaked our thirst from the horse trough, the Primus Pilus and I led the way to the sanctuary that the Sasanians had surrounded, making sure to keep to the back alleys until we emerged onto the street leading to the temple. Up ahead we saw the immortals sitting around cooking fires, while four men took turns in striking the doors with axes.

"When is it going to happen?" Hostilius asked, making sure to keep his body pressed against the stones of the building bordering the street.

"Any time now", I whispered.

Just then, the Sasanians battering down the gates of the temple issued a collective cry of victory as the doors swung inward with a load clap. The four men immediately drew their blades and stepped away from the entrance to the temple, while the remaining immortals assembled in front of the doorway.

"Give yourself up and I will be merciful!" the commander of the Sasanians boomed.

In reply, an arrow whistled from the darkness inside and slammed into the helmet of the man beside the commander, splitting the riveted plate.

The officer issued a string of curses in his native tongue and the Sasanians filed into the room, brandishing torches and curved swords. Two men remained to guard the gate. The last of the immortal guards had hardly entered the temple when the ones outside the door crumpled to the ground, arrows lodged in their skulls.

On my signal, Hostilius and I led the praetorians forward at a jog. Reaching the entrance, we pulled the gates shut just as the first puffs of greenish yellow smoke billowed from inside.

Hostilius wedged a spear between the thick copper fittings of the gate to ensure that none would escape. "Even if it doesn't kill them, it'll take care of the lice that infest them."

Before Vibius and Gordas had escaped through the tunnel, they threw the caskets of pine tar and bags of sulphur into the bonfire that we had made at the entrance to the passage.

Ironically, it was the same mixture that the Sasanians had used to kill Julius Terentius and his men all those years before.

The Primus Pilus impatiently tapped a finger on the hilt of his blade. "It's about time they started to beg for mercy", he said.

"Be patient", I said. "When they realise that the mixture cannot be extinguished, they will come."

Two hundred heartbeats later, the first of the Sasanians started banging on the wood, pleading for their lives.

I counted to a hundred and reached out to open the doors, but Hostilius placed a hand on my wrist. "Let's just wait fifty more counts", he said. "Lice takes a while to succumb to fumes."

I shrugged and stepped to the side.

Chapter 36 – Mercury

It took the best part of a third of a watch to retrieve the dead and injured from inside the temple and to relieve them of their weapons and armour. A dozen of the enemy warriors had succumbed to the noxious gases and we left them where they fell. Having lost consciousness, some were dragged out by their feet, while others were manhandled from the temple, gasping for breath and rubbing their swollen and inflamed eyes. Once the enemy were all bound and under guard, we retired to the large tent that must have belonged to the commander of the immortals. Although we were all exhausted, I knew that there would be little opportunity for rest as the night was already morphing into the grey time of the wolf.

"When do we ride for Palmyra?" Vibius asked.

"As soon as we have released our prisoners", I replied.

"You would release them?" Gordas asked.

"Neither Rome nor the Sasanians are in a position to wage war on one another", I replied. "I will not give Bahram an excuse to be a fool."

As the sun appeared above the eastern horizon, we herded the bound immortals to the river. One by one I had their bonds cut, and sent them wading through the waist-high water. When only the commander of the foe remained on the western bank, I gestured for a guard to bring him to me.

The praetorian pushed the Sasanian to his knees, the tip of his *gladius* pressed against the small of the man's back.

"When do you expect Zenobia to arrive?" I asked, and gestured to the spare mounts of the Sasanians that were kept under guard nearby. "Answer truthfully and I will allow you to ride back to your king so that your honour may remain intact."

For a span of heartbeats he wrestled with himself, but wisely abandoned defiance for the sake of salvaging his honour. "I sent my swiftest rider with three spare horses to deliver the message to the queen", he said, eager to avoid the terrible humiliation of returning to his king on foot. "I expect her to arrive today."

Satisfied that the officer was being earnest, I cut his bonds. I nodded to the praetorian guarding the horses, and he slapped the rump of the nearest animal, driving the whole herd into the river.

When the warrior was out of earshot I turned to my friends. "We had better leave as soon as possible", I said. "If the Sasanians' missive reached Zenobia she would have ridden east without delay."

"I agree", Hostilius replied. "Zenobia would sell her own children into slavery for the opportunity to get her hands on you, Domitius."

A third of a watch later, having packed our gear and filled our waterskins, we departed from the temple complex inside Dura. We had yet to exit the Palmyrene Gate when Gordas gestured to a cloud of dust rising in the west, not far beyond the wall. "It seems that the queen is more eager to get you under her blade than you thought, Eochar", he said.

"We will allow the warriors of Palmyra to pass", I said, and turned Intikam's head into a side street. "Once they are gone, we will escape to the desert. Zenobia and her men would have ridden hard to reach Dura. Our horses are rested and Waddah will lead us to the wells."

While we waited for the riders to arrive, Hostilius and I dismounted, backtracked a block or two along the main thoroughfare, and gained the roof of a large *domus* bordering the street.

We did not have to wait long for a commotion, which hinted that a large warband had entered through the gates of the fortress and were making their way towards us. A hundred heartbeats later, the first riders rode into view. I peered down at the column of camels, immediately recognising the features of the olive-skinned warrior riding in the vanguard.

* * *

Amr dismounted and inclined his head in greeting, perplexed that we had been hiding atop a roof. "It is good to see you, lord, but it seems like you were expecting someone else."

"We are waiting for her highness, the queen of Palmyra", Hostilius replied drily, his words drawing a frown from the *Tanukh* lord.

After we had told all, it was Amr's turn to bring us up to date. "We led the immortals deep into the desert, to the soft sands that horses struggle to traverse. When the men who pursued us noticed the black hurricane rising in the east, they turned tail and cantered back the way they had come. The *khamsin* caught up with us while we were still amongst the dunes, where the storms are worst. In an attempt to save themselves my men scattered across the wasteland in search of shelter. Once the sandstorm had passed I gathered five hundred of my finest warriors to ride to your aid, the others I sent home to see to their families. If it pleases you, lord, my men and I will escort you back to Palmyra."

I regarded the warriors of the desert lord, all tough men familiar with the ways of war. "There has been a change of plan", I said. "We are no longer riding west, but will rather wait for the queen to come to us."

* * *

Zenobia showed her cunning by not approaching Dura by way of the Roman road. It was the start of the last watch of the afternoon when a sentry, posted to the eastern wall overlooking the Euphrates, arrived at the agora. "Lord", he said, inclining his head to Amr. "Three hundred camel riders have arrived at the ford. They are watering their animals in the river."

Amr made no secret of his hatred for Zenobia because of the treacherous way in which she had lured and murdered his uncle, Jadhima. "Is the whore amongst them?" he asked.

"Bat-Zabbai and Zabdas lead them, lord", the warrior replied.

The Arab lord took me aside once he had dismissed the sentry. "Bat-Zabbai owes me a blood debt", he reminded. "I wish to be the one to claim it."

"The queen rebelled against Rome", I said. "It is our way to bring criminals like her to the Eternal City so that they may suffer the humiliation of being paraded through the streets in chains."

I could see that the thought of Zenobia's humiliation greatly pleased Amr, but he dug in his heels. "I have sworn an oath before the gods", he said.

"Allow me to display her to the people of Rome", I suggested. "When it is done, I will send her back to you and you may do with her as you please."

Amr did not seem elated by my suggestion, but he conceded with a nod.

"It's all good and well arguing about the division of the spoils, but we still have to catch her", Hostilius said. "Zenobia's a clever one, we will have to be cunning."

* * *

A third of a watch later, Hostilius, Vibius and Amr rode beside me with ten of his most imposing *Tanukh* warriors following close behind. The Primus Pilus, Amr and our escort were attired in the immaculate armour of the immortals who had died in the temple, and mounted on the large geldings employed by the royal guard of the Sasanians. Their full-face helmets obscured their features and ensured that they would not be recognised by either Zabdas or the queen. I, on the contrary, wore a torn purple cloak over a tattered, dirty tunic to give the impression that the Sasanians have had their sport with me. To appease my friends, I wore my Scythian scale vest underneath my tunic. My hands were seemingly tied to the saddle horn, but that, too, was a ruse.

We picked our way down the ravine towards the narrow floodplain bordering the river. When Zenobia and her men noticed our approach we reined in and Vibius continued alone, coming to a halt midway between us and the Palmyrenians.

Having come to the conclusion that my friend was an immortal guard, a rider detached from the warband. Vibius, who had learned to speak Persian on the lap of his minder, conversed with the Palmyrenian and walked his horse back to us. "The queen is eager to purchase our prisoner from the king of kings", Vibius said. "Apparently she has brought a princely sum of gold with her."

I raised an eyebrow. "Diocles told me that the campaign against Palmyra is proving to be more costly than he had anticipated. Mayhap we can bolster the treasury if you sell me for a goodly sum."

Vibius, Hostilius and Amr nudged their horses forward, the Primus Pilus holding the reins of Intikam. I sat slumped in the saddle, like a broken man would, making sure to keep my head down and averting my gaze.

Almost simultaneously, Zenobia, Zabdas and two burly royal guards detached from the Palmyrene warband. The queen of Palmyra was as well-groomed as ever and rode beside the commander of her army, flanked by two mounted axemen who followed a pace or two behind.

"Why do you bring an unequal number of warriors to a parley?" Vibius growled in Greek tainted with a Persian accent. "Have you no honour, queen of Palmyra?"

Zenobia flashed a disarming smile, displaying her perfect teeth. "Surely the royal guard of Shahanshah Bahram does not count a woman as a warrior?" she replied. "Besides, we are not enemies but allies in the struggle to rid the world of the terrible yoke that is Rome."

Vibius inclined his head in acceptance of her words. "King of Kings Bahram requires twelve talents of gold as payment for delivering the king of Rome into your hands", he said. "May our lord be immortal."

"You wish to empty the coffers of Palmyra", she countered.

Vibius gestured to me. "With the Roman Emperor out of the way, you will be able to regain your lost lands", he said. "Before spring arrives, the treasury of Palmyra will be overflowing with gold and silver."

Zenobia was no doubt keen to conclude the arrangement. "Agreed", she said, her gaze focused on me, the ultimate prize.

Vibius smiled and nodded.

"I will inspect the prisoner", she said, and made to pass through the gap between Vibius and the *Tanukh* lord.

I kept my head down and said a prayer to Arash, thanking the god for our good fortune.

As the queen brushed past Amr, he reached out and grabbed her from behind, pulling her from the saddle. Zenobia issued a screech that would have made a siren proud, and Zabdas and her two guards sprang into action.

But we had the advantage of being forewarned.

Hostilius rammed his gelding into the flank of the guard on the right and the Palmyrenian's horse staggered under the impact. The Primus Pilus lifted himself from the saddle and brought his sword around like a club, intent on caving in the warrior's helmet. Struggling to control his mount, the guard tried to parry with his axe, but Hostilius's blade bit into the iron vambrace protecting his forearm. Such was the power behind the blow that, although it did not split the iron, it shattered the bone underneath. The man was not chosen to be a guard of the queen for no reason. Adroitly he flipped the weapon to his left hand and swung it at Hostilius, who ducked underneath the path of the blade.

Fortuna favoured Vibius, probably because his opponent was distracted by the Primus Pilus's attack on his fellow warrior. My friend's sword thrust was aided by the momentum of his horse and the tip of his blade severed the links of the axeman's chainmail, slipped in deep between his ribs and pierced his heart. The corpse fell from the saddle and aided his comrades in death by ripping the sword from Vibius's fist.

Zabdas jumped at the opportunity. His stallion shot forward and he used the speed of his horse to add power to a backhanded cut, his blade slicing into the scales protecting Vibius's right shoulder. The Palmyrenian's iron came away red. Spurred on by Zenobia's screams, her lover struck again, this time a thrust intended to pierce my friend's heart.

Having lost his sword, Vibius managed to get his dagger in his fist. In a desperate attempt to avoid being skewered by the powerful Palmyrenian, my friend lashed out with his short blade and violently twisted his torso to the side. The thrust barely altered the path of Zabdas's blade, but just enough that the honed edge scraped against Vibius's armour, peeling away the scales without piercing his flesh. The manoeuvre saved Vibius's life, but left him unbalanced, and he tumbled to the dust.

I had been party to countless battles and skirmishes and had witnessed even more. Before Vibius hit the ground, Intikam was powering forward, his hooves striking the sand like the hammer of Vulcan.

Zabdas jerked on his reins to position himself so that he could bring his sword arm to bear and impale my prone friend. His blade was already drawn back and his lip curled up in a ferocious snarl when my massive stallion slammed into the shoulder of the smaller horse of the Palmyrene general. The animal stumbled to the side, and before it could right itself, Intikam bowled into it a second time, sending the horse and its rider sprawling to the ground.

Zabdas, like most Palmyrenians, was a skilful horseman and he rolled away to avoid being crushed by his mount. He gained his feet with the grace of a feline and his dark eyes turned to Vibius, who lay fifteen paces distant, softly groaning and still disorientated from the fall.

I swung down from the saddle, stepped into Zabdas's path and slipped my blade from its sheath just as the rest of Zenobia's warband issued a collective war cry and surged towards us. From behind me the cry was answered by Amr's camel lancers who spilled from the concealment of the ravine.

"You have made a mistake", Zabdas spat, and lengthened his stride. "Only a fool relinquishes his horse to fight on foot."

I did not rise to his words, but closed my fist around the leather-bound hilt of my eastern sword and breathed deeply to prepare myself for what was to come.

The Palmyrenian lunged as soon as I was within reach of his weapon. The thrust was well executed - the power being generated by his legs, back and hips, and flowing along the arm into the sword.

A lesser swordsman would have retreated outside the range of his weapon, but I had trained with a master for more than three decades. I took a short step back with my left foot, twisting my torso to the right as I did so. I bent my knees, brought my blade up in a middle guard, and allowed the edge of his iron to scrape along the scales of my armour, my blade already rising.

A fraction of a heartbeat before his arm was fully extended, I was in position. My sword moved from high to low, using my legs and the powerful sinews in my back to endow the blade with incredible speed.

The honed edge split the air as fast as lightning and struck Zabdas's fist that was clutched around the hilt of his weapon, sending at least three fingers flying.

The sword dropped from his grip and he staggered backwards, his eyes wide with shock.

My weight was already transferring from my legs and hips into my sword. Moments later, my blade, crafted from sky-iron, sliced through the thick mail protecting Zabdas's torso. The razor edge did not stop moving until it bit deep into the bone of his spine.

I heard a terrible scream from behind and saw Zenobia scrambling towards me, her long black hair loose as she had lost her helmet in the struggle. Behind her Amr was clutching his face, blood pouring from his hand.

"Whore!" he boomed, and spurred his horse to ride her down.

"You will never have the chance to parade me before the scum of Rome!" she shouted. Before Amr could reach her, Zenobia dropped down onto a knee, plucked a hidden dagger from a riding boot, and plunged the long, thin blade into her own neck. Defiantly she stared into my eyes and toppled to the ground, coming to a rest beside the body of Zabdas.

His blood up, Amr vaulted from his horse and repeatedly stabbed the body of the woman who had murdered his beloved uncle. When his rage was spent, I put an arm around his shoulders and steered him away from the corpse.

Having witnessed their queen's demise by her own hand, Zenobia's men reined in. They stared at us for a span of heartbeats before jerking their horses' heads around and melting into the desert. Amr's warriors did not pursue.

Hostilius, who, after a long struggle, had landed a killing blow to the guard, dismounted and strolled closer, assessing the scene of Zenobia and her lover's closeness in death. "The good news is, she wanted to be Cleopatra", he said. "But I fear that she's going to start smelling before we can get her to Rome."

Amr stood five paces away, his eyes averted in shame. "Something came over me", he said. "I do not know what."

"It matters not", I said, and gestured for him to approach. "At least we have quelled the rebellion", I added, and placed a hand on his armoured shoulder.

Vibius approached on shaky legs and pried the dented helmet from his head using both hands. He touched his ear and his hand came away bloody. "Could have been worse", he mumbled.

The *Tanukh* lord stared at Zenobia, which prompted the Primus Pilus to ask, "What are you looking at?"

Amr kept his gaze fixed on the queen. "It's just that I never realised how much Bat-Zabbai resembles my wife's servant, Makkai", he mused. "They are of an age as well."

I shared a look with Hostilius and Vibius, and then Mercury, the trickster god, whispered into my ear.

Chapter 37 – Coin

Three days later, Hostilius, Gordas, Vibius, Cai, Diocles and I reclined on couches arranged on a roofed portico of the palace overlooking the famed colonnaded main street that led to the Temple of Bel, the chief deity of the city. The giant marble columns lining the thoroughfare were fitted with pedestals on which rested bronze statues of the men and women who, over many centuries, had toiled to make Palmyra the great city that it was.

Upon our return to Palmyra the elders had opened the gates, singing the praises of the emperor for delivering them from the heavy yoke imposed by Queen Bat-Zabbai. I did not allow the army to loot the city, but to keep the legionaries content, generous amounts of gold gained from the treasury were distributed amongst the soldiers.

"Where is Queen Zenobia?" Vibius asked with a mischievous grin.

"Probably somewhere between Emesa and Antioch", I said. "Her coach is kept under strict guard by two hundred of my most trusted praetorians."

Hostilius shook his head in disbelief. "Five hundred *Tanukh* warriors witnessed Amr burying his dagger in Queen Zenobia", he said. "Word will get out."

"Who will be naive enough to believe the tales of a bunch of desert dwellers above the sacred truth from the conquering emperor's own lips?" Diocles asked. "We will attribute such rumours to the envy of the *Tanukh* clans. Besides, Makkai has such a striking resemblance to Zenobia, not even her own mother would know the difference."

Vibius raised his cup in a toast. "Long live Zenobia", he said.

"The important thing is that the East has been brought back into the fold of the Empire", I said.

"And that it was achieved without destroying the cities", Diocles added. "The tax base is largely intact."

"You have been too merciful, Eochar", Gordas cautioned. "If you do not put the fear of the gods into these people they will break their oaths as soon as your army marches over the horizon."

"That is why I will appoint a prefect to oversee the East", I replied. "Someone I can trust, who is familiar with the ways of the land."

"There is none outside this room that fits that description", Hostilius said.

I stood, accepted a scroll from Diocles, and handed it to Vibius. "Congratulations Prefect Marcellinus", I said. "You are hereby appointed to rule the East on behalf of the Emperor of Rome."

Vibius grinned, and in that moment he did not appear much different than the raw recruit who I had met in the legionary camp outside Sirmium, more than thirty years before. "I will need a good aide", he said. "Maybe Diocles will be interested in the position?"

"It depends on the pay", Diocles jested.

"I will pay you to take him if the East can't afford him", Hostilius suggested, and turned to my aide. "But then you will miss out on Domitius's triumph, won't you, Greek?"

"They say that women throw themselves at the generals who are part of the Emperor's retinue", he said. "Seeing that I am unmarried, I would not wish to miss it."

"We are still far away from a triumph", I reminded my friends. "Only when Postumus's Gallic Empire is reincorporated will Rome be whole again."

"So you are considering a triumph?" Vibius asked with a sparkle in his eye, knowing how I despised glory.

"Maybe", I conceded, "but then just to keep Diocles happy."

"You know how Greeks love being the centre of attention", Hostilius said, slapped Diocles's shoulder, and drained his cup.

* * *

Later that evening, when all had gone to their furs, only Cai and I remained on the portico, slowly sipping on cups of priceless *basarangian* from Zenobia's private cellar.

"Empire nearly whole again", Cai said. "How you feel now that goal within reach, Lucius of Da Qin?"

I took a sip from my cup and thought on Cai's words while I watched the moon rise over the Jewel of the East.

"I am starting to believe that it can be done", I said. "And that is why I feel like Ancaeus, the son of Poseidon."

My mentor stared at me quizzically.

"Before Ancaeus set out on a perilous journey, a seer prophesied that he would never get to drink the wine from his newly planted vineyard. On his safe return, the hero poured himself a cup and confronted the oracle. He pressed the vessel to his lips and was about to taste the wine when he was called away to defend his vineyard against a wild boar. Needless to say, he was killed by the beast before being afforded the opportunity to sample the fruits of his vineyard."

"You concerned that you will never get to taste fruits of labour, Lucius of Da Qin?" Cai asked.

While I considered the Easterner's words, I marvelled at the beauty of the colonnaded streets that were bathed in the light of Mani.

"No", I added after a span of heartbeats had passed, "I fear that I will find that the taste of the wine is not to my liking."

A smile settled on Cai's normally expressionless face and he chugged the last of the purple-black liquid remaining in his cup.

* * *

To be continued.

Historical Note – Main characters

Main characters of the series

Eochar - Lucius Domitius Aurelianus, or Aurelian, as he is better known, I believe, was the most accomplished Roman to ever walk this earth. Some would disagree, which is their right.

In time, all will be revealed, but for now I will leave you with a few quotes from the surviving records.

From the English Translation of the (much-disputed) *Historia Augusta Volume III*:

"Aurelian, born of humble parents and from his earliest years very quick of mind and famous for his strength, never let a day go by, even though a feast-day or a day of leisure, on which he did not practise with the spear, the bow and arrow, and other exercises in arms."

"... he was a comely man, good to look upon because of his manly grace, rather tall in stature, and very strong in his muscles; he was a little too fond of wine and food, but he indulged his passions rarely; he exercised the greatest severity and a discipline that had no equal, being extremely ready to draw his sword."

"..."Aurelian Sword-in-hand," and so he would be identified."

"... in the war against the Sarmatians, Aurelian with his own hand slew forty-eight men in a single day and that in the course of several days he slew over nine hundred and fifty, so that the boys even composed in his honour the following jingles and dance-ditties, to which they would dance on holidays in soldier fashion:

"Thousand, thousand, thousand we've beheaded now.

One alone, a thousand we've beheaded now.

He shall drink a thousand who a thousand slew.

So much wine is owned by no one as the blood which he has shed."

Marcus - Marcus Aurelius Claudius was an actual person, famous in history, and I believe a close friend of Lucius Domitius.

Cai is a figment of my imagination. The Roman Empire had contact with China, or Serica, as it was called then. His origins, training methods and fighting style I have researched in detail. Cai, to me, represents the seldom written about influence of China on the Roman Empire.

Primus Pilus Hostilius Proculus is a fictional character. He represents the core of the legions. The hardened plebeian officer.

Gordas – The fictional Hun/Urugundi general. Otto J Maenschen-Helfen writes in his book, The World of the Huns, that he believes the Urugundi to be a Hunnic tribe. Zosimus, the ancient Byzantine writer, mentions the Urugundi in an alliance with the Goths and the Scythians during the mid-third century AD. (Maenchen-Helfen's book is fascinating. He could read Russian, Persian, Greek and Chinese, enabling him to interpret the original primary texts.)

Vibius Marcellinus was an actual person. He will feature more later.

Segelinde – the Gothic princess, is an invention. However, Ulpia Severina, the woman who was married to Aurelian, is not.

Lucius's Contubernia – Ursa, Silentus, Pumilio and Felix. They were not actual people, but represent the common soldiers within the Roman Legions.

Diocles – was an actual man. The son of a freedman who became one of the great men in history.

King Bradakos of the Roxolani never lived.

Characters that make a guest appearance.

Zenobia, or Bat-Zabbai as she was known in Palmyra, appointed her son, Vaballathus, as ruler of the East after the death of her husband, Odaenathus. Sensing the weakness of the crumbling Roman Empire, she invaded Egypt and her armies conquered almost all of Asia Minor. Some view Zenobia as a heroin who stood up to the power of Rome. Others believe that she was party to the murder of Odaenathus and drank the blood of Jadhima after she had him killed. You decide for yourself.

Zabdas was Zenobia's chief general.

Amr was a lord of the *Tanukh* and the first semi-legendary king of the Lakhmid Kingdom. He rose to power after his uncle Jadhima was murdered by Zenobia. According to Arab legends he stabbed the corpse of Zenobia after she committed suicide.

Postumus was a Roman legate of Batavian descent who emerged as the dominant figure on the Rhine during Valerian's reign.

Cannabaudes (the Crow) was the king of the Goths and a thorn in the side of the Roman Empire. Apparently, Aurelian slew him with his own hand.

Julius **Placidianus** was the prefect of the *vigiles* in Rome. Some believe that Claudius Gothicus promoted him to praetorian prefect while others are convinced that **Heraclianus** was still prefect during the start of Aurelian's rein.

Historical Note – Palmyrenian storyline

State of the Roman Empire at the time of this book (September 271 AD to July 272 AD)

Once the war against the coalition of Germanic invaders had been successfully concluded and the traitors and rioters in Rome dealt with, Aurelian turned his attention east.

Zenobia (the widow of Odaenathus) who ruled through her young son, Vaballathus, had slowly but surely been expanding the Palmyrene Empire. Until the middle of 271 AD, the soldier emperors had been occupied with repelling Germanic and Scythian invaders.

Aurelian's campaign got under way late 271 AD/early 272 AD. There is no record of the composition of the army he took east, but I believe that he would have recruited heavily from amongst the tribes who fought from horseback, i.e. the Scythians and Berbers, who were known to fight as mercenaries (*foederati*) in the Roman army. Besides, it was standard practice for Roman historians to ignore or play down the role of barbarian auxiliaries and *foederati* when recording history, as they preferred to let the glory accrue to the Roman soldiers and generals.

It is recorded that Zenobia sent a delegation to the breakaway Gallic Empire. Historians also make vague mention of the Romans turning back the Sasanians who were on their way to assist Zenobia. If this was indeed the case, envoys would have visited Ctesiphon. Hormizd, Shapur's favoured son, ruled the Sasanian Empire for only one year. The history is silent on the cause of his death. There is no evidence that he was murdered, but, in my opinion, it is plausible that either Kartir and/or Zenobia could have had a hand in his demise.

Hormizd was succeeded by Bahram, Shapur's eldest son from a low-status wife. Unlike Shapur and Hormizd, who were tolerant towards other religions, Bahram backed Kartir, the high priest of the Zoroastrians, who started a campaign of religious persecution.

Did Zenobia send a delegation to Cannabaudes of the Goths? Probably not, but she may well have incited the Goths to attack Aurelian's army while on their way east.

Come the spring of 272 AD Aurelian marched his army east. The Historia Augusta says that along the way he "… ended many great wars… " and "… on the other side of the Danube he even slew the leader of the Goths, Cannabas, or Cannabaudes as he is also called..."

There is no record of Aurelian crossing the Danube to assist the Scythians against the Goths, but it is possible that he joined the tribes of the Hungarian plain in an effort to halt the advance of Cannabaudes.

In any event, Aurelian crossed the Propontis from Byzantium and landed unopposed in the province of Bithynia. On his march to Syria most towns welcomed him with open arms until he reached Tyana. Heraclammon was the name of the man who betrayed Tyana. Who knows, he might have been an agent of Zenobia...

Aurelian continued his march and encountered the Palmyrene army just north of Antioch, the capital of the East. Not only was the emperor outnumbered, but also outgunned by Zenobia's heavy cavalry. He won the battle by employing a strategy of feigned retreats to tire the cataphracts of the enemy.

Having tasted defeat at Antioch, Zabdas and the queen retired to Emesa where they rallied their forces. Again, Aurelian faced superior numbers of heavy cavalry. Initially the battle favoured the Palmyrene army, but when the emperor's cavalry was almost overwhelmed, he dispatched a large contingent of infantry to assist his horsemen against the Palmyrene riders.

The gamble paid off and turned the tide in Rome's favour. Apparently Aurelian's Lebanese clubmen proved extremely effective against the cataphracts of Palmyra.

Zenobia and what remained of her forces retreated across the desert to Palmyra. With the help of the *Tanukh* (Arabian tribes) Aurelian followed the queen of the East and besieged Palmyra.

The emperor wrote to her, requesting her surrender, but she informed him that her allies were on their way.

It seems that the Sasanians did send an army to lift the siege, but somehow Aurelian managed to turn them back. I used the colourful history of Dura Europos, the fort on the western bank of the Euphrates, to paint an interesting scenario.

On being informed that her allies had been routed, Zenobia fled to the Sasanians, but was captured when she was about to cross the Euphrates. Arabian history tells us that she committed suicide and that Amr stabbed her corpse.

After appointing his trusted general, Marcellinus, as prefect of the East, the emperor marched his army back to Europe.

Historical Note – Random items

- The main religion of the Sasanian Empire during the time of this book was Zoroastrianism. Kartir was the high priest, but I doubt whether he was the keeper of the veil. After Hormizd's short reign, his brother, Bahram, took the throne. With the support of the new ruler, the high priest started to root out other competing religions.
- Although fire is not worshipped in Zoroastrianism, it is seen as a link between the physical and spiritual world. No ritual is conducted without it. Interestingly, the name of the country Azerbaijan is believed to be rooted in this religion as in a free translation it means '*he who keeps the fire*'.
- A large mosaic of the nine muses had indeed been unearthed at Trier (Augusta Treverorum), but I do not know whether such a design adorned the floor of the imperial audience hall.
- Apparently Zenobia did send a delegation to the Gallic Empire to form an alliance against Rome, but it came to naught.
- The large private gardens of wealthy Romans were mostly divided into three parts. The *xystus*, an

expansive terrace, the *ambulation*, a larger area with ornamental plants and trees used for relaxed walking and the *gestation*, an oval piece of ground used for activities on horseback.

- According to the Historia Augusta, Aurelian preferred to live in a villa in the Gardens of Sallust where he constructed a portico to train on horseback.
- Somnus is the Roman god of sleep. He resides in the underworld and his brother is the god of death (Mors). According to the Roman poet, Ovid, Morpheus is a son of Somnus.
- Little is known of the numerous people referred to as Taifali. Otto Maenchen-Helfen believes that they were Sarmatians. The tribe is first mentioned in the third century as allies of Cannabaudes, the Goth. A hundred years later they occupy Oltenia, the plain south of Transylvania and north of the Danube.
- Some say that the Vulcan Pass was named after the Roman god Vulcan after a medieval army's campfires ignited deposits of coal. Others believe that it is named is derived from '*Vlk*', the ancient name for wolf in the local tongue.
- The remains of ancient ramparts and ditches (The Devil's Dykes) have been unearthed on the western

edge of the Great Hungarian Plain. No one knows who built the fortifications, but most believe that it was a collaboration between the Romans and Sarmatians to protect the access to the Carpathian Basin. Hungarian folklore says that King Csörsz of the Avars built it, while others say that it is the devil himself who dug the ditch.

- The rampart of the Devil's Dyke varied between 2.5 to 3.5 metres in height, the ditch between 2 to 4 metres in depth and between 5 to 9 metres in width.
- The stakes in the Devil's Dyke is based on the well-preserved Roman stakes found at an excavation site at Bad Ems, Germany. The 'barbed' spikes were hammered into the soil at the bottom of a V-shaped ditch.
- Archaeological finds in Ukraine have confirmed Herodotus's statement that Scythians used human skin to craft quivers. In this case, only the top part of the quivers were covered with human skin.
- Statius Alexander was indeed a *speculator* attached to the XIII Gemina sometime during the third century. *Speculatores* were Rome's equivalent of modern-day special forces.

- Mount Hasan in Asiatic Turkey (Argeos in days of old) is an inactive volcano that rises a thousand metres above the surrounding landscape.
- Antioch Lake (Lake Amik) on the Orontes Plain, north of Antioch (Antakya), was drained during the middle of the twentieth century. According to historic records the lake was massive, thirty-two kilometres (20 miles) long and eleven kilometres (7 miles) wide. The lake that was fed by not only the Orontes, but also a few minor rivers, had a complex structure, and was surrounded by wetlands.
- The Axumite Empire was a contemporary of the Roman and Palmyrene Empires. The claims made by the Historia Augusta that Zenobia had been supported by Axumites, had to a certain degree been vindicated by the discovery of epigraphical evidence indicating that Palmyra had close ties with the Axumite Empire.
- Elagabal (or Ilaha Gabal) translates to *God of the Mountain*. This god, who was worshipped in Emesa, is believed to have pre-Arabic origins from Canaan.
- A Roman *urna* equates to about thirteen litres.
- Some believe that under normal conditions a Roman legionary would have required eleven litres of water per day when on the march. When the temperature is

higher, the requirement increases. I guessed this figure to be about thirteen litres, or one *urna*.

- The ghaf is the national tree of the United Arab Emirates.
- The first use of chemical weapons is attributed to Shapur of the Sasanians, who burned sulphur and bitumen to gas the Romans in the tunnels underneath the walls of Dura Europos.

Historical Note – Place names

Augusta Treverorum – Trier, France.

Tyras River – Dniester River, Ukraine.

Olbia – Parutyne, Ukraine.

Oltenia – The Wallachian Plain, west of the Olt and north of the Danube.

Alutus River – Olt River, Romenia.

Tibiscus River – Timis River, Romania and Serbia.

Roman fort at Rittium – Surduk on the Danube, Serbia.

River of the Oak Forests – Surgani River, Romania.

Pass of the Wolf – The Vulcan Pass in the Carpathians, to the north of Oltenia.

Ulpia Traiana – Sarmizegetusa, Romania.

Tissus River – Tisa River, Romania. (In this case, the Bega, a tributary of the Tisa.)

Ratiaria on the Danube – A mile west of Archar, Bulgaria.

Rhabon River – Jiu River, Romania.

Ciabrus River – Tsibritsa River, Bulgaria.

Byzantium – Istanbul, Turkey.

Chalcedon – a district of Istanbul, Asiatic Turkey.

Ancyra – Ankara, the capital of Turkey.

Salaberina – near Kepez Pepe, Asiatic Turkey.

Tyana – Kemerhisar, Turkey.

Cydnus River – Berdan River, Turkey.

Black Mountains of Amanos - Nur Mountains, Turkey.

Antioch Lake – Amik Lake, Turkey.

Antioch – Antakya, Turkey.

Orontes River – Asi River, Syria and Turkey.

Apamea – Thirty-five miles northwest of Hama, Syria.

Antilibanus Mountains – Anti-Lebanon Mountains.

Emesa – Homs, Syria.

Palmyra – Tadmur, Syria.

Dura – Ruins of Dura Europos near Al-Salihiyah, Syria.

Author's Note

I trust that you have enjoyed the sixteenth book in the series.

In many instances, written history relating to this period has either been lost in the fog of time, or it might never have been recorded. That is especially applicable to most of the tribes which Rome referred to as barbarians. These peoples did not record history by writing it down. They only appear in the written histories of the Greeks, Romans, Persians and Chinese, who often regarded them as enemies.

In any event, my aim is to be as historically accurate as possible, but I am sure that I inadvertently miss the target from time to time, in which case I apologise to the purists among my readers.

Kindly take the time to provide a rating and/or a review.

I will keep you updated via my blog with regards to the progress on the seventeenth book in the series.

Feel free to contact me any time at hectormillerbooks@gmail.com - I will respond.

www.HectorMillerBooks.com

Printed in Great Britain
by Amazon